MW00437018

Sailor Take Warning

Sailor Take Warning

A novel of suspense

Richard Bolt

Encircle Publications, LLC
Farmington, Maine U.S.A.

Sailor Take Warning © 2018 Richard Bolt

Paperback ISBN 13: 978-1-948338-17-2
E-book ISBN 13: 978-1-948338-19-6
Kindle ISBN 13: 978-1-948338-18-9

Library of Congress Control Number: 2018937487

ALL RIGHTS RESERVED. In accordance with the U.S. Copyright Act of 1976, no part of this publication may be reproduced, distributed, or transmitted in any form or by any means, or stored in a database or retrieval system, without prior written permission of the publisher, Encircle Publications, Farmington, ME.

This book is a work of fiction. All names, characters, places and events are products of the author's imagination or are used fictitiously, and any resemblance to actual persons, living or dead, or to actual places or businesses, is entirely coincidental.

Editor: Cynthia Brackett-Vincent
Book design: Eddie Vincent
Cover design: Christopher Wait
Cover images © Getty Images/Thinkstock

Published by: Encircle Publications, LLC
PO Box 187
Farmington, ME 04938

Visit: http://encirclepub.com

Printed in U.S.A.

Acknowledgements

I owe much to the support and companionship of my writing group: to Vicki Sanders for her remarkable editing skills and apt suggestions; to Bill Regan and Jane Roy Brown for their helpful and wise commentary, always rendered with tact and patience; to consummately imaginative storyteller David Gardner for his invaluable observations and encouragement. Special appreciation is due as well to Sharri Whiting De Masi and the late Gregory Williams, past members of our group, both of whom contributed richly to our meetings.

A note of gratitude is due Barbara Shapiro for the lessons imparted in her writing classes. She skillfully laid bare strategies and techniques essential to crafting a compelling narrative.

Special thanks to Katharine Wroth who meticulous copyedited the entire text, and who offered suggestions that markedly improved the book.

Lastly, and most of all, I am grateful to my wife Olga Baloueff and our sons John and Nicholas for allowing me to take the time in our family's life to write this story.

Dedication

To Olga, with much love

Red sky at night, sailor's delight;
Red sky at dawning, sailor take warning.

- Ancient proverb

Introduction

*S*ailor *Take Warning* is set in the early 2000s, a time when America's Cup racing yachts still looked like traditional boats, not multi-hulled, wing-sailed catamarans on hydrofoils. This story, in part, pays homage to that earlier time when the sailing smarts of the seasoned skipper were at least as valued as sheer design technology.

Chapter 1

I didn't know it was a body when I first saw it.

I'd been up all night in my office at MIT's Cognitive Computing Laboratory trying to finish a research proposal. With dawn coming on, both my thoughts and my ability to express them had become pretty muddy. When you're a 38-year-old associate professor instead of an 18-year-old freshman, pulling an all-nighter doesn't come that easy. To revive my flagging brain, I'd put on my parka and headed for a brisk pre-dawn walk around the Charles River basin.

From the MIT campus in Cambridge, I'd gone over the Harvard Bridge to Boston, west along the river past Boston University, then back to Cambridge over the Cottage Farm Bridge where a right turn onto Memorial Drive gets you headed back to MIT. Heading east on this last leg of my circuit, I stopped about a hundred yards beyond the Pierce Boathouse to catch my breath and take in the scene before me.

Above, the dawn sky had a roseate cast. A raw December wind swept toward me from across the Charles. The river was partly frozen—thin sheets of gray-green ice alternating with large patches of open water. A covey of squawking gulls crowded the edge of a mid-river floe.

On the opposite bank, below Boston's landmark CITGO sign, I could just make out two tiny figures swinging along the jogging path. They and I seemed the only ones up and about at this hour, though the dearth of people in sight was not surprising early on a Sunday morning.

1

Directly below me, a sheer eight-foot drop to river level, a pair of heavy timbers floated in the choppy water. Each was about a foot wide, and maybe fifteen feet long. Joined at the far end, the timbers formed an upside-down "V," the point jutting away from me out into the river, the two butt ends secured to the embankment wall by a pair of rusty iron shackles.

A patch of wet cloth bobbed up against the far tip of one timber. It was of shiny material, a deep maroon. Its surface bellied up, and rippled in the wind.

I idly tried to make some sense of the fabric. A tarpaulin blown off a boat? A sleeping bag someone had tossed over the railing? An old raincoat? A brief lull in the wind collapsed the cloth enough to reveal a dark blob at its farther edge. A blob that began to look for all the world like a head with a glistening cap of black hair. My pulse leapt as my brain put it together: a parka, with someone inside floating face down.

My first thought was to call the police. But, as I turned to go, I thought maybe that person was still alive.

I looked around. No one in sight except the joggers across the river. A lone car sped by, tires beating on the damp asphalt. Not many motorists at seven a.m. on a Sunday. If there was going to be a rescue, it was up to me, and I had better move fast.

I swung myself over the railing and set my feet on the narrow granite ledge between me and the sheer drop to water level. The timbers looked big and buoyant enough to support me.

Gripping the bottom rung of the railing, I lowered myself as far as my arms could reach. Crevices between the wall's granite blocks gave me toe- and handholds to go the last couple of feet to the nearest floating timber.

I dropped to my hands and knees and crawled out toward the body. As I neared it, I could make out "Massachusetts Institute of Technology" stitched in script letters across the back of the parka.

I grasped the collar of the parka with both hands and, with a great heave, pulled the body's head and shoulders up from the water and partly onto the timber. Water sheeted over the top of the head, plastering the thick, dark hair down flat. I clung tightly to the collar with one hand, and with the other I pushed the hair back from the face.

Good God! I knew this body! It was Justin. Justin Marsh, my graduate assistant.

I squeezed his cheeks. They were hard and rubbery, and icy cold. Water gushed out of his mouth as I turned his head to look for a pulse from his jugular, just to make sure of what I already knew. He was gone. I couldn't help him.

His eyes were tightly closed. With my free hand I pushed back the lid of his left eye. Why I did that, I don't know. Maybe I still hoped to see some glimmer of life.

The socket was empty.

I lurched back, letting go of the collar, and Justin's head and shoulders sloshed back into the water. Waves of nausea passed through me. I could scarcely think. All I knew was that somehow I had to lash his body to the timbers so the wind wouldn't push him out into the river.

I yanked the nylon waist cord out from my windbreaker. A heavy iron ring, maybe six inches across, protruded from the point where the two timbers joined. If I could just get the cord under Justin's arm, maybe I could tie him to the ring.

Making a loop of the cord and holding it in my hand, I stretched out flat along the timber. I scooped my arm beneath the water where I judged Justin's left forearm must be dangling. I made several tries, plunging my arm and shoulder deep into the water. I shuddered as my hand at last found his. The fingers were rock hard and bent like claws. I worked the cord loop under and around them, and pulled up.

I had looped the arm. Rising to my knees, I gave the cord a tug to get it up firmly under the armpit. I knotted the cord down snugly on the arm, then fastened the other end of the cord to the iron ring.

For some terrible moments, I stared at Justin's body, wrapped in its sodden clothing. He was someone I had known. Spoken with. Worked with. Now, in this icy water, he'd become a *thing*...

3

I crawled back along the timber to the embankment wall, then climbed back to street level and raced across Memorial Drive to the lobby of MIT's Ashdown House, and, for the first time in my life, dialed 911.

Chapter 2

I'd been sitting for about an hour at Cambridge police headquarters at a wooden table that was bare except for a single sheet of paper dense with typing. Opposite me was Detective Lieutenant Ronald Haggerty, a tall, raw-boned redhead with pale blue eyes and just a trace of brogue in his voice. Why the trace I couldn't guess; he didn't look very old country to me. Maybe it was his version of ethnic pride.

It was a little past nine-thirty and I was into my third cup of coffee. My hands holding the cup were still shaking with chill and shock. Haggerty picked up the sheet of paper and insisted I would have to tell him yet again exactly how I discovered Justin's body. I did that, while Haggerty's glance alternated between fixating on me and following the paper's text.

I finished my account, and Haggerty set the paper back on the table. I could see him staring at my trembling hands. "That'll teach you to find bodies in the Charles at six in the morning," he said. A tight smile played on his face. Had he concluded I had nothing to do with how Justin got there? Maybe, but nonetheless he continued to take me through his litany of questions.

"Ok. Quickly from the top. Name?"

"William Rundle."

"You're a professor at MIT?"

"Yes. Associate professor."

"What part of MIT?"

"The Cognitive Computing Lab. Over on Amherst Street."

"Cognitive Computing Lab? What goes on there?"

"It's all about putting human-like intelligence into machines."

"Machines?"

"Into computers. Sometimes we say 'machines' for 'computers.'"

"And what were you doing out on Memorial Drive so early on a Sunday?"

"I told you," I said, my tone of voice getting testy despite my efforts to rein it in. "I'd been up all night working on a research proposal. Had to set it up for Jean-Paul...er, Professor Etherington."

"Who's he?"

"He's director of the lab. The walk around the river was to unwind before heading home."

Haggerty's eyes narrowed. "Just a bit more and we'll be done." He took a dark gray pen from his shirt pocket and toyed with it for a moment, screwing and unscrewing the cap. Then he asked, "Just how well did you know Mr. Marsh?"

"I knew him fairly well. He was starting his third year as my graduate research assistant."

"When did you last see him alive?"

"At the lab, last night. I'd popped into his office just before midnight."

"How'd he seem?"

"A bit tense."

"Tense? More than usual?"

"Maybe a little more so."

"Why might that be?"

"I've no idea."

"Didn't you ask him?"

"Ask him what?"

"Why he was wound up. More than usual."

"No. He had his moods. I didn't ask."

"But you knew him well?"

"Yeah. But I'm sure there are sides to all my students' lives that I don't know about."

Haggerty kept loosening and tightening the pen's cap.

"How'd you get along with him?"

6

"Fine. We got along fine."

"No tensions, pressures between you two?"

"No. Not really. Just the usual push and pull between student and advisor."

Haggerty stopped playing with the pen cap.

"What do you mean 'push and pull'?"

"Nothing. Just you've got to lean on the students from time to time to get them to make deadlines."

Haggerty resumed twisting the pen cap. I studied the backs of his hands: huge, bony, white-knuckled, and mottled with freckles. "So, Professor Rundle," he asked, "why did you 'pop' into Marsh's office?"

"I wanted to check on some supporting material I needed for my proposal." I thought a moment, then added, "He'd been late in producing it, and I…"

"So you were leaning on him for some stuff?"

"Well, yeah…"

"Leaning hard—like you and he were having a fight about it?"

"No. Not a real fight. He just seemed distracted lately, and I guess I had to prod him to get a move on."

"Distracted?"

"Yeah. Like his mind was somewhere else."

"Where else?"

"I don't know where else. I just needed to have him get some things done and he was being very slow about it."

Haggerty again stopped toying with his pen and leaned forward. His eyes bore relentlessly into me.

"So how do you 'prod' students? Threaten to flunk them? Take away their financial support?"

I stared back into Haggerty's eyes. Where was he trying to take all this? Yes, I'd kind of blown up at Justin last night. To my regret, because it was to be the last time I would see him alive.

"Nothing like that," I said, trying to disperse the suspicion I seemed to be generating around myself. "You just tell them what you expect of them and give a firm time-frame for when it's all due."

7

Haggerty leaned back, recapped his pen, tapped it a couple of times on his lower front teeth.

"Ok," he said softly. He rose from his chair, went over to the window and looked out. Over his shoulder, he asked, "You mentioned he had a girlfriend. How did that go again?"

I repeated what I'd told him before about Karen Hewitt. Karen lived with Justin in an apartment near Inman Square. I'd first met her two years back when I ran into the pair of them eating lunch in Walker Memorial cafeteria. Some days later, they'd invited me to dinner at their place. Like Justin, she'd been an undergraduate at Dartmouth, majoring in European history while he majored in physics and math.

I wondered whether the police at this very moment were knocking on her door to tell her about Justin. Were they already plying the poor girl with all kinds of questions?

"Can I use a phone here to call Karen?" I asked. "She's got to be worried, his being away all night. And someone has to tell her what happened."

"I've sent an officer over there. She'll break it to her."

"And grill her like you're doing to me?" I started to rise from my chair. "Don't you people…"

"Easy, there." Haggerty gestured for me to settle back onto my chair. His voice was calm and gentle, but the look in his eye signaled he meant for me not to move. I settled back.

"And what about his mother? I should be calling her, too."

"We're handling that," Haggerty said. "We got the number from the MIT police."

"Wouldn't it be better if I, as Justin's advisor…I mean, to get a phone call early in the morning from the police? She's a widow, and lives alone."

"Look, we've got it all covered. 'We people' have a lot of experience in breaking news of this kind."

I guessed what he really wanted was for his office to talk with Justin's mother and with Karen *before* I did. Was he thinking I'd had something to do with Justin's death and would try to influence them some way or other?

8

Haggerty resumed his questioning. "About Karen Hewitt and Justin Marsh—you were telling me before that they got along fine?"

"Yes. For the *n*th time, yes! Look, you're going to check it out with her, aren't you?"

I glanced at my watch. I could barely focus. Beyond the shock of finding Justin's body, I hadn't had any sleep for maybe thirty hours now.

Haggerty turned, and gave me a stern look. He walked slowly back to the table. "We will," he said. "In good time."

"I'm sorry," I said. "Look, I'm wrecked. I've got to get some sleep. OK?"

Haggerty nodded and pointed to the typed paper on the table with my statement about finding the body. He tapped his teeth with his pen. "Look it over," he said. "Sign it, if it's right."

I forced my eyes over the lines. It looked like what I had said. I groped in my shirt pocket for a pen, but none was there. Haggerty handed me his, the one he'd been tapping his teeth with. I signed the statement.

"Sleep tight," Haggerty said, as I pushed the paper and pen together across to him. He called for a squad car, and had me driven back to pick up my car in MIT's East Garage.

I drove back to my apartment on Irving Street. Inside, I kicked off my shoes and fell across my bed into a fitful sleep—a sleep haunted with images of Justin's sodden face. His empty eye socket. His eyelid like a slit in a sheet of rubber...

It was half past noon when I got up. I showered and shaved, pulled on a terry robe, and scuffed in slippers out to my kitchen.

I toasted a couple of slices of date nut bread and spread them with a thin layer of cream cheese. While the dark roast coffee was brewing, I poured out a glass of orange juice.

My favorite wake-up meal.

I couldn't touch it.

Good God, how could something like this have happened to Justin? Sure, there were MIT students who jumped out of dorm windows or into the Charles to do themselves in, even set themselves on fire—as a result of family trouble, grade pressure, drug usage, depression, psychosis, whatever. There'd been too many student suicides happening as of late, at least six students over the last few years, finally forcing the Institute to do something about improving its mental health services.

There are students who tumble off roofs, balconies, or down elevator shafts as the result of a dare, or while trying to pull off some prank, or "hack," as such are dubbed locally. Then, every year a few students get knifed, mugged, beaten up, or raped. Boston and Cambridge have some tough people. Techies, even those on the wrestling team, don't stand a chance against someone weaned on street fights and wielding a knuckle-knife with a six-inch blade.

Appalling, I reflected, how little MIT seemed to do to protect its own. A student from Norway knifed to death on Memorial Drive in broad daylight by a townie thug. A freshman dying from acute alcohol poisoning—all part of a fraternity rush ritual. Here was a school with some of the world's brightest kids, but which, for all I could tell, maintained a fastidious hands-off policy when confronted with mayhem and reckless behavior right on its doorstep.

I poured a mug of coffee, wandered out into my living room, and stood at the bay window. The waist-high sill of my basement apartment was level with the ground, and I could see the stalks of last season's hollyhocks leaning raggedly against the windowpanes. The reddish dawn had turned to a uniformly gray day.

Ok, I told myself, maybe the Institute's not to blame. Maybe Justin simply had the bad luck to confront a lethal mugger. A lethal mugger who had taken his eye…

But why take out his eye? To mutilate? Maybe. But why so cleanly, then? Why not just gouge it out?

Was it some kind of ritual murder? I couldn't imagine Justin being into any cult thing. Though he could have been jumped by somebody who was into weird rituals and, well, needed an eyeball.

Could there be some other reason to kill someone for an eye? I vaguely recalled an old James Bond movie wherein one of the bad guys used a false eye implanted with a simulated retinal blood-vessel pattern to crack a White House security system. Like matching fingerprints, the pattern of blood vessels lining the back of the eye are unique, and a retinogram taken by an ophthalmic security camera can separate you out from the several billion other souls on the planet.

In the Bond thriller, the faked retinogram was of the President of the United States and the stakes were a couple of nuclear bombs. Could Justin's retina serve as a key to open up some national secret? I dismissed it. This was life, not a 007 movie.

I rang Karen Hewitt's number—the same number I'd occasionally rung Justin on over the months. No answer. What a shock it had to have been to have the police break the news to her. Despite what Haggerty had said about their experience in such matters, I could only hope they did it with at least a modicum of compassion.

Hanging up, I rang 411 to get Justin's mother's phone number. She lived in Hamilton, on Boston's North Shore. Kindly, dignified, and very much the old-money Yankee gentlewoman, I'd met her several times when she'd come down to visit Justin.

Lilian Marsh answered, her voice stoic and subdued. Immediately after I identified myself, she broke in to say the police had informed her that morning of Justin's body being found, and that I'd been the one to discover it. I told her that I was so sorry for Justin, and for her. She said that Karen Hewitt had driven up to her house, was there now, asleep from a sedative the Marsh family doctor had given her, and that she would be keeping Karen there overnight. I repeated my condolences, and we rang off.

I took a sip of my coffee. It had gone cold, so I dumped it in the sink and started a fresh pot brewing. I had to concentrate. There were still some non-trivial loose ends to tie up on my research proposal before I could send it on to Jean-Paul.

Much too on edge to go back to MIT, I powered up my home computer, logged in by modem to my office workstation, and downloaded the proposal draft. I steeled myself to finish it—and to divert my mind from the image of Justin's ruined face.

It was about three in the afternoon when I concluded the proposal draft was as good as I could make it, and I emailed it to Jean-Paul prefaced by a cover note telling him about Justin.

Where might our peripatetic lab director be right now? Paris? No, I recalled from his emails he'd left Paris on Wednesday for Geneva en route to Milan for a meeting with Olivetti. Wherever he was, though, he'd go over the proposal text word for word preliminary to either ripping my effort to shreds or proclaiming me a hero.

I made myself a Scotch and water and set my alarm clock for six-thirty p.m.

Tonight, it was dinner in Concord. Provost Langdon Hale was hosting his traditional pre-Christmas gathering—largely MIT people, plus a few Boston-based entrepreneurs the Institute was trying to put the bite on for capital gifts. Every year about thirty MIT faculty and staff were picked more or less at random to be invited, along with their spouses or "significant others." My name was among those that came up for this year's affair.

Hale's gatherings were purportedly in the interest of "furthering a sense of community," which I suppose was reason enough to accept. But with Hale rumored to be on the short list for nomination as MIT's next president, it became even more of an invitation that could not be gracefully refused. What made it an occasion for me, though, was that I was taking Irina along as my significant other.

Irina was special. I'd first seen her in Harvard Square, two months ago, as she was stepping off one of the MTA buses in the midst of evening rush hour. Her dark blonde hair skimmed the collar of her camel hair coat, and framed her alert, serious, and exceedingly lovely face. I had to meet her.

But how? Stan Kittridge, my old Cambridge roommate, was a whiz at striking up conversations with women anytime, anywhere. His secret: just start talking. If the woman is willing to meet you, any topic not too inane will do.

I had trailed along after her as casually as I could while still keeping up with her brisk walk, out of the Square and down John F. Kennedy Street. When she entered a drugstore, I halted at the door. I thought, OK, Bill, fantasy's over. You don't have Stan's flair. You'll blow the whole thing. Forget it.

Just then, she re-emerged and literally bumped into me. After mutual begging of pardons, I feigned quasi-recognition.

"Say, you teach French at MIT, don't you?"

Why those words came into my head I don't know. Maybe I sensed a European air about her. In any case, I was amazed at my audacity.

She stopped, took a step back, and inspected me quickly but carefully. Looking me directly in the eye, she said, "No, but I do speak French."

"I'm sorry. I thought you looked like someone I've seen about MIT."

"Well, I have some friends there. Perhaps you saw me with them." She spoke with an accent, a bit French, a bit something else.

"I'm terribly sorry to have bothered you. Good evening," I found myself saying.

She smiled and nodded. "Oh, it was no bother. Good evening." With that, we walked off in opposite directions.

After maybe ten steps, I halted, turned about, and looked back down the street. She had vanished into the crowd. But we were talking! That's what I'd wanted! I was the one who choked. It was I, not she, who had cut it off. Well, maybe I'd blown it, but at least I had my opener for next time. If there was to be a next time.

I made a point, each workday afterwards, at evening rush hour, to retrace my steps as on the day I first saw her, looking for her in the commuter crowd. So many people. Would I see her again? Would I recognize her?

I needn't have worried. I could, and can, spot that bouncing hair and buoyant walk a mile off. It was two weeks to the day at 5:21 p.m., to be exact, when I ran into her again at the bus stop on Massachusetts Avenue opposite Leavitt and Pierce's tobacco store.

I had my opener. "Say—wasn't it you I thought taught French at MIT?"

"Yes," she said, "it was." And yes, she replied to my next question, she did have time for a coffee at Au Bon Pain…

Chapter 3

"Maybe it was gulls?" said Irina, as we sped through the swirl of snow northward on Route 2 toward Concord and Provost Hale's party. "Couldn't gulls have done that?"

"Maybe. But it was so clean, like his eye was taken out surgically. Or, his eyes. I don't know about the other one."

"But how did he *die*? Was it drowning, or something else? Didn't they tell you at the police station?"

"No, they didn't tell me much of anything. I did see a mark—kind of a bruise or discoloration—on the side of his face, though, when they pulled him out of the water. But it wasn't clear what it was. The police let me stand by, but they wouldn't let me up too close."

"Didn't you see the bruise when you first found Justin?"

"No. It was on the side of his face away from me, the right side."

"Do you think he may have jumped in?" Irina paused, and her voice darkened as she resumed, "I mean deliberately. The mark on his head could be from hitting the stone wall. Or something floating in the water."

We stopped at the traffic light where Route 2 cuts to the left and the old Cambridge Turnpike, straight ahead, continues on to Concord Center. I mulled over what Irina had said. The light changed. I stepped on the accelerator and headed toward the Center.

"Irina, I don't think he took his own life, if that's what you mean. I don't think he was depressed, or anything like that. Besides, what about that missing eye?"

"Maybe he had a false eye, and it came out when he hit the water.

14

I know it's far-fetched, but it's possible."

"But wouldn't I have noticed he had a false eye? I saw the guy pretty much every day for over two years. Wouldn't I've noticed his eyes didn't move together, or didn't converge normally?"

"It depends on how the eye had been damaged and how the prosthesis was done whether it would move along with the sighted eye. A friend of mine in church choir has a false eye, and you would never know it unless he told you."

"Well, Justin never told me anything like that."

Having exhausted theories about how and why Justin might have died, we drove on in silence. The swirling snow made the world magical, like being inside one of those crystal globes with tiny white chips you shake up and then watch settle. We entered Concord Center, the Ralph Waldo Emerson homestead on our left, a row of colonial vintage homes on our right. Holiday candles and an occasional Christmas tree glowed warmly through multi-paned windows. The houses grew grander and set farther apart as we headed west on Main Street, past Concord Academy, toward Musketaquid Road and the Hales' house.

We were met at the door by a uniformed maid who led us into a foyer carpeted with oriental rugs and lined with Federal period oil portraits, some of which I took to be of early Hales. We handed our coats over, and were directed into an Olympic-sized living room with yet more oriental carpeting and oil portraits, antique mirrors with gilt frames, and a grand pair of Philadelphia highboys.

There were maybe forty people in the room, dispersed in small clusters. The gathering was oddly quiet, given the number of conversations going on. The room's sheer size, I guess, made people feel they were in church.

Irina and I surveyed a tray of champagne glasses offered by a tall, balding, beak-nosed man dressed just like a butler in the movies. "Pink that end," he said glancing at one end of the tray, and shifting his eyes, "White here. Either is excellent." We both took white.

We sipped, and glanced about. The most animated group, hence the easiest to join, was over by the fireplace where Langdon Hale himself was holding forth with six or seven guests. I reached for Irina's hand, and we walked toward the group. As we neared, we heard Hale say, "…and, could you imagine, he had to sweep the stuff all back into the bag, right in front of the press corps and all. And only a few pounds of it…"

Hale's eyes met mine. "Halloo, Bill!" he whooped softly. I knew him only slightly, in spite of having met him and his wife at numerous faculty functions. Ever courtly and affable, he parted the knot of guests about him and swept us into their midst. His eyes quickly lighting on Irina, who was trailing behind me, he added, "And who, pray, is this lovely lady with you?"

"Provost Hale, may I introduce Irina Tatarinoff. She's an associate at the Davis Center for Russian Studies at Harvard." A flurry of nods and handshakes ensued as the rest of the introductions went on. I knew about half of those in the cluster.

Hale continued, "Bill, we've been chatting about the new trade talks with Japan, and whether something good might come of it all. That incident where our embassy man had to pack up that rice didn't help things, certainly."

I knew what he was referring to. Amid renewed trade tensions, Japan had suddenly imposed a strict ban on foreign rice. The Friday papers had carried a front-page picture of a U.S. envoy at an international food fair near Tokyo. Wearing an apron emblazoned, "Great Food from USA," he was bent over a display table and engaged in pouring a small bowl of American grown rice back into a cloth bag. Ringed about him were stony-visaged officials from Japan's Agricultural Ministry who had just ordered him to pack it up or face criminal charges.

"What do you think, Bill?" Hale went on. "Do you think the American people and Congress have finally had it on 'free trade' in certain sectors and want to back off for a while?" He bit into a small cracker with caviar.

"I hope, like everyone, that Congress will act in a sensible way," I said noncommittally.

One thing I'd learned in academia about discussing anything

ideological is—don't. But, while I was reluctant to touch anything political, someone else wasn't: a young Japanese, Kenichi Tsukamoto, who was on an exchange fellowship with the Institute's Department of Ocean Engineering, while also taking a course in interactive graphics at the Cognitive Computing Lab.

"Ah, but what you Americans don't understand," Tsukamoto launched in, "is that rice, in Japan, is not just something you eat. Rice is an ancient and profound part of our culture. It is a gift of the gods. A few years ago, we let you bring some into our country, you know, to be friendly. But the kind of rice you grow in Louisiana or wherever else, if I may be allowed to say so, is something for your 'Uncle Ben,' and not suitable for Nippon."

A pall fell over the group. Though he spoke politely, and in perfectly inflected English, there was something ominous about Tsukamoto's manner. Tautly muscular, with a wide firm jaw and an unmanageable shock of thick black hair above his steel-rimmed glasses, he was a forceful, even threatening, presence.

Hale, ever the diplomat, cut though the silence. "Well, I'm sure Japan has every right to grow its own rice, if that's what the people of Japan want. But, if anything like open markets are to prevail, it's perhaps understandable why the American Rice Council is pushing on our Congress to push on Japan." He quickly added, "Not that I agree with that strategy myself, you understand."

Tsukamoto glanced condescendingly at Hale, turned to face our group, and went on, "It is amazing how Americans can regard things American as important, but things that are foreign to you are just that—foreign. But how would you all feel if something very American was taken away from you, if something American were violated, like you would violate our island's market for its own rice."

He paused and cast his eyes about our circle. "For example," he went on, "think of your America's Cup. Your famous sailing trophy. What if Japan were to grab that away? What then?"

"Well, it has already been grabbed away," Hale said with an uneasy smile. "The Aussies took the Cup in '83. Got it right back in '87, though," he added with an equally uneasy laugh.

17

Tsukamoto replied, "Ah, but your 'Aussies' are safe enough to lose to. They are white. They speak English. They are from England, like the colonial Americans." He had assumed an almost combative posture vis-à-vis Hale. An older Japanese man, at the edge of our circle, gazed down at the floor, a look of distress on his face. Tsukamoto went on. "The Australians are relaxed, like Americans," he said sneeringly. "They are 'sportsmen.' They are 'gentlemen,' who 'play the game.' I suppose you don't think a Japanese crew can be like the fine sportsmen at the New York Yacht Club?"

I was astonished Tsukamoto would be speaking to the provost as brazenly as he was. Everyone around the fireplace was silent, tense. Hale seemed, for once, at a loss for words. The air seemed filled with static electricity. I noticed Irina slipping discreetly out and away from the circle.

It was Sarah Hartwell who broke the silence, a fortyish woman in a tailored suit, who conducted MIT's Science and Technology Policy Seminar and wrote semi-monthly op-eds for the *Boston Globe*. "I quite agree with you," she said, directing her gaze at Tsukamoto. "It's all part of Western cultural arrogance, of which the United States is the chief exponent." She glanced about more widely. "You've all heard about ASAT?" she queried. "At least I hope you have. It's been in all the papers."

A few of the group mumbled they'd seen or heard something about it, but most met her remark with puzzled looks.

Hartwell went on, "Well, ASAT is a monstrous piece of anti-satellite technology the U.S. has been building in southern New Mexico. It's this big chemical laser. If the thing works, its supposed to send a beam of concentrated light into satellites to bring them down." She threw up her hands. "We're right back in 'Star Wars,' as if that Reagan creature were still around."

"Shooting at satellites?" muttered a short, balding man standing next to Hale. "What's that all about?"

"The intent is—supposedly—to be able to knock out enemy spy satellites in time of war," said Hartwell. She wrinkled her nose, and went on, "As if we're about to be invaded any time soon. I mean, whose satellites are we planning to shoot down? Good God, no. It's all part of our wanting to dominate the world, even if it means making space a shooting gallery."

"Just a moment," piped up Greg Evans, "a moment, *if* you please." Stocky, ruddy-faced, his straight sandy hair falling to one side, Greg was the same age as me. My best friend at MIT, I'd known him since we'd been grammar school buddies in Boston's Charlestown section. Like me, he was an associate professor at the Cognitive Computing Lab, with an office just a couple of doors down from mine. We'd collaborated on a number of software projects, especially over the last four years or so. Ordinarily a calm guy, he had a hot button when it came to anything political.

"Satellites are crucial to the military," Greg went on. "To our military, and the military of any potential enemy. Which side 'sees' the best has got one hell of an advantage over the other. More and more countries are launching observation satellites, even military satellites that can screw up how *our* satellites work. You may not like it, Ms. Hartwell"—he drew out the Ms. like *Mizzzz*—"but space is already a theater of military operations."

"All I can tell you," Hartwell replied, as Greg swirled the drink in his hand and rocked back and forth on his heels, "is that we need to get negotiations started for a world-wide treaty to permanently ban such technology. You may not be exactly thrilled with that, I imagine." She thrust a finger in Greg's face. "Say, are you one of those physicists? Maybe you even worked on those kinds of lasers?"

"Maybe, and may have," replied Greg as he continued to rock and swirl his drink. "Maybe, and may have."

Win Roberts, a full professor in Brain and Cognitive Sciences, interjected, "Look. What Sarah is saying is that space is for everyone, not just a playground for the U.S." He pushed his ever-present Greek fisherman's cap farther back on his head, and went on, "God knows how our country is crippled with paranoia. It's clearly in our interest, and in the interest of humanity, to get a treaty going that keeps space out of the hands of nuts. And, I'm sorry to say, just now, we're the nut cases."

Greg's face began to redden even more than usual. Hell, I thought, once he smells a Cambridge liberal he goes berserk. And here he was, facing two.

I racked my mind for something to say to switch the subject. Meanwhile, Greg went on, "What's in our interest is to be sure our country is safe from nuts who may want to blow out our communications, or lob a bootlegged nuclear bomb down on Manhattan. You can do either of those neat things from satellites. And even two-bit countries are putting up satellites, or can contract out to some other country who can."

Greg's voice was becoming heated, edgy. Blood was in the water, and the sharks were circling. Economics Professor Lydia Korf, a slight woman with graying bangs and gold-framed reading glasses dangling to her bosom from a thin black ribbon, took the next bite.

"Er...Mr. Evans...Mr. Evans," Korf interjected, with emphasis on the mister. "This contempt for other countries is exactly what our young friend from Japan"—she nodded toward Tsukamoto—"was talking about with regard to the rice issue. It seems it doesn't matter *what* the issue is, we—the U.S.—have got to be top dog. But that anti-satellite laser that Sarah's so rightfully concerned about, we have to kill it, and kill it now, even if we scuttle our program unilaterally. If we want to be friends with the rest of the world, that is, not just lord it over them."

You had to know Greg exceptionally well to spot it, but I could see his right hand wiggle-waggle briefly and ever so slightly, as if he were erasing a blackboard—an unconscious tic developed over years of classroom teaching and triggered upon hearing something illogical, something flat out wrong, or, in the case of Ms. Korf, something he didn't agree with and regarded as totally inane.

Greg gave her a tight smile and countered, "Look, this isn't a friendly world. I wish it were. Remember what happened to the World Trade Center last year on 9/11? God knows what's in store for next year. You got all kinds of people out there who would like to do us in, if they could. The ASAT program is designed so that, in some ways at least, they can't."

"Mr. Evans," resumed Sarah Hartwell, "the U.S. would have more friends around the world, and at home even, if it would just drop its imperialism—cultural, economic, and military. Look at our domestic imperialism toward minorities, the homeless, migrant farm workers. These are national shames. And what about Mexico, Central and South America? Don't tell me we don't have our own 'empire' in our own back yard. And now we want to make space our empire as well." She smiled a tight smile at Greg. Greg was not smiling back.

Good God, I thought, Greg's a centimeter away from shouting. He was up for a promotion, I knew, because I'd been asked to write a supporting letter, one that would eventually cross the provost's desk. Langdon Hale's a fair guy, but you just don't play out a scene like this in front of someone who has to sign off on your promotion.

"Ms. Hartwell! Ms. Hartwell!" Greg barged on, again drawing out the Mizzzz. "Your whole attitude and that of that flaming liberal rag you write for—what is it? *The Boston Globe*?—is that America is what is wrong with the world!"

That was it. Greg was embarrassing himself, the lab, and everyone here standing around him. I felt I had to do something. Anything.

I broke in firmly, "Did you people hear an MIT student was found dead this morning? I…er… I pulled him out of the Charles near Pierce Boathouse, just after dawn."

I hadn't wanted to mention it. It came out automatically, the only thing I could think of to break up things. It did, like a cold bucket of water. All eyes turned to me.

"Yes, Justin Marsh," said Hale, his face suddenly become solemn. "The Cambridge police left me a brief phone message mid-morning, while Cassie and I were at services. They just said it was an Institute faculty who discovered the body. So, it was you who found him?"

I gave a condensed version of how I'd found Justin, omitting the raw details.

Hale said, "Every year, I guess, the Charles claims someone from Tech. Out of four-thousand odd kids you're bound to get a few who become severely depressed, and one or two who go over the edge. Hard to take…"

Everyone was silent. Then Hale, forcing a smile, said, "Heavens, this is supposed to be a party. Please, let's not turn too gloomy. Or," he added, giving Greg a wry glance, "too…too…whatever."

Our circle at the fireplace began to disperse about the room. I was troubled I'd used Justin to save Greg's social neck. Why wouldn't he learn to leave politics at home?

I filched two champagne glasses from a passing tray and went over to where Irina was talking with a plainly dressed middle-aged couple who looked ill at ease amid the grand surroundings.

"Bill, let me present Maureen Murphy and her husband Frank," Irina said as she accepted the glass I proffered. "They've both worked at MIT for thirty-five years now," she continued. "Mr. and Mrs. Murphy, let me present Bill Rundle."

Maureen Murphy gave me a timid smile and extended a pale, puffy hand. Frank was heartier, with a florid, blotchy complexion and a rock-like grip. "Buildings and grounds," he said, "and Maureen here's on the morning counter shift at Walker Memorial cafeteria."

The Murphys were part of that vast army who washed windows, cut grass, painted walls, delivered mail and whatever else at MIT. Hale, I imagined, had invited them to have some MIT "support people" present at his gatherings, his way of endorsing egalitarianism. All well-intended, perhaps, but maybe an ordeal for those who had to be on exhibit.

Irina, I knew, had gravitated to the Murphys instinctively to help them feel more comfortable. Born in Paris of Russian parents who were themselves the children of émigrés, and having lived there up through her college years, Irina could not bring herself, in the U.S., to feel other than a foreigner. Though a naturalized American citizen, her accent—a blend in equal parts of French and Russian—was a constant reminder to herself that she might be *in*, but never would be really *of*, America, in the same way that the Murphys might be, for an evening, in the MIT of Provost Hale—but only for an evening.

The four of us chatted about how MIT had changed over time. How it had been pretty much all men when the Murphys had arrived, though there were beginning to be more women, and now there were so many. How Frank would, nowadays, be cutting down trees and shrubs he had planted in the loam so long ago. How Maureen was still arriving at Walker Memorial cafeteria way before breakfast time to put the juice out and start the sausage and bacon going for the early arrivals.

Our chat with the Murphys was interrupted by a maid at the doorway, gently ringing a lead-crystal bell while announcing that dinner was served. We followed the rest of the guests out into the foyer and across the hall to where the evening banquet had been set up.

Eight circular tables were set in two rows of four down the length of what probably had once been a ballroom, a wing jutting out from the main house. Three sets of French windows, separated by fluted pilasters, accented the walls on either side of the room. An 18th century painting of three exquisite women in pastel gowns filled the wall over the fireplace at the far end.

Irina and I had been placed at separate tables, but I could see her clearly from where I sat, the rakish set of her dark blond hair, the Tatar eyes mischievous, yet warm. At my table, I knew no one except Lydia Korf—and her only by sight and her reputation as an Institute scold, and Hale's wife, Cassandra, or Cassie, as she insisted on being called. The Hales had planned the seating to maximize mixing; I could see Mr. and Mrs. Murphy split asunder, and peering across the room at one another with anxious faces. Even the Japanese coterie had been dispersed about the room.

At our table, Cassie went through introductions: "…And over there is Polly McBride, whom I hear—may I tell, Polly?—just got tenure in Aero and Astro." A modest smile broke across the face of the chubby strawberry blond opposite me. "And," said Cassie as she clutched my arm playfully, "at my right is Bill Rundle who's not up for tenure yet, but they'd better give it to him or they'll break all the ladies' hearts at MIT. Can't understand," she added *sotto voce*, "how any guy that good-looking is still unmarried."

Cassie's words triggered a harsh memory…

I had been married, when I was twenty-six, to Valerie Matignelli, whom I'd met at an MIT dance party. Less than three weeks had gone by when I'd proposed, and for all of seven months we'd been immensely happy in our top floor apartment in Somerville while focusing—the only distraction being one another—on finishing our doctorates, hers at the Institute in molecular biology, mine in experimental psychology at suburban Brandeis University.

Valerie was tall, with hazel eyes and dark lustrous hair—from her Calabrian grandmother, she said—that tumbled down her back nearly to her waist. Possessed of a wondrously athletic yet womanly body, she loved to ski, and more than once I had nearly broken my neck trying to keep up with her.

Would that I had…

We were at Maine's Sunday River ski resort when it happened. A Saturday night, my birthday. We'd been celebrating with friends and I'd more than enough to drink, so Valerie insisted on taking the wheel for the trip back to our lodge.

Snow was falling, the road was poorly lit, and as our Honda Civic swept around a sharp curve an eighteen-wheel lumber truck smashed into us head-on. Valerie—on the driver's side, in place of me—was killed instantly, crushed before my eyes in a tangle of steel and glass. I'd gotten barely a scratch.

In the years since, haunted by that night and convinced I might be calamitous for any wife, I'd never let the few short attachments I'd had get so serious that re-marriage loomed as a possibility. Never, that is, until Irina—if ever I could find it in me to ask her to entrust her fate with me…

I came back from my pained reverie in time to nod hello about the table, and to hear Cassie continue, "…and finally, across from Bill is John Creedon. John's been so generous to MIT with donations from all that money pouring into his coffers from making… from making…" She tossed her wonderful head of blue-white hair and asked laughingly, "John, just what are those things you make?"

"Well, our newest products are super-conductor circuits for laser systems," replied Creedon affably. He was slender, with regular, finely honed features set under black wavy hair just beginning to gray. His rich tan signaled someone who didn't depend upon the local sun.

That tan may have been what set me off in a *déjà vu*. I'd seen him before; in fact, I had met him. It was two years back and so slight an encounter that I was sure he didn't remember it at all. We were at the Broadmoor Hotel in Colorado Springs, site of the Western Interface Conference, where I'd given a talk on graphical dialogue systems. Creedon was to be the keynoter that evening, already a legend in the world of high-tech, with his patents, his booming company, his jet-set personal style that even included bankrolling an America's Cup yachting syndicate—his gilt-edge Weston Group. All day long the small talk had been about him, and there he was, before me, as I stepped into the hotel elevator.

In contrast to the staid suit he now had on, he'd worn white ducks and a tailored blue blazer. He was as tan then as now, with an equally bronzed blond on his arm, stunning in a sleeveless white dress. I must have been staring, since they were both looking back at me across the elevator car with the cool self-possession you see in the faces of models in ads for expensive Scotch. I said to him, "Excuse me, but I think I recognize you from your photos. You're John Creedon, aren't you? I'm Bill Rundle from MIT. I'm looking forward to your address tonight."

He extended a firm handshake, fixing me with steady gray eyes.

"Nice to meet you," he said in a clear, crisp voice. "I was over at MIT just last week talking with Seth Mowrer. Know him?"

"No. It's a big place. Heard enough about him, though." Seth Mowrer was a star professor at MIT's Sloan School of Business. Nobel Prize in Economics. Advising trade ministries. Heading presidential commissions. No, I couldn't say Seth Mowrer was a buddy of mine.

"Exciting place, MIT. Don't get by there often enough." Creedon smiled graciously as he and the tanned blonde exited at the fifth floor.

I pulled my mind back to the dinner table at the Hale home. But my eyes must have glazed for a microsecond or two, because Creedon said, "Have we met before? You look as if you…"

25

I told him we'd met at the Interface Conference, briefly amidst the event's flurry. "Well, hello again, then," he said pleasantly.

Polite chatter continued as the appetizer, a cold asparagus soup, was served. I could see Greg Evans across the way chatting peaceably enough at his table. Maybe he could manage to keep it all in for the rest of the evening.

"Are any of your company's products—ZIDEX isn't it?—used by the military, Mr. Creedon?" asked Lydia Korf, who was seated next to me.

"Well, some of our stuff could be, I suppose," Creedon said. "Super-conducting laser technology might have uses such as in imaging for reconnaissance."

"Could those imaging systems be used with ASAT anti-satellite technology? Could your technology shoot down satellites?" asked Professor Korf.

Dear Lord, I prayed silently, let us not go down that path again.

Creedon replied, "Well, what I've heard of ASAT is that the lasers they use are much more powerful, to say the least, than what my firm deals in. Imaging systems—using our lasers—can be used in satellites for surveillance. For instance, such systems could help monitor a nation's compliance with provisions of a disarmament treaty." Creedon paused, and added, "Including our own compliance."

Professor Korf seemed pleased and mollified by Creedon's last point. He had read her well.

It was nearly eleven when the gathering at the Hales' finally broke up, and people headed for their cars. Irina and I had almost reached ours when a voice ahead of us called, "Hey, can you guys give me a lift back to town?"

It was Greg Evans, waving a hand across to us over the raised hood of his elderly Pontiac. With his other hand, he pointed down at the silent engine of his car. "It was threatening to die on the way out here, and it just made good on its promise."

I told him we'd be happy to give him a ride back to Cambridge, and that we'd enjoy the company.

"Let me just tell the Hales that the abandoned wreck in their drive will be towed tomorrow morning," Greg said. "I'll be right back."

A moment later Greg reappeared, crossed the walk, and tumbled into the rear seat of my Jeep Cherokee. We pulled out of the Hales' drive, and headed toward Route 2 back to Cambridge.

"God, that's awful about Justin," Greg said over my shoulder. "I can't believe he's not going to be there when I go to the lab tomorrow. How could it have happened?"

"One of our theories is that it's an accident," I said. "For some reason he was out there sitting on the railing and lost his balance and fell in."

"Sitting on the railing—this time of year?" said Greg. "Or even just tumbling over it? That's hard to figure. With the height of the railing and the width of the ledge, you really'd have to make an effort to clear it all and land in the water."

"That's just it," I said. "Making the effort suggests that it's a suicide. But Justin? I can't see it. It's got to be an accident, or…"

"An accident?" Greg cut in. "But Justin was a good swimmer, wasn't he? Remember the lab outing up at Crane's Beach last summer? Hell, the guy could swim like a fish."

"There was a mark on the side of his head," I said. "A welt, or a gash, or something. If he fell accidentally, he might have hit his head on the embankment wall and been out cold when he hit the water."

We drove on in silence. A truck bore down behind us, its high beams flooding the Cherokee. It sat right on our tail. I was in no mood to accelerate, so I slowed to force it to go around me. It did. Out of the corner of my eye I could see the driver extending his arm in a vigorous middle-finger salute. Merry Christmas to you, too, fella.

"You're going to miss Justin particularly, aren't you, Greg?" Irina said softly. "You had so many projects going on with him."

"Yeah…yeah, that's for sure," answered Greg. "He was the key grad assistant in our virtual reality simulation stuff. He could do it all—the math, the graphics algorithms, the acoustics. Anything you gave him, it came out golden. It's not only the personal loss, but it'll be a long time before we get another student like that."

Greg was silent for a moment, and then went on, "Bill, remember the tug of war you and I had about who'd Justin hitch up with for his thesis topic? But I guess we'd have ended up all of us collaborating, with both you and I on his doctoral committee."

"Yeah, that would have been pretty good," I said.

The snow, light and intermittent all day and evening, had turned to a hard rain. I turned up the wipers to full speed. We passed the Cambridge Gateway Inn motel and Lanes & Games on the right as we neared the end of Route 2 at Alewife Brook Parkway.

Greg leant forward and said, "So they—the cops—think he fell in, and hit his head on something on the way? But wouldn't that wake him up? The water, I mean. Like a pail of water in the face?"

I wished Greg hadn't returned to the subject of Justin. But I couldn't blame him. I was just as curious about the truth of what had happened.

"Yeah, I asked about that at the station," I answered. "They said it depends on where on the head he was hit, and how hard. He could have been out cold, and then, with a few breaths, be drowning without really coming to. But they won't know exactly what happened until they do an autopsy."

We swung by Fresh Pond Shopping Center, and through the traffic rotary just beyond. "There's a nasty detail I left out," I told Greg. "About Justin, when I found him. His eye was missing."

Greg recoiled. "God, that's weird," he said. "I mean it would have to be some bird or fish, wouldn't it? For something like that to happen?"

"I don't know. I don't even want to think about it."

We drove down Concord Avenue to Garden Street, then headed for Harvard Square. The rain beat down. On our right, a skinny dog cowered against the wall of the Sheraton Commander Hotel.

"Anyway, it's all up to the police at this point," I said. "I don't know what they make of the eye business. Maybe they'll call it an accident 'til they get something that makes them think otherwise."

We stopped at the light on Mass Ave., then continued on to the underpass to Broadway. At Prescott Street, we took a left, and pulled up in front of Greg's apartment building.

"Do you still get free rent for doing duty as your building's jan... er, custodian?" I asked Greg, tongue in cheek.

"Don't knock it, Bill," Greg replied as he swung out of the rear door. "With Cambridge rents up where they are, I'm happy to haul out the ashes."

Irina jumped out her door into the rain, and gave Greg a hug and— bidding him a Merry Christmas—three kisses in the Russian style, on alternate cheeks. Greg leapt for his doorway with its granite staircase and wrought iron balustrades. He disappeared behind the outer door as Irina got back into the car.

We drove back the way we came, toward Harvard Square.

"This thing about Justin must be awful for Greg," Irina said. "They worked so closely. I hope it doesn't get him too down."

I pulled the Cherokee over to the curb on Mass Ave. across from the Leavitt and Pierce tobacco store. Irina and I got out, and we crossed over in the pelting rain to the door of her building, a red brick presence owned by Harvard but managed by one of Boston's big name real estate outfits.

We entered, and walked up the staircase to Irina's door. She unlocked it and turned to me. "I'd ask you in," she said, "but it's late and I still have a couple of hours of work to do for tomorrow morning's meeting at the Davis Center."

I brushed her hair with my hand. "I missed you at my table," I said. "Missed you, too," she answered. I kissed her gently. She went into her apartment and closed the door behind. I went downstairs to my car and drove back to my apartment on Irving Street.

I got in bed. Despite my lack of sleep and the long evening, I was too keyed up to nod off. If I closed my eyes, grotesque images of sodden hair and empty eye sockets arose in the darkness about me. And when, for a moment, I let my arm trail off the side of the bed, I could feel again the brush of an icy hand with fingers like the tines of a garden rake.

I got up, heated some milk, and laced it with a generous belt of Myers dark rum. Taking the concoction in hand, I decided to distract myself with a quick look at my email. I went to the Macintosh on my living room desk, powered it up, and logged in.

I riffled through some messages about pending visits by lab sponsors, a couple of announcements of upcoming conferences, a listing of when next year's faculty meetings were scheduled. The seventh message stunned me.

from marsh@ccl.cognition.mit.edu
to rundle@ccl.cognition.mit.edu
sent Mon 19 December 00.10.00
received Mon 19 December 00.30.33
message id <936748304-66.7>
status: R

Dr Rundle:

If you get this something has happened to me. You are the only one I think I can trust with this. Keep it safe till I get in touch...

Justin

Appended to the message was a file bearing more than six thousand lines of letters and digits, mixed together and totally incomprehensible—but just may have cost Justin his life.

Chapter 4

"The usual, Bill? Deep dish raspberry and cheese croissants for two?"

It was 11:27 a.m. Monday after Hale's party, and Harry Mirsky had just swung into Au Bon Pain in Kendall Square at the corner of Main and Hayward Streets. I'd asked Harry to meet me there at eleven; he was late, as usual, but I didn't mind. If anyone could help me figure what it was that Justin had sent, it was Harry.

Harry plunked his briefcase on the chair opposite. He doffed his light brown parka and draped it half over the briefcase, half trailing on the floor.

Pale from a life indoors, more than just a bit overweight, with thinning shoulder-length sandy hair, scraggly beard, and wire-framed half-spectacles, his looks suggested Benjamin Franklin gone to seed. His rumpled white shirt—replete with multi-hued ink stains despite an ever-present pocket protector—topped baggy khaki-colored twill trousers that billowed out beneath his ample waist.

Before I could reply to his inquiry, he sped toward the counter. "You want decaf, right?" he hurled over his shoulder. I nodded, but he was already placing the order.

Harry is a genius. An I.Q. genius, that is. He had goofed off in high school, and even was one of those shaggy guys, so he said, who hung around on street corners revving up motorcycles—Harleys with ape-hanger handlebars and exhausts that blast out 120 decibels. His mother was a widow and in despair for her only child, who never went to synagogue and never did anything with his mind except for

31

an occasional game of chess with a neighbor, a retired lawyer who lived two houses down.

But that retired lawyer had been a rated player, and Harry used to beat him all the time. He told Harry, so the story goes, maybe—just maybe—you have a mind. Why not take some aptitude tests? Twenty miles from where Harry lived was Northwestern University, where, for a small fee, you could get the psychology department to give you a test battery.

Harry took the battery, for the hell of it. He scored—so Harry said the Northwestern guidance counselor had put it—forty points above the highest score that could be related to a meaningful I.Q. That top meaningful I.Q. was 169, and Harry had left it in the dust.

Well, he entered Northwestern on a scholarship, packed all of undergrad college into a year and a half, and finished his Ph.D. in applied math at U. of Pennsylvania at the age of nineteen years, three months. After that, he landed an instructor's job at MIT, first in the math department, and then in the Electrical Engineering and Computer Science department. That was thirteen years ago. Now a full professor, he held a joint appointment at EE & CS and at the Cognitive Computing Lab, where we'd become colleagues and friends.

The nice thing about Harry was that, for all his smarts, he had no pretensions of being a Von Neumann or an Einstein. "I'm not a real genius like those guys," he'd say. "A third-rate genius, maybe. But with what you get for your money nowadays, that's not so bad."

What Harry could do, though, was take a lot of complexity in his head at one time, keep it all straight, and work it every which way about. The kind of friend to have when stuck with the kind of puzzle Justin had just presented me.

He returned with a loaded tray, pushed his briefcase off onto the floor with his knee, and settled in the chair across from me.

"Jeez, that's tough about Justin," he said. "I still can't believe it."

I'd sent a broadcast email to lab personnel first thing in the morning, and Harry had seen it along with my note asking him to meet me. He pushed my coffee across the table toward me, along with my raspberry cheese croissant. Clearing his throat, he asked, "Ok, what's this message stuff?"

I reached in my case and removed a printout of Justin's message— the coded part only, without the personal note at the top. It was over 190 fan-folded pages. I set it before Harry. "This is either gibberish," I told him, "or pretty damned important. Nothing in between. Take a look."

Harry took the printout and began to pore rapidly over the pages. He said nothing, just chewed on his croissant. Several minutes went by. He asked, "Can I mark this up?" I said OK.

He pulled a ballpoint pen out of his pocket protector and began to make little slashes in green ink here and there among the lines of print. He jotted loops around swatches of letters, dividing them into groups. He made little balloons around some of the groups, and connected them with lines. Maybe five minutes went by like that. Finally, he looked up. I leaned forward in anticipation.

"You know, Bill," he said, waving the last morsel of his croissant, "walking over here, I really got sad about what's happened to Kendall Square." He popped the last of the croissant in his mouth. "Like they really destroyed this whole area when they brought down the old F&T diner. Do you remember that place?" He glanced over his shoulder and out the window. "Used to be up the street there a bit?"

"Yeah," I nodded. "But please, Harry, focus on the…"

"The old Fart & Talk," Harry cut in. "Now, there was a greasy spoon for you. But a great one. You know what my favorite was?"

I knew better than even to try to reply. He skipped a beat, and plunged on.

"Well, it was hot pastrami on a bulkie. Get that, a hot pastrami on a bulkie. These Yuppies or whatever that go around here with their low-fat diets, why, they'd shoot the thing on sight. You got grease all over your fingers, your chin, all over your shirt. Your pants, maybe. God, they were something. With a dark brew. I used to like Bass Ale and Guinness Stout, mixed half and half. What'd they used to call that?"

"Harry, I think it's…"

"Oh, yeah—'Black-and-Tan.' 'Half-and-Half,' though, if you're using Harp's." He plunged back into the printout, flicking marks down the page with the green pen.

Ten more minutes went by.

"Bill…" he murmured, looking up.

Finally. He'd cracked it. Great.

"Right, Harry, I'm listening," I said. I braced myself.

"Bill, can you get me another one of those raspberry cheese croissants? They're lousy. But great, anyway. You know what I mean? Like Drake Devil Dogs? Lousy-great. They may never make the junk food hall of fame, like Devil Dogs, but I'll take another anyway."

He reached into his pocket, took out a wrinkled wad of dollar bills, and thrust it at me.

"And another coffee," he added. "Get yourself whatever, too."

I pushed his money back, and went to get Harry his croissant and coffee. I got just water for myself. I sat down, pushed the tray under his eyes so he could see to refuel.

Another five minutes went by. Harry kept munching and swigging his coffee while he made more loops and slashes on the fan-folded printout, which now hung festooned between our table and two spare chairs.

We were beginning to get stares from other customers. One of the clerks behind the counter was saying something to the manager, who was looking our way. Maybe they were grousing about MIT kooks, or worse, perhaps getting set to throw us out.

The lunch crowd was beginning to gather, too, and tables were filling up. I waved to Greg Evans as he came through the door with a couple of his grad students. "I'd invite you guys to join us," I said to Greg as he and the students sidled by on their way to the counter, "but we're…in the midst of something."

"I can see that," said Greg, his eyes taking in the mounting clutter of printout. "Talk to you later," he called with a bemused smile.

I was getting uneasy. "Harry…"

The munching and marking stopped. "Yeah?"

"Talk to me. Tell me what you're thinking."

Harry shifted his bulk in his chair. He reached and brushed some crumbs of croissant from his beard.

"OK," he said finally. "I can tell you what it's not. It's not some long thing in plain English—like Winston Churchill's autobiography, or whatever—that just happened to get garbled by transmission glitches. It's not some random memory dump. It's not an encoded image."

"Great. But any idea what it is?" I said. I felt moronic pressuring him. Neither I, nor anyone else I knew, or knew of, could even begin to do what he was doing.

"Yeah. It looks like some combination of program and data. Not absolutely certain, but pretty much." Harry's eyelids squinted together, his eyes becoming slits, a kind of don't-shit-me look he must have perfected in his motorcycle days. "Do you mind telling me again where you got this?"

"Harry, it's like I told you. It arrived in my email shortly after midnight. It's from Justin Marsh."

The slits became even narrower.

"Not from Justin, I mean. From his computer. He must have rigged it to send me this if he didn't log onto his machine at certain intervals."

Harry sat back. "Well, at least this is something from Justin and not some hot code you boosted from Microsoft or Cisco or whomever."

Harry looked at his watch. Re-capping his pen, he said, "I need to work it over more. Can I take the printout with me? Do you have it on a floppy disk as well?"

I took out a disk copy I'd made of the code and handed it to Harry. He folded up the printout, assured me he'd not let it out of his sight, and jammed it, along with the disk, deep in his briefcase. He stood up, brushed the croissant debris from his lap, and helped me pile up the paper plates, cups, and napkins.

"You going back to the lab?" I asked.

"Naw, I'm heading over to Tech Square. Walk you part way, though."

We left Au Bon Pain, and headed up Main Street.

"You know, I wasn't able to buy one of those booths," Harry said.

"What booths, Harry?"

"Those old wooden booths. From the F&T, when they were going to rip it all down. I wanted one for my kitchen. Or maybe the dining room. Anyway, when I got around to asking them they said it was all spoken for—the bar, the booths, everything. The F&T regulars beat me to it. All I got was one stupid brick for a paperweight. Grabbed it the morning they knocked the walls down."

We'd reached the Kendall subway station entrance by the MIT Press bookstore. "Hey, I'll be in touch," Harry said, and he cut across Main Street toward Legal Seafood and his office in Tech Square.

Back at my office at the Cognitive Computing Lab, I tried to focus on work. I printed out a copy of the proposal I had sent yesterday afternoon to Etherington and began to comb it for glitches. It kept me distracted till about 2:30, but my mind kept coming back to Justin, his battered face, his cryptic message.

I dialed the number where Justin and Karen had been living, and Karen answered. Her voice seemed collected. She said the police had come by Sunday morning, had told her everything including my finding his body, and had questioned her at length.

I recalled Haggerty's words. Nice going, I thought, you guys with all the experience with breaking such news…

I asked could I come by and talk with her? Was she up to it? She said yes, but that I should come by right away, because she was leaving around four o'clock for Hamilton to visit again with Justin's mother. I set out to East Parking Garage, got in my car, and headed for Karen's.

Chapter 5

Karen and Justin had been living in a green triple-decker on Antrim Street, just off Inman Square, a mixed neighborhood of academics and blue-collars. I pushed the button under the tag "Hewitt/Marsh" and, at the buzzer, opened the door and climbed to the second floor. The hallway was immaculate: painted an off-white eggshell, accented with rich, dark wainscoting. At the second landing, I went down a short hallway where Karen was waiting, hand resting upon the open door.

Tall, maybe five-ten, with striking blue eyes, she wore her long, dark hair as she usually did, twisted in a thick braid. She had on blue jeans and a black ribbed turtleneck. She looked very beautiful and very sad.

She stepped back and, beckoning me inside, gently closed the door.

"Come into the kitchen. Please. I'm making coffee," she said. She led me into her kitchen and gestured for me to sit at an oak trestle table opposite an antique cast-iron stove. She poured out two mugs of coffee from a tall, tapered pot—the kind you see sitting on campfires in Western movies—and set one of them on the table in front of me. She sat down opposite, one hand cradling her coffee, the other shading her eyes. When she took her hand down, I could see fresh tears, which she quickly wiped away.

"Karen," I said, "I am so sorry about Justin."

"Oh, God," she said, "it couldn't have been easy for you, finding him like that." She put down her coffee mug and reached across the table and put her hand on my arm. "What...what did he look like? When you found him, I mean? I want to know."

As gently as I could, I described how I had found Justin. I decided not to tell her about the missing eye. For now, anyway. Would she have known whether he had a false eye? Probably. But I couldn't bring all that up.

She rose from her chair and walked in a slow circle about the kitchen floor. She pulled a small handkerchief from out of her jeans pocket, dabbed at her eyes, and sat down again.

She said, "Why would anyone kill him?"

"Karen, the police think he might have..."

"Oh, no!" she said angrily. "Justin didn't kill himself. Somebody did this to him. I don't care what the police say." She took a moment to compose herself. "I'm sorry," she said, "I didn't mean to jump at you like that."

I nodded, and looked away. Then she said, "You knew him. You found him. Tell me, do you think he killed himself?"

I looked back at her. "No, I don't," I said. "I think it was murder. I think someone killed him."

She rose in her chair, and said heatedly, "Then why don't you do something? Why don't you tell the police? Why don't *they* do something?"

"Karen," I said, "I think they do suspect Justin was killed, that it wasn't an accident. It's just the way they talk, the way they do things. They're looking into it." I didn't say so to Karen, but one of the directions in which they'd probably be looking was at me.

Karen settled back into the chair across the table from me. I asked her, "Think hard. Is there anyone, anyone at all, who might have reason to—to want to harm him?"

She got up and, carrying her coffee mug, again circled the kitchen. "The police asked me that, again and again. There just isn't anybody. Anybody." She looked at me pleadingly.

"What about other things he was doing, besides his research assistantship at the lab?" I asked.

"I don't know what to tell you," she said. "There was mostly his work at the Cognitive Computing Lab. And worrying about a thesis idea. And he and I. Our relationship was…well, strong, but not all that smooth at times." She went over to the window and stared out at a leafless tree in the yard. "We were planning to go to New Orleans for spring break. To get away from Cambridge for a while."

She continued to look out at the bare branches, her arms wrapped around her waist as if warding off the cold. She went on, "But there isn't anyone or anything, like you're asking. There wasn't anyone who would just kill him. I mean, anyone who knew him or had something against him. It's got to be muggers…people who'd… who'd…" Her voice choked off. She bent forward and, with closed eyes, rocked slowly back and forth in front of the window.

We were both silent for what must have been only a minute or two, but seemed infinitely longer. A large buff-colored cat with a graying muzzle wandered slowly into the kitchen from the hall, and over to a small aluminum no-spill bowl on the floor by the refrigerator. It licked half-heartedly at the rim of the dish. I watched it pick at the pellets of food.

Finally, Karen turned to me and spoke. "Last summer and into the fall, he worked at some place out on Route 128. It was for maybe twelve weeks. At night. Sometimes he'd work all…" She paused, looked away, and looked back. "I know what you're thinking. With his research assistantship, he wasn't supposed to be doing outside work, was he?"

"No, I guess he wasn't," I said. "Volunteer work's OK, but not jobs for money."

"This wasn't for money. He said it was a non-profit project, and he was donating his time. He wouldn't tell me what the project was about. Just that it was very important to him, and he'd show me it when it was all done."

"What was the name of the place?"

"One of those high-tech companies. Its name sounded—well, high-tech. I could never remember the name of it."

"What about phone calls? Were there people who called him a lot, or at odd hours—people you didn't know?"

"Not really. A few months back, there was this man who'd occasionally call at night, maybe nine-thirty, ten o'clock. I'd just tell him—he'd never give his name—to try the Cognitive Computing Lab. He'd just say thanks, and hang up."

"Did he have the number? I mean, the very first time he called, did you have to give him the number at MIT, or did he already have it?"

She screwed her face up. "I don't know. It's hard to…I think he didn't ask…but I'm not really sure."

"What was his voice like?"

"Kind of…well, not too young. Not a student, I mean. Very precise speech, like he could have been British. It was a nice voice, very pleasant."

"How long did the calls keep coming?"

"There were just a few, like I said, late last summer. Then they stopped."

"Did you tell all this to the police?"

"Yes. They asked about phone calls, just like you did now."

I felt uncomfortable putting Karen through the same hoops. I felt uneasy, too, that I was exploring the same paths the police were. I probably shouldn't be doing it. But this was about Justin, not some stranger I'd read about in the newspaper.

I pushed my coffee mug away and rose from my chair.

"Karen, I should go. I'm sorry to have put you through this, asking these questions."

She reached across the table and took my hand.

"It's OK. He talked a lot about you. He felt you were always square with him. He felt he could trust you." I thought of what Justin had said in his email message. "Yes," she repeated, "he felt he could trust you."

We both walked slowly down the corridor to her apartment door, arms linked. The buff cat trailed after us, meowing softly.

We reached the door. "Do you have anyone to talk to?" I asked.

"Yeah. There's Francie and Skip, upstairs. They own the house. She's at the Sloan School. He's an architect. That's why the house is kept so nice. They've been real kind. Then there's my mother. I've been on the phone with her a lot. And now I'm going back up to Justin's mother. She's comforting me and trying to be brave, but it must be so hard on her, being alone and losing her only child."

We gave each other a kind of father-daughter hug.

I said goodbye, and started down the stairs. At the foot of the staircase, I turned and glanced back up. Karen was holding the cat like a fur muff. As I was closing the outside door behind me I heard Karen call out, "ZIDEX."

I swung the door back open.

"That's the place Justin worked at out on Route 128 last summer. I just remembered. It's ZIDEX. Z-I-D-E-X."

"Thanks," I said, and shut the door.

Chapter 6

I drove back to MIT from Karen's apartment. So Justin had worked at ZIDEX. That was John Creedon's company, somewhere out in Waltham, where his people, among other things, made the laser technology he had spoken about with Cassie at the Hales' dinner party. I'd have to think up some pretext to contact Creedon, chat him up, and turn the topic to Justin and what he might have done at ZIDEX. Most likely, given his corporate responsibilities, Creedon wouldn't be aware that a certain MIT grad student named Justin Marsh had worked for him last summer; he could, though, connect me with someone at ZIDEX who would know.

I parked my car at East Parking Garage and headed out past the Ralph Landau Building, its sharp triangular edge thrusting forward like the prow of a cement ocean liner. I crossed Ames Street by the MIT Media Lab, an I. M. Pei confection sheathed in two-foot square aluminum tiles, then turned left and on down Amherst Street to the Cognitive Computing Lab, and took the elevator to my office on the third floor.

A cluster of pink "While You Were Out…" slips was taped to my door. One, from SUN Microsystems, asked whether I still wanted the quote on their new workstation. (I did.) Another from the Boston Computing Society wanting to know if I would speak at their February meeting. Honorarium: a free supper. (I'd think about it.) Another, from Channel 8, wondered whether I'd do an interview for their "Science Scene" series. (Oh, why not?) Another was from a former student asking for a job reference. (A talented, positive person—happy to do that.) Yet another was from an assistant professor at U. of Colorado, up for tenure—would I be a reference? (Not all that impressed with his work and articles; I'd have to think of a graceful way to say no.)

Then I spotted one that said Harry had called at 4:05, and would I please call back.

I punched out his extension number, heard four rings, then Harry's recorded message. Hell, I'd missed him, I thought, but then his voice broke through, asking—he could see my extension number come up on his phone's display—"Bill, it's you, right?"

"It's me, Harry. Anything yet?"

"Yeah, I got something. Not all of it yet, but it's coming. It's a program, plus a lot of data packed in below it. The data drives the program."

"Can you tell what kind of program?"

I heard an exasperated grunt on the other end of the line.

"Bill, the sonofabitch is encrypted. That's why it's been taking so long. I can tell what's going on with the thing generally, but some parts are real ballbusters."

"But any clue at all to what kind of program it is?"

"It's an expert system. One that's been modified a lot to be heavy on input/output. But, yeah, I think it's an expert system."

Expert systems are programs that embody knowledge about some area, like medicine or petroleum geology. Typically, they consist of an "inference engine"—the instructions that perform the program's logic—and a "knowledge base"—the set of rules that embody the expertise. Expert systems in medicine often produced better diagnoses than some human doctors did. Other expert systems helped petroleum prospecting firms sift through geologic and seismic data to decide where to drill for the next big gusher.

I pushed Harry for more. "What does it do?" I asked. "What's it 'expert' about?"

Silence. I could hear what sounded like a pencil tapping in the background.

"Harry?"

More silence. More tapping. Then Harry said, "You know, Rundle, you piss me off. You give me this thing at eleven or so just this morning. I've had this seminar from one-thirty to three. It's maybe five or thereabouts now. Who else do you think could crack this friggin' thing, anyway?"

Big egos need grooming at times. "Harry, you're maybe the only person who could even begin to pull it apart."

"Betcha ass," he replied. "Well, maybe not the only one. Maybe there's two, three others. There's this guy at Stanford; not too convenient for you, though. Someone else at Carnegie-Mellon. Nah, she's in Israel now, on sabbatical. Even less convenient. So, maybe a couple of others could figure this out from scratch. Maybe not. Anyway, I'm the nearest."

I could feel his dander dropping.

"And my fee's reasonable," he added. "Like maybe I won't even charge you for this. Like it's more fun than the Sunday *Times* crossword."

Harry could do the Sunday *New York Times* crossword in thirteen minutes on average, in ballpoint. Most of those minutes were consumed simply by the effort of jotting the letters on paper, writing as fast as he could. I tell anyone who's not impressed, clock yourself next time you do one. And do it in ink.

"Harry, I appreciate this. I truly do."

"Yeah?" Pause. "Well, OK. Like be patient, huh? Be in touch." I heard a click, then silence.

My thoughts drifted back to my visit with Karen Hewitt. I could see her face in my mind's eye, its gentleness, its anguish. Yes, why don't the police do something? Why don't I do something?

I picked up the phone and called Lt. Haggerty. It was about 5:15, but maybe he hadn't left police headquarters yet. I was correct on that, but dead wrong if I was thinking he'd let me in on anything.

"Rundle, this is a police matter. We'll handle it."

"I'm just curious if there were any new developments. He was my student, you know."

"I know that."

"Could you tell me just one thing?"

"Depends. What?"

"Why was the eye socket so clean? It looked like it had been taken out by a surgeon."

Silence.

I tried another tack. "Was it just one eye gone, or was it both? I saw only one gone. The left one."

Again, silence.

"Do you think he was a suicide? Or was…"

"Rundle, all of this is under investigation. You know as much as we do." He paused. "Maybe more," he added.

I pushed on. "Lieutenant, did he have water in his lungs? I mean, if he didn't, then he was killed before he was in the river."

All that came over the phone was a silence like a scowl. Finally, Haggerty said, "What do you spend your evenings doing, Rundle? Watching reruns of *NYPD Blue*?"

I said nothing, and Haggerty went on.

"For your information, Rundle, his lungs were full of water."

"Then it has to be a suicide—right?"

"It's not that easy. There was water in his lungs all right, but it may not be Charles River water. The lab's still checking on that."

"Then how could…"

"Right. How could?"

We were both silent for a moment, then I said, "I told you all I know, Lieutenant. You have my statement."

"Yeah, we have all that. If you think of anything that should be added, contact me."

My mind raced. Should I tell Haggerty about Justin's message? My guess was he'd just take it, clam up, and I'd never know what it was of Justin's I'd betrayed. Justin had told me to keep his file safe, whatever "safe" might mean. No, I'd wait. When Harry had the puzzle unraveled, and I knew what it was all about, perhaps then I'd pass it on.

The entire business was fraying my nerves. Charges of "withholding evidence" flashed through my mind. What kind of hole was I digging for myself?

Haggerty's voice broke through my agitated thoughts. "I've got to cut out. Call me right away, you think of anything."

"I'll do that."

"Anything, anything at all."

The phone clicked.

His pointed refrain of "anything" unnerved me further. Good God, I thought, was Haggerty psychic? Could he hear deception in my voice? Or did he know there had been a message, knew or guessed that I had it, and was just stringing me along, letting me tie myself in incriminating knots?

I glanced at my watch. Five-thirty. Time to pack it up.

I quickly sorted the papers on my desktop into file folders: to do, to answer, to file. I put a blue folder on top—the one that held my much-neglected book draft. Working title: *Talking with Machines*. My resolution to put at least an hour per day in on it had been repeatedly bumped by appointments, meetings, demos, visitors, proposal writing. I resolved to resolve for New Year's that next year would be The-Year-the-Book-Gets-Done.

I heard a soft rustling behind me. I wheeled around just in time to see a large gray envelope sliding under my door. Lettering on it announced "MIT - Interdepartmental." I took it to be a routine, late in the day delivery—most likely the MIT Industrial Liaison Office sending confirming agenda for some upcoming visit by industry VIPs, or maybe the lab's business office copying me on a sponsor contract. I rose from my chair and fetched the envelope from the floor.

It was taped shut, with "Personal" and "Confidential" carefully lettered on it in red marker. I pulled off the tape and opened the clasp. Inside was a single sheet of bond. The typed note read:

```
12/19


Professor Rundle:


Put all of what Justin Marsh sent you
on a high-density floppy disk, or disks
```

```
if more than one is needed. Use PC
format. Make three sets. Seal each set
in 8" x 10" mailer. Leave the outside
of the mailer unmarked.
Delete ALL copies of what Marsh sent
you from your own files.
Leave one set of disks at each of
these locations:
1) Barker Engineering Library, 7th
floor carrel in area where Scientific
American journal bound back issues are
kept;
2) under the Isaac Newton Tree in the
courtyard north of building 10;
3) on the moat wall of the MIT Chapel,
on the side facing Kresge Auditorium.

Place them, YOU ALONE, walking
delivery route in 1, 2, 3 order, per
above. Walk between 10:00 and 10:30
a.m. tomorrow morning.
Repeat: do this alone. TELL NO ONE.
Follow instructions to the letter.
Else, you will come to grievous harm.
```

I dropped the letter, dashed to the door, flung it open, and looked both ways. No one.

I turned right, and ran to the end of the corridor. Turning the corner, I saw a figure halfway down the hall, pushing a small cart toward me. Gil Francis, one of the night custodial crew. I ran up to him.

"Gil, did you see anyone in the hall just now?"

"Hi, Bill! No, no one around here. All out Christmas shopping, I guess."

"You didn't see or hear anyone?"

Gil looked intently over his wire frame spectacles, which—as always—sat crookedly on his face. As with a picture frame hanging askew on the wall, you had to fight the impulse to straighten them.

"Nobody, just like I said. Somethin' wrong?"

"No," I lied. "Just thought I heard some funny noises."

I thanked him, and walked back toward my office. I'd had a fifty percent chance of running in the right direction to catch whomever, and had run the wrong way.

Just beyond my door, I saw light coming from Greg Evans' office. Maybe he'd seen someone or something. I went up to his doorway. I could see him inside, bent over his desk, unpacking a cardboard carton. Styrofoam peanuts tumbled everywhere.

"Just in time, Bill! My new laptop. Guy just delivered it. You know, this has…"

I cut him off. "Did you see anyone go by in the hall?"

"Yeah. The delivery guy."

"No, not a delivery guy. Someone else. Someone who looked like they…" My voice trailed off. I had no idea how they might look.

"Bill, what's up?" Greg asked, his face full of concern. "You look like you've seen a ghost."

I must have looked a bit frantic. Problem was I *didn't* see the ghost. "You sure you didn't see or hear anyone going by in the hall?"

"Nobody. Just the guy who delivered this, a moment before you came in here."

Whoever it was had completely eluded me.

"Thanks, Greg. Sorry to be so—so wound up." I turned and started out the door.

The delivery man.

I wheeled about. "The delivery man, Greg! Did you ever see him before?"

Greg, startled, looked up at me again.

"No," Greg answered, a puzzled look on his face. "He was just some guy from UPS. Did you know, a lot of the UPS guys are women now?"

"Are you sure he was from UPS?"

Greg wrinkled his face. "You know, I didn't really notice. He was medium height, glasses, stocky build. Kind of oriental looking. Eurasian, maybe."

"Did he have a UPS uniform on?" I asked again.

Greg squinted at me, then replied. "Bill, you know, I don't think he did. Just some kind of dark shirt and dark pants. Down jacket."

"So he could have been just anybody with a package who wanted to get into the building?"

Greg gave me a what-the-hell-is-eating-you look. I couldn't blame him.

"Yeah, I suppose…" Greg paused, then continued in a sympathetic tone. "You know, he may actually have had a UPS uniform on. I don't even know what the hell their uniforms look like. You know, there are these studies on eyewitness reports. This psychologist at University of Washington—what's her name? Anyway, she shows how people say they've seen all kinds of things that really weren't there. And they miss things that were there. Even when they really believe they were paying attention."

"Thanks, Greg. Sorry to sound so strange."

He looked at me solicitously. "You've been through a lot, Bill. It's OK to act a little, you know, funny at times."

"Yeah. I guess I'm pretty wound up."

Greg brightened, and turned back to his carton. He lifted out his new laptop computer, sealed in plastic sheeting, either side still stuck in pressed-pellet packing supports. "Say, you want to see the back-lit screen on this baby?" He pulled off the packing and started to slit the sheeting with his letter opener. "It's really something. I tried out a demo model in this really bright room. Didn't wash out. It really stands up."

"Thanks, but no. I'm closing up for the day."

I left Greg to gloat over his laptop by himself and went back to my office, where I noticed I'd left the door open. What else might have happened while I was running around the halls, talking with Gil and Greg?

Nothing looked touched. The note about the three packs of Justin's code was still there, lying in the center of my desk where I'd dropped it. I folded it up carefully, put it in my briefcase and headed back to my place on Irving Street.

The phone was ringing as I entered. It was Irina.

"Bill, you'll be able to come to South Hadley on Wednesday afternoon, do you think? Remember? My father's birthday?"

Wednesday was the day after next. Maybe Harry would have a handle on Justin's code by then. Maybe before then.

"I haven't forgotten. I think I can come. I have to check."

My voice must have sounded distracted, as Irina said, "Bill, you sound so strange. Is something wrong? What is it?"

"Nothing. Everything's OK. It's just I'll have to let you know for sure about Wednesday. Can I let you know Wednesday morning?"

"Ok. I'll be at the office at Harvard."

There was a skeptical note in her voice, despite my assurances that all was well with me. Irina and I had known each other long enough that she could tell—despite any denials on my part—that I was, as she put it, "cooking something." I wasn't lying to her, but she could sense I was holding something back.

"Try to call me at eleven," she added. "I have these back-to-back classes and meetings. Or leave a message."

We rang off.

My night was nearly sleepless, my mind weighing my options. Maybe I should take the whole thing to Haggerty after all—Justin's code, the threatening letter, everything.

But Justin had entrusted that code to me as if his life had depended on it. And, for all I or anyone knew, it had. Now, someone who in all probability was Justin's killer was threatening me to hand over the code.

Harry, I said to myself as I finally drifted off, please hurry up and figure out what the hell's in that code so I can do the right thing with it.

Chapter 7

Next morning, Tuesday, I made the deliveries.

But not before I'd inserted some junk lines in the disks in random locations, and edited out runs of characters here and there. Whoever it was would have Justin's code, but with its complement of assorted gaps and glitches, it ought not run too well, if at all.

I dropped a pack of the high-density floppy disks at each of the three locations specified in the typed note. The timing in the drop-off schedule, of course, was deliberately designed to foil any attempt I might make to spy who would be making the pickup.

For instance, I could be placing disk packet number three on the Chapel moat wall while whoever could be picking up floppy packet number one at Barker. And, if I was tempted to rush back to Barker to see who it was, they could be retrieving packet number three from the moat. Short of enlisting confederates to do my spying for me—which I did not want at this point to risk—I was stymied.

I couldn't escape the feeling that I was taking an awful chance with my own neck. What if whoever was out there checked over the code and discovered I'd sabotaged it? On the other hand, maybe whoever it was, though they knew what the code was for, hadn't the slightest clue about how to make it work, glitches or not.

In any event, the doctored copies were on the way, and maybe they'd buy some time until Harry could identify what the code was all about and I'd be clearer on what to do with it.

One last wrinkle—the note had said to destroy all my copies of Justin's code. I'd given Harry a printout of the code plus a floppy disk of it; all of Harry's computers were pretty secure, so the material would be safe with him. Still, I was loath to not somehow retain a copy myself—after all, Justin had charged me with the code's safekeeping.

I had no idea how whoever it was might verify whether I had destroyed my copies. I calculated, though, that whoever was probably high-tech oriented; accordingly, I'd go very low-tech with a hidden-in-plain-sight strategy.

I downloaded Justin's code onto a couple of scruffy looking floppy disks, their paper labels erased and written over again many times. I jotted "Quarterly report draft - Parts 1 & 2" on them in pencil, dated them mid-last year, and bound them with a broken rubber band I'd knotted together.

On a side shelf by my desk was a wire basket jumbled with ballpoint pens, printer cables, boxes of staples, glue sticks and highlighters, rolls of tape, plus a smattering of new and used floppy and ZIP-drive disks—just the spot. I tossed in the pair of disks, gave the tray a shake, and positioned it back on the shelf. Lastly, I electronically expunged and scoured clean any trace of Justin's code on my office computer, and made a mental note to do the same on my home computer.

The rest of the day dragged by with excruciating slowness. At one-thirty, some visitors from Union Bank of Switzerland came by to see a demo of my group's "Graphical Inquirer" information organizer system. When they'd left, I took a turn working on my book draft. Later, a bit past three, some visitors from Fujitsu appeared to see the same demo. All this took me up to four p.m.

After the Fujitsu group left, I phoned Irina and told her of the posthumous note from Justin, the threatening envelope under the door, the delivery of the disks, and the copy I'd reserved for myself.

It was a lot to unload on her all at once.

"Oh, God, Bill, I can barely take this all in. Whatever there was in Justin's message, there's someone determined to get hold of it. Maybe you should bring it all to the police before something bad happens."

"I can't, Irina. I don't know what it is Justin sent me. I gave Harry copies. He's trying to figure out what it is."

"Bill, you don't know what can…"

"Justin told me to keep it safe, whatever it is. I'm going to do that, at least till I find out what it is."

Irina was silent a moment. "I suppose I can't talk you out of it. OK, you're keeping a copy—but is that a good way to hide it? I mean, just there in a basket in your office?"

"I suppose it's a bit like stuffing the rent money in the cookie jar. But sometimes simplicity trumps complexity. I'll bet whoever's after it is deep into technology and thinks—if they come searching my office—it'll all be buried in my computer somewhere under a layer of passwords."

"Bill, be careful. This is all…"

"I know. Scary. Don't think I don't feel it, too. Anyway, I'll call at eleven tomorrow, like we said."

We rang off, and moments later, at about 4:15, I phoned Harry. He didn't answer; there was just his leave-a-message recording. I'd just have to rein in my curiosity until he called me.

At five, I went home. It had begun to snow an hour before, and it was falling even harder when I arrived at my door at Irving Street. I phoned Harry again, got his recording again, and left another urgent request to phone me, ASAP.

To distract myself, I took up my guitar and went through a set of diatonic scales prescribed as exercises in a book by Andrés Segovia. I went through the entire cycle, and started through it again.

My fingers began to ache. Dammit, Harry. Call. Call now.

I took out my folio of pieces by Francisco Tárrega, and turned to his *Mazurka en Sol.* I'd learned half of it by heart. Maybe I could learn the other half by the time Harry called.

I must have been hacking away at the *Mazurka* for forty minutes or so when the phone's ring startled me back from the lush, languid world of Tárrega.

"Harry," I barked into the receiver.

"Rundle, this is Ron Haggerty. I guess that's Harry Mirsky you were expecting to hear from. Early last evening an MIT cop found him unconscious in the lower level of East Garage over by Vassar and Main. Some kind of mugging. The MIT cop called our guys, then took him over to Mass General."

"Is he OK?"

"They tell me he's been in and out of consciousness all last night and most of today. He's awake now. He's been asking for you. The nursing staff called MIT police because they'd brought him in, and they bounced the call to me."

"What happened to him? What do you mean 'some kind of mugging'?"

"He'll tell you all about it. Can you get over there now?"

I said I could.

"Fine. Now, listen. After you see him, call me. I have some things to ask you about Mirsky, about his being roughed up."

I could feel my facial muscles tensing up. *Talking with you is like talking to a black hole, Haggerty. You just suck in information and give nothing back.*

"You were expecting him to call you," Haggerty said. "Why?"

I searched for something plausible to offer up to him.

"We were going to meet for dinner. He was supposed to call me to set where we'd meet." It sounded lame, but I didn't much care.

"Is dinner always such an urgent thing with you?" Haggerty asked.

"What do you mean?"

"You nearly took my ear off when you came on the phone."

I didn't say anything.

"You'll see him?" Haggerty went on.

"I'm going right now," I replied.

"You'll call me right after?"

"Sure. Yeah, I'll call."

Haggerty gave me his direct number. We both hung up. I hurried over to Massachusetts General Hospital.

They'd put Harry in a double room on the fifth floor of the White Building. The near bed was empty, with Harry in the far one. The head of his bed was cranked up at a forty-five degree angle. A sling cradled his left arm. A bright lamp on a bracket reaching from the wall to bedside illuminated his face.

He looked like hell. Both cheeks above his beard bore purple welts. He squinted out through plum-colored eyelids. There were two inches of stitches above his left eye. A white bandage was wrapped around the top of his head.

"How are you feeling? Do you feel like talking?" I asked.

"Sit down. I'm glad you came. Did the cops tell you to come over?"

I pulled a chair up to the side of Harry's bed.

"Lt. Haggerty called me. Said you were over here. What the hell happened?"

"I left the office and went over to East Garage to get my car. Maybe quarter to six. I'm parked down in the basement. Pretty dark there, some of the bulbs were out. Anyway, these two guys in stocking masks jumped me. Strong bastards. Wiry. Martial arts types. They used my head to practice their kick-boxing skills."

"What were they after? Were they just trying to rob you, or what?"

"They wanted what you gave me. They wanted the printout. I told them I didn't have it. They grabbed my briefcase and tore it apart. But I'd shredded the printout before, and didn't have it. The only copy of Justin's stuff I have now is on my office workstation. And don't worry, my workstation is secure. It's got even hairier crypts on it than Justin's code, though that one's a doozy."

While Harry was talking, I studied the bruises and bandages, the stitches on his forehead. I asked, "Tell me the truth, Harry, how do you really feel?"

"Right now, OK, I guess. My head was hurting all over. The docs gave me something that seems to work, but my ears are still ringing. They thought my jaw was broken, but then they decided it wasn't. Hey, don't they wire your mouth shut for weeks to set your jaw? Imagine that. I'd be scared shitless I'd swallow my tongue. Teeth getting fuzzy with crud 'cause I couldn't brush. Why don't they simply pin it with a titanium rod? Oh, and I chipped my elbow on the pavement."

"Haggerty told me you were unconscious when they found you."
I was in fear for Harry's head—his mind—the way you'd feel for a
pianist who'd caught his hand in a doorjamb.

"Yeah. Concussed. They say I was out for maybe ten, fifteen
minutes even after they found me. Deep gash, too. They sewed it
up." I glanced again at the neat row of stitches over his left eye.

I asked him, "Harry, what's the cube root of 537?"

Harry looked at the ceiling. He hummed softly. He counted the
fingers on his left arm with his free right hand. Then he shot me a
quizzical look.

"Jeez! I don't have the vaguest idea."

"Oh, shit," I said. Well, how about—the fifth root of 32?" To
anyone even mildly versed in math, this was like asking to add one
and one. In fact, the answer was two.

A look of pained concentration passed over Harry's face. Seconds
passed. Ten seconds. Fifteen. More grimaces. Then he brightened.

"Two. Hey, it's two." His face burst into a wide grin. "Yeah, I'm
sure. It's two."

Good God. He's really damaged, I thought.

I pulled my chair closer to his bed. "Harry," I said, "I'm sorry this
all happened. I'm sorry as hell. This is something I got you into. It's
my fault for involving you in whatever's going on."

Harry reached up and swung the lamp away from his face. The
softer light from the ceiling fixture made his face look not quite as
bad as before. Like he'd gone maybe three rounds with a brick wall,
not ten or twelve.

"Look," he said, "I'm almost done with Justin's code anyway. So
what the hell—let's go all the way. Make all the pain worthwhile."

"Sorry, pal, but I'm turning this one over to the cops. To Lieutenant
Haggerty. I should have done it from the first."

Harry's voice lowered to a growl, an affectation from his
motorcycle days.

"The hell you are, Bill. I started this puzzle, and I'm going to finish
it. Nothing's more frustrating than a case of *puzzlitis interruptus*.
Listen, I already phoned a student to bring my laptop over here so I

can pull in Justin's code. I'll have all I need to wind it up. It may take another day, maybe two, but I'll have it beat."

"Harry, you can't..."

"Balls. I'm that close." He held up his right hand, thumb and forefinger a millimeter apart.

I got up to leave. "Why not?" I said. "I can't stop you anyway."

What had I let him in for?

I headed for the door, and was almost at the threshold when Harry began to drone, "Eight point...one...two...eight...one..." The numbers tumbled out, about a half second apart: "...three...nine... seven..."

I turned around. "What's that?" I asked.

Harry interrupted the number sequence. "What the hell do you think it is?" he answered. "Cube root of 537. How many places do you need, anyway?"

"Harry! For Christ's sake, why didn't you just say your head's OK..." My voiced choked off.

Harry closed his eyes and settled back into his pillow. "Hey," he said, "spare me any tears. I gotta rest, you know. Get the hell out of here before I buzz for the head nurse."

When I got home the phone was ringing. It was Haggerty.

"Why haven't you called me?"

"I just came back. I was going to call." Truth was, it had slipped my mind that he had told me to call him after seeing Harry. I could think of nothing but those bandages and stitches, how I'd gotten him into all this.

"Did he say who did it?"

"Didn't he tell you guys all that already?"

"I'm asking you, Rundle. Did he tell you anything about who did it?"

"Couple of guys in stocking masks. They knew martial arts."

"Orientals?"

"He didn't say. But you don't have to be oriental to know that stuff."

Silence. Then Haggerty resumed, his voice a notch lower. I guess he didn't appreciate the tutorial.

"Why did they beat up on him?"

"Are you thinking this is connected with Justin Marsh's death?"

A pause. "*You're* the connection, Rundle. I don't know whether these two things are connected, but they're both linked to you."

"Harry doesn't know why. Maybe they were just muggers," I said. "That happens sometimes in the East Garage. There's some pretty secluded corners in there."

"Rundle, they didn't take his money. They had a clear shot at his wallet when he was out cold. But they didn't take it."

Silence.

"Rundle. Why did they attack him? What did Mirsky tell you?"

I answered testily, "I told you what he told me. He doesn't know why."

I was digging myself in deeper, and Harry, too, I supposed. But I wasn't going to say any more until I knew what it was that Justin had entrusted me with.

More silence. Haggerty was big on the pregnant pause. Then he spoke, his voice even lower and closer to the phone.

"Rundle, when I phoned you before you thought it was Mirsky calling. You were juiced up for that call. It wasn't just about dinner. There are some things you're not sharing. There are penalties for withholding evidence. Can go up to five years sometimes. Think it over. I'll be talking to you."

The line clicked.

Chapter 8

It was the next morning, about 10:15, when I walked up to the curb at the street crossing from MIT's East to West Campus and waited for the light to change. Towering above the knot of people waiting on the opposite side was the massive portico of the Institute's main entrance at 77 Massachusetts Avenue: four Ionic columns capping a broad, two-tiered flight of stairs. Cut in large Roman letters on the architrave above the columns was:

MASSACHVSETTS INSTITVTE OF TECHNOLOGY
WILLIAM BARTON ROGERS FOVNDER

As the light changed, a voice behind me called, "Bill, wait up! Headed back to the lab?"

I turned. It was Greg Evans. "Yeah, back to the lab," I mumbled, and we stepped out together. As we crossed, my eyes darted in and about the approaching band of students, in the vain hope of seeing Justin among them.

Simply, and in ways I couldn't fully explain to myself, I felt responsible for his not being alive. At the very least, I blamed myself for not catching the signals, for not sensing something dire coming. I'd been putting pressure on him to deliver stuff for my proposal when—obviously, in hindsight—something much bigger was eating away at him. And I'd totally missed it.

Greg's voice broke into my thoughts. "Hey, I forgot to thank you for rescuing me at the Hales' party Sunday evening. I'd had a couple by the time you joined the circle, and I guess I was just pissed off at all those liberal fanatics." He smiled wryly, then his face turned solemn as he asked, "Have you heard any more about Justin? I saw the article about him in *Tech Talk* and one in the *Globe*, too."

We reached the opposite curb and started up the stairs. "All I know is what the campus police said in *Tech Talk*, that it looks like a mugging, just a particularly vicious one."

We entered Building 7 and headed across the lobby.

"What about the funeral arrangements?" asked Greg. "Justin comes from the North Shore, doesn't he?"

"Yeah, from Hamilton. The funeral's tomorrow morning. I'm driving up."

"I'd like to come. My mind would be there anyway..." Greg's voice trailed off. Then he added, "Is there room in your car? I had my heap towed in from the Hales' place, but they say it'll be in the shop a few days. They have to order parts."

"Sure. Irina may come, too, if she can get away. Karen Hewitt phoned me yesterday to say she's going up in her van, and that she's taking a bunch of Justin's friends from the lab. Other students are organizing a couple of cars, and I may be packing two or three overflows into the Cherokee, but I'm sure we can squeeze you in. I'll send you an email about where and when to rendezvous."

"Thanks. Jeez, it's weird to be burying someone so young. It doesn't feel right, does it?"

"No," I agreed. "It doesn't feel right. I still can't bring myself to believe he's really gone."

We started down what's known at MIT as the "Infinite Corridor," a hallway stretching straight through the Institute's main complex for about eight hundred feet. Featureless except for office doors, bulletin boards, and occasional photo-collages of past MIT greats, its main fame among students is that, twice a year, the corridor's axis aligns with the setting sun as it plunges below the skyline of West Campus. The event becomes tongue-in-cheek paganism as students momentarily hush and draw aside to let the sunbeams stream laser-straight down the hall.

"Did Justin have much family?" Greg asked. "I only met his mother, and her just once—when Justin first came to the lab."

"He was an only child. And his father's dead. He was a stockbroker or something like that, and left Justin and his mother pretty well off."

"So it's just her alone now…"

"Yeah. Lots of money, a big house, and no one to share it with."

Greg asked, "Isn't there some relative of Justin's that was a pretty well-known sportsman? Helmsman, sailor, something like that?"

"I think there is—an uncle who used to do ocean yacht racing. Justin mentioned him a couple of times. He said the uncle was not very well, so maybe he'll be at the funeral, maybe not."

We reached the halfway point through the main building corridor where it opens onto a spacious foyer looking out upon Killian Court. To our right, posters tacked on the fronts of a row of student-staffed desks publicized a gay/lesbian rally, the Chorallaires in a Bach recital, and a performance of *The Taming of the Shrew* by the student Shakespeare Group.

Crossing the foyer, my eye swept over the lines inscribed in the marble of the far wall:

> I see proceeding from our technology of the
> future a vast army of vigorous young men
> able to play their part manfully and effectively
> anywhere in the world.

> Richard Cockburn MacLaurin
> President of MIT 1909-1920

I had to fill in from memory some of the quote, though, since a bushy plant—a large weeping fig—had been placed strategically before the wall, obscuring maybe a third of the passage.

Noticing where my gaze was trained, Greg quipped, "That wording would never pass these days, would it, Bill?"

"No, Greg, probably not."

"*Definitely* not."

"Yes, definitely not."

Poor Greg. It couldn't be easy being a conservative in what was dubbed "The People's Republic of Cambridge." On any Sunday morning in the cafés about Harvard Square you could spot people—either alone or in small knots—poring over the editorial pages of *The New York Times*. ("Checking out what their opinions for the week ought to be," Greg would say.) Occasionally, Greg would be among the readers, seated alone, his copy of *The Washington Times*—never *The Washington Post*—bravely unfurled. I remember him saying once that to be seen browsing through that conservative sheet could be a good way to meet the occasional woman who, in the midst of Cambridge *profound*, dared to lean to the right. I suspect that, given Cambridge, it was the very occasional soul.

"Bill, at Hale's party—did you get to talk with anyone interesting? I mean besides me and those cranky liberals I blew up at?"

"Well, I had a great time chatting with Cassie and the people at her table, catching up on Institute gossip and all. And, oh yeah, there was this guy at the table—John Creedon. He has a high-tech firm out on Route 128. You've probably heard of him."

"Oh, so it *was* Creedon I spotted at your table. I thought I recognized him from his salon-cut hair and the drape of his jacket. Sure, I've heard of him. As a matter of fact, I did some work for him some time back." Greg's face pursed into a frown. "He's…well…I guess you could say he's a slick operator."

"Greg, do I detect a sour note? That you don't like the guy?"

"Naw. I guess it's just my Charlestown background rearing up when I see someone with a well-cut, money look. Which Creedon has in spades. Hell, you know the feeling."

I knew the feeling all right, having grown up in Charlestown a block away from Greg. You've got to get over the poor boy feeling, though—especially if, like Greg and I, you had a doctoral degree and were teaching at MIT.

"Did he have much to say?" Greg asked.

"No, just polite chit-chat. He seems to have been giving a lot of money recently to the Institute—at least I gather that from something Cassie said."

"Well, them that has is them that can give. Anyway, you have to make it before you can give it, and Creedon has a way about him."

We reached—oxymoronically speaking—the end of the infinite corridor, and stepped into the brisk air.

"Are you tied up just now, Bill?" Greg asked. "I can show you my gang's latest project if you've time."

I glanced at my watch. Five of eleven. "I guess I have time. I need to check my email to see whether Jean-Paul got my proposal draft, but that can wait a bit."

"Was that the proposal you were working on with Justin?"

"Yes. Yeah, the one for the National Science Foundation. I wrote most of it, but he was doing a lot of the boilerplate—you know, the specs, the diagrams, that kind of stuff. He was kind of slow coming with it. He seemed preoccupied with something."

"Like what?"

"He never said. Well, I guess I never asked him. Anyway, it's all moot now. And the draft's gone out to Jean-Paul."

"So Justin sent you all his stuff?"

"No, not all I needed, but most of it. I got it the day before he… died."

I decided not to mention the posthumous message and the code, though Greg—along with Harry Mirsky—was one of my closest friends at the Institute.

"But, like I said," I added, "it's all moot now."

We turned down Amherst Street and entered the Cognitive Computing Lab. "Ok," I said, "what is this stuff your gang is doing that you're going to show me?"

Greg pointed down the stairs to the set of double doors on the lower level that was the entry to "The Block." "It's in there. I think they're working on it right now." Greg waved me on, and we descended the stairs and went on through the doors.

Dubbed "The Block" because of its near-cubical shape, the lab's experimental media theater was a space sixty feet by sixty feet square, and fifty feet high. It hosted a myriad of lab events: laser light shows, student exhibitions, music concerts. Often, it was set up with twenty to thirty electronic booths to showcase projects for sponsor visits.

The floor, covered with dark gray carpeting, was raised to permit computer cabling to be deployed beneath it. The walls, covered with a soft tufted fabric, also dark gray, were unadorned except for a catwalk up near the ceiling that extended all the way around the room. A gantry crane for suspending lighting, moving scenery, or what have you, hung at ceiling height from a steel beam rafter. Scattered about the periphery of The Block were tables cluttered with electronic equipment, stacks of newly arrived computers in unopened boxes, odds and ends of stage scenery, and—the nucleus of the room's occasional lunchtime student musicale offerings—a Bösendorfer grand piano.

Alongside the wall to our left, and bunched around a large shiny object, were a half dozen of Greg's students, all of whom I recognized. As we approached they let out a "Ta-Da!" in unison and stepped aside to reveal a miniature blimp, about seven feet long and a foot-and-a-half in diameter. Outrigged on either side was a small electric motor with a four-bladed propeller.

"How's that?" asked Greg with evident pride in his group. "They made it themselves out of Mylar stretched over aluminum wire. Pretty good, huh?"

"It's great!" I answered. I'd seen some toy helium blimps maybe three or four feet long, but this model was king-size and sculpted with finesse to resemble an old-time zeppelin. "Correction…it's terrific!" I went on. "But what are you all going to do with it?"

Tamara Boyd, a tall, auburn-haired girl with wire-framed spectacles, and one of Greg's star pupils, stepped forward. "The blimp's going to be navigating a three-dimensional virtual ocean environment modeled in the space of The Block," she explained. "The challenge is to model fishlike behaviors in the blimp. There'll be a shoreline, reefs, currents to get around in—as well as predators the blimp'll have to avoid, and prey it'll have to find for food. We'll be making a bunch of smaller blimps to simulate the little fish it's got to catch."

"What's that gadget on the nose of the blimp?" I asked.

"It's a laser," replied Tamara. "It runs on a charge built up on a capacitor—takes about ten seconds to build it up for a single shot—and then it can fire at special spots on the target fish to 'spear' them—kind of like a game of laser tag."

"Isn't it dangerous?"

"No. It's not very powerful. It's about like one of those laser pointers used in lecture hall." She shrugged. "I suppose you could put in more batteries and rig a bunch of capacitors in series to build up a bigger charge. But it was tough enough to get COUHES—that's the Committee on the Use of Human Experimental Subjects—to let us, if there were going to be people nearby, use even the single capacitor setup."

My attention drifted away from Tamara and her discourse on the shiny blimp. I knew what Greg was trying to do—distract me from my deep funk over Justin's death. He'd done something similar when we both were eight and my mother had passed away and he'd tried to help me through it by showing me his comic collection and set of model planes. He'd done it again years later when he helped me get through the weeks and months of despair and self-loathing the winter after Valerie's death.

The blimp demo over, Greg and I took the elevator up to the third floor.

"Thanks," I said to Greg as he turned the key in his door.

"Hang in there, Bill," Greg said as he paused on his threshold. "I'm only a couple of doors down if—you know—you feel like talking."

"Thanks, again," I said, and went on to my office.

I logged in to check my email. A note from Harry said that he'd need all day, maybe more, to put the pieces of code together. It was just eleven o'clock, so I rang Irina to say that I was on for the trip this afternoon to South Hadley, and that I'd pick her up at three and we'd head out.

Chapter 9

"Who'll be there?" I asked, as we entered the Mass Turnpike in my Cherokee for the trip westward to Irina's parents' house.

"Well, there'll be my brother Vladimir and his wife Geneviève. They live in Paris, where he's with the Citibank branch there. She's an associate editor with *Le Monde*. They've flown in for Papa's birthday, and they'll be staying through the Christmas holidays."

"That it?"

"Just one more, Sergei, my cousin. A third cousin, to be exact. He's twenty, lives in Russia, in St. Petersburg. Right now, though, he's at Harvard on an exchange fellowship studying physics and math. He's on the Russian sailing team on their America's Cup entry *Orel*."

"He's at Harvard? We could have taken him out with us."

"I asked him, but he had a final exam today." She glanced at her watch. "He's in it right now. He'll be driving out afterwards, so he may be a little late for dinner."

En route, I rang Harry at Mass General on my cell phone, but he just growled a few times and hung up. We took Exit 5 from the Pike just a bit after five o'clock, and it was already dark as we headed up Route 16 to South Hadley.

The Tatarinoff dining room was a warm blend of wood paneling, heavy damask table linens, and soft yellow candlelight. Standing, we all looked toward an ancient icon suspended in a corner of the room while Irina's father led us in a preprandial prayer. Once seated, we toasted with chilled vodka poured from a bottle of *Stolichnaya* frozen in a block of ice.

Dinner started with *ukha,* a clear fish soup with lime and dill. While we ate, Irina's parents—her father, Basil, who taught Slavic Languages and Literature at nearby Mount Holyoke College, and her mother, Natalia, who co-managed a small art gallery in South Hadley Center—animatedly inquired how I was, and how my research was going at MIT. Irina's brother, Vladimir, at thirty-three, a couple of years older than she, offered economic gossip on what might be the fallout from conversion to the Euro, while his wife, Geneviève, contributed the latest press speculations on certain stubborn rumors still surrounding the death of Princess Diana.

Next in the meal came *zakuska*—small dishes of herring, anchovies, and red and black caviar, together with a platter of *pirozhki*—small finger-length pastries filled with minced fish, mushrooms, and hard-boiled eggs. "I hope you're not becoming overwhelmed with the fish-based dishes," Natalia said to me smilingly. "Irina suggested we offer you a traditional Russian meal, and meat dishes would not be served in Advent."

"Not at all," I answered truthfully. "Fish is a favorite of mine."

I couldn't help but notice the distinctive little silver porringer holding the black caviar. Ostensibly very old and finely made, it had tiny claw-and-ball feet and a high, satiny burnish. The only piece of its kind on the table, I remarked on the intricate crest engraved on its side and asked Irina's father if there were some story behind it.

"What you see," he said, "is a relic from bygone Tatarinoffs. The ancestor of our family was a Tatar chieftain, Arslan Murza Tokhin-Tatarin. In 1389, at the head of his band of three hundred mounted Mongol warriors, he swore fealty to the Grand Duke Dmitri Donskoi. In return he received vast lands, three cities, a boyar's daughter for a wife, and the Grand Duke himself as godfather upon his— mandatory—conversion to Christianity."

Just then, the doorbell sounded. "That must be Sergei. I'll get it," said Irina, as she rose from her chair.

While Irina answered the door, her father continued, "Arslan's descendants, now the Princes Tatarinoff, settled mostly in what is now the province of Tula. Over generations, their individual holdings became increasingly small. In some nobilities, like that of England, all lands went to the eldest son. But with a princely family in old Russia, every child is a prince or princess, and the land is divided accordingly."

Irina's father smiled and chuckled softly. "Well, most of these 'princes' soon became just plain farmers," he continued. "It was not uncommon that when someone with Tatar blood came into town in his ragged coat, matted hair, and dingy felt boots, a dray horse before him and a pack of dogs behind, the townspeople would yet tip their hats and say, 'Good morning, Prince' and 'How are you today, Prince.'"

As her father's anecdote ended, Irina returned to the dining room with a tall, slender young man in tow. He had piercing blue eyes and long, straight blond hair, wisps of which fell left to right across his forehead. He headed straight for Irina's mother, said what I took to be "good evening" in Russian, and kissed her three times, in the Russian manner, on alternate cheeks. He said a similar good evening to Irina's father, Irina, Geneviève, Vladimir, and lastly—without the kisses—to me.

There was yet another birthday toast, proposed by Sergei, and the singing of the traditional Russian benediction *Mnogye Leta* or *Many Years*. After mutual bringings-up-to-date, the table conversation turned to Sergei, his studies at Harvard, and his crewing on *Orel*.

"In the dead of winter," he said, "of course *Orel* cannot sail in the waters around St. Petersburg. So it was flown in a gigantic military transport—a surplus Antonov 124, similar to your US Air Force *C-5*—to Sydney in Australia. It is there now, being re-fitted. Soon, *Orel* will be in the water again, and her crew will begin winter training. I shall be taking next semester away from Harvard and re-joining them for the trial runs."

I mentioned as how I'd be spending a few days in Sydney in early January, attending a computer conference. Sergei said I should let him know where I'd be staying, as perhaps he could show off *Orel* to me. "The name of our boat, *Orel,* means 'eagle,'" he added. "It is named for the first ship ever in the Russian navy."

Then, addressing everyone, Sergei asked rhetorically, "Now, does our 'Eagle' really have a chance to take the America's Cup?" He tipped his head back, glanced about the ceiling. Lowering his head, he went on, "We are a good team. We have a good yacht beneath us. This combination will take us far. Yes, I believe we have a chance to take the cup from the Americans."

His face took on a serious cast.

"Of all the yachts to be competing to make the challenge to you Americans," he said, glancing at me, "there is only one that could be a serious threat to our chances. But only if that yacht has a crew with the best of all sailing skills."

"And which entry do you think that might be?" asked Irina's mother from the end of the table.

"It is *Chrysanthemum.* The Japanese entry. We all know—it was yesterday morning in *The New York Times*—that Team Nippon is rated to have the best boat."

"*Chrysanthemum* is designed by computer, by the very same design technique that you people at MIT developed in your Ocean Engineering department." He again glanced toward me and went on, "But you have this 'open door' policy at MIT, and everyone can walk and look over your shoulders. So Team Nippon has taken every advantage of that. They even have some design students who are planted there. Moreover, Team Nippon has even improved the aft hull design. Yes, the Japanese are famous for copying, but they are no fools, either. They can put new things together when they really want to." Again glancing at me as somehow representing at the table both the U.S. and MIT, he said, "Between you and the Japanese, you both surely have the best yacht design."

"So does this mean it's now really a matter of having the best crew?" asked Irina's father.

"Yes, it all comes down to how the boat is sailed," said Sergei. "They—the Japanese—have been training a lot. I have even heard at one point they had hired an Australian to help them."

Sergei paused a moment while Irina and her mother cleared the appetizer plates away and brought on the main dish, which was—no surprise—broiled salmon. Irina laughed softly. "You're really getting your vitamin E this evening, Bill!"

A toast of *Stolichnaya* about the table, and Sergei resumed his account.

"We on *Orel* have a great crew. We work very hard. But the key is strategy and tactics. It is knowing how to play the wind, when to jibe and come about. It is all split second. You need a plan, too. You have to sense what the other boats are doing, and you have to devise on the spot a way to cope. It is not just how well your boat is designed, or whether your crew is strong and working hard. Above all, you need sailing skill. You need a first rate 'skipper,' and a first-rate tactician. They are the brains of the boat."

"But your Captain Yermalov," Irina's mother interjected. "You admire him, you told us. Isn't he one of the best?"

Sergei replied, "Oh yes, Yermalov. He is a navy man. But he has no real experience in ocean yacht racing. An amateur, I suppose. Anyway, he is the best we have."

"The Japanese," said Irina, "they may have an exceptional boat. But do they have a good skipper as well?"

Sergei's hand tightened on his vodka tumbler. He stared icily ahead.

"If the Japanese have the better skipper, they will win. They were training with the Australian. They may have paid him as much as a million dollars, the rumor goes. The Japanese have no ocean yachting tradition. Neither does Russia, for that matter. But if, on top of a good boat design, the Japanese have the better skipper, the combination will be too much and they will surely win."

"Now this Australian…" said Irina's father, "is he all that…"

"There is a small chance he may not actually join Team Nippon. There is a rumor, too, that some other Australians are trying to talk him out of training the *Chrysanthemum* crew."

"Well, then," Irina's father went on, "things will become more equal, perhaps."

Sergei snapped, "It's all a cover. The Australian can come or go, who knows. He may or may not be all that good." He lowered his head and his voice trailed off. "But there is someone—something—even better."

Sergei stopped talking. He stared down at his plate. There was silence around the table.

I looked over at Sergei and tried to catch his eye, but he kept his head lowered. I asked, "How do you mean 'something' better?"

Sergei continued to stare at his plate. "I—I don't know. Let us just say that some people can be very resourceful." He raised his head, looked about the table, and with a forced smile said, "It is enough talk of boats. We are going to win, that is all. We are going to win." He turned to Vladimir and Geneviève, and inquired, "How is your apartment in Paris? It must be exciting to live there…"

After a dessert of *babka yablochnaya*—translatable as apple Charlotte with apricot sauce—Sergei excused himself to drive back to Boston, citing an urgent paper he had to finish. Irina and I, like Vladimir and Geneviève, would stay the night in South Hadley with Irina's parents. After some coffee, and a bit more conversation, the evening ended.

"I'll show you where you'll be," said Irina. "It's Papa's study. There's a couch there that folds out into a bed."

Irina took my hand and led me down a long narrow corridor toward the back of the house. On one side, the corridor wall bore a row of Baskt prints of costumes from the Ballet Russe, plus a grouping of antique maps. On the other side, the wall was densely hung with old photographs of bemedalled men in uniform and stately women in court dress, interspersed with finely wrought miniatures done variously in watercolor, oil, silhouette, or cameo.

"I hope you forgive Papa for talking so much about politics." Irina glanced at the pictures on the wall. "And about the family."

"There's nothing to forgive," I replied. "It was fascinating."

She brought us both to a halt by a doorway halfway down the hall and to the left. "This is where you'll be," she said. She looked lovely in the soft light from the sconce by the door.

71

"I didn't know you were a princess," I said.

She tilted her head to the side in mock hauteur. "Couldn't you tell?" she said. She broke the pose, turning her head front. "All of that's in the past. It makes a diverting story, but we have to live in reality." She linked her arm through mine and pressed close to me. She added, "But reality is not so bad, I think."

I drew her closer, and kissed her. "Not from where I'm standing, it isn't," I said.

Suddenly, over Irina's shoulder, I discerned a young-old face staring directly at me. Sergei's face. Sergei's face in a faded sepia photograph in a heavy gold frame. Irina must have felt me startle, because she asked, "Is something wrong? What is it?"

"That face." I turned her to look at the photo. "That's your cousin Sergei. But this picture has to be a hundred years old."

She looked at the picture, then at me. She broke into a broad smile.

"It is Sergei. Not the Sergei we had dinner with, but another Sergei. His great-great-grandfather. Their names are the same, Sergei Vasilievich Tatarinoff. The photograph was when he was a cadet at the St. Petersburg Naval Academy. He got his commission as an officer, and later he served on the battleship *Orel* in the Russo-Japanese War. He was killed in the battle of Tsushima Straits in 1905. He was only thirty-one years old. The *Orel* was captured by the Japanese, along with some other ships, and was put to service in their navy. It was all a big humiliation for the Russian side, I'm afraid."

I stared at the photograph of Irina's relative. "The resemblance is amazing," I said. "It's like your cousin had dressed up and got one of those instant nostalgia photo shops to make a do-your-own daguerreotype shot of him. But didn't all your family leave Russia after the Revolution? How come he lives in St. Petersburg?"

"Sergei's grandfather was in World War II, with the American army. He fell in love with a Russian woman, a displaced person. They got married, and for a variety of reasons she wanted to return to live in Russia. It was all very painful for the family because she was a party member, a Soviet."

Irina glanced over to the Sergei on the wall. A troubled look came over her face.

"What is it?" I asked.

"Sergei has this romantic idea—an obsession, really—of trying to get the new Russian government to restore an estate the family had. A manor house in Krasnoe, near Tula. We have pictures. It was very large, with a lot of land, including the village."

"I thought the Tatarinoffs were down and out with the dray horses and dogs."

"Oh, that's Papa's way of dealing with it all. The house at Krasnoe's probably been used for a cow barn the past eighty years. Or maybe it was just burnt to the ground."

With that, we kissed again, and I went into her father's study.

The foldout couch was very comfortable, but sleep eluded me. I turned on the lamp on the side table. In the half-light I could see a dozen or so framed photographs on Irina's father's desk, yet others tiling the wall behind his high-back chair. A distinctly Russian trait, that desire for immersion in images of family and friends.

One of those pictures haunted me. One not here in the room with me, but out in the hall. Sergei.

I recalled the intensity of the live Sergei at the table. The Russo-Japanese war had destroyed his ancestor, his namesake. Humbled his country. The Japanese had newer ships, better guns.

An image came floating back in my memory from a class I'd taken as an undergraduate, an image of Donald Tyler Caldwell, my old history professor, recounting an anecdote about that disastrous naval encounter. "There was a saying at the time that on board every Russian ship at Tsushima was an Englishman," he had told the class. "Not only had the British closed Suez to the Russian battle fleet, forcing them to go the long route around Africa, but they hadn't allowed the Tsar's ships to re-fuel at their coaling stations en route to the Sea of Japan."

Could the present-day Sergei be also on a romantic quest to avenge his namesake, to do it at sea, and before all the world? The name of the Russian entry—*Orel*—was even the same as the ship his ancestor had died on. To what lengths might he go—might he already have gone—to assure that Team St. Petersburg would win?

I put out the light and let my head fall back upon my pillow. Early next morning, Irina and I would be heading back on the Mass Turnpike for Justin's funeral in Hamilton. The thought brought back repressed visions of Justin's sodden face and its missing eye. Like some bizarre kaleidoscope, his face whirled and cascaded about in my mind's vision, intertwined with those of the two Sergeis, as I lapsed into a fitful sleep.

Chapter 10

The early morning traffic on the Mass Pike had been mercifully light as Irina and I drove back to Cambridge to pick up Greg and three graduate students from the lab. From there, we made it to Hamilton in good time for Justin's funeral Mass.

The service was a mixture of solemnity and prayerful hope, even joyful in its way. On the ride to the burial site, though, the starkness of death, its finality, reasserted itself.

Saint Julian's Cemetery at Hamilton was an old one, dating back to before the Civil War. It was not quite as lavish in funerary statuary as Mount Auburn Cemetery in Cambridge, but, in the older part where Justin's mother's family were entombed, it was nearly so.

It was raining hard. Irina, Greg, and I stood clutching umbrellas at the periphery of the sizeable knot of people who were in attendance. There had been no need to break through frost-hardened ground to make a final resting place for Justin; instead, his casket stood on a wooden platform before the aboveground family tomb. The name emblazoned in block letters on the nine-foot high structure was not Marsh, but Eames—his mother's side of the family.

The Episcopal priest officiating intoned a few prayers, his voice barely audible above the patter of rain on the umbrellas. I looked over at Justin's mother, her handsome profile firmly set, her only admission of emotion a faint redness about her eyes. Why New England ladies of the "old school" have to put on such impassive fronts, I don't know. Maybe they all imagine how Katharine

Hepburn might behave at a funeral—Yankee gumption, and all of that—and comport themselves accordingly.

A distinguished-looking man in a pale yellow rain slicker was seated in an electric motor-chair next to Justin's mother. From the length of his legs and height of his torso I judged that, were he able to stand, he would have towered above her and most of the present company. His head was bent over in evident sorrow, and he had allowed his umbrella to tilt to one side so that the pelting rain ran in rivulets through his graying hair.

Later, the entire funeral party was invited back to the Marsh home, a large, rambling two-hundred-year-old structure painted a shade of pinkish purple that only ancient New England manses seem to be able to pull off. Family and friends filed in, leaving quivers of umbrellas in the commodious clay pots set just inside the front door. We all proceeded into the living room—nearly as large as that at the Hales'—where a pair of fireplaces and a long table laden with silver coffee urns and trays of sandwiches awaited us.

Justin's mother, together with other family members, formed a receiving line, and all of us—friends, neighbors, and MIT acquaintances—began to file by them.

Moving through the line, I shared mutual introductions and commiserations with Justin's relations, and in due course came to the distinguished man in the motor chair. "Hello. I'm Bennett Eames, Justin's uncle," he said as he grasped my hand with a grip that, in contrast to his low, halting voice, was surprisingly strong. "We became very close after his father died when Justin was only six. I'll surely miss him."

"I'm Bill Rundle," I responded. "I was his advisor at MIT. We'll all miss Justin at our lab."

"'Rundle,' you say. Wasn't it you who—who found him?"

"Yes. I found him that morning." In response to the questioning look in his eyes, I said, "No, I guess the police don't know anything more about what happened."

Eames held onto my hand.

"Can you come by my house sometime? I want to know—

anything you can tell me."

"Yes. I'll come by, if you like. I don't know what I can tell you, really, but I can come by."

"Good. Thank you." Eames glanced at Karen Hewitt, who was standing immediately to his left. "You'd met Karen before, with Justin, I trust?" I nodded. "She can tell you how to get to my place."

I assured him I would come, and he released my hand.

Next, and last in line, was Justin's mother.

She took both my hands in hers. "Professor Rundle," she said, "it's comforting to see you. Justin thought so well of you. He felt you were someone he could really trust."

The words of Justin's email echoed in my mind as she spoke.

"I suppose," she continued, her expression softening, "in the world of academia it's reassuring to have a mentor one can have complete confidence in." She smiled. "Anyway, you were that for him, and we all thank you for it."

Her eyes misted as she added, "Thank you, too, for—for finding him." Her reserve and mine broke momentarily and, awkwardly and a bit off balance, we embraced. Wordlessly, we let go, and I moved on while she resumed the air of formality she shared with the grand living room with its oriental rugs, Wedgwood vases, and antique silver.

On the drive back to Cambridge, the rain fell even harder, washing the muddied snow from the sides of the road. For most of the trip we all were silent, though now and then one of the students would relate some memory or anecdote concerning Justin.

"Justin was real great at getting us organized and out of the grad school rut," said Miriam Katz, who was seated in the middle of the rear seat. "Remember how he got the softball league going. Jeez, we were awful, but it was so much fun."

"Yeah. And remember how he got our rowing regatta started last spring?" said Orrin Clafin, a tall, gangly young man in a gray duffle coat who was squeezed in the front seat between Irina and me. He let out a muffled laugh. "What a bunch of clowns we were, trying to launch the shells in the Charles…" He stopped, then muttered,

"Sorry, gang. I didn't mean to talk about the Charles...where Justin and all..." His voice trailed off.

Everyone was silent again, until Claudia Rossi, one of the grad assistants working for Harry Mirsky, spoke in a low, deliberate tone from the left rear of the car. "I hope to hell they find out who did it."

"What do you mean, 'Who did it?'" asked Orrin.

"Where have you been?" Claudia hurled back, her voice rising. "Who killed Justin is what I mean!"

"Yeah," joined in Miriam. "Yeah. Why don't they really look into this? The Cambridge cops, I mean. All they seem to be able to do is tag cars and bust up frat parties. But when it comes to a real case, they're completely out of it."

Greg—stuffed into the right rear seat—called across to Claudia, "Is that what the lab students are saying, that Justin was murdered?"

"It's not what they're saying, necessarily. But it's what most of us are thinking. I mean, isn't it obvious that Justin wasn't the kind of guy to just go and kill himself?"

"Wasn't he pretty moody, though, this last month?" said Orrin. "I mean, he wasn't like he always used to be, since maybe after Thanksgiving or so. The last couple of weeks, anyway. You know, kind of glum and looking washed out."

No one spoke for a moment, then Greg asked, "Hey, Claudia, what does Mirsky think? Does he think Justin was...I mean, that something happened to Justin?"

"Harry's in the hospital, Professor Evans. Remember?"

"Oh, that's right. So much has been going on..."

Miriam spoke up, "Maybe there's some new gang lurking around Kendall Square. It's happened before. Like that outbreak of muggings that went on for maybe a month, spring before last, until the cops broke this bunch up." She paused a moment, then added, "OK, I take it back about the cops. Well, maybe not *all* of it back. Anyways, they did a good job on that."

"You know, Miriam could be right," said Orrin. "I mean about some gang doing this. Both of these things happened at night. When it was dark, anyway. Justin at the river. Professor Mirsky getting beat up in the parking lot. Yeah. Maybe there's some new gang targeting Tech people. Didn't the MIT cops issue some advisory?"

"They did. I saw it in the emails," said Greg. "You know, it's really too bad there's stuff happening after dark on the streets around the Institute, with students headed for the library, going for pizza, whatever."

Everyone fell silent for the rest of the trip. I dropped Greg and the students back at the lab. Irina and I debated a moment whether we'd go to a Starbucks for coffee, but with the rain not letting up and the gloom of Justin's funeral still full upon us, we opted not to. I took Irina to her office at Harvard, and drove back to the lab.

Back in my office, I stared out the window toward the vacant tennis courts on Ames Street and beyond to the gray waters of the Charles. The view was as fittingly somber as my mood, the rain now turned to swirling snow.

Chapter 11

Later, the afternoon after Justin's funeral, I phoned Harry Mirsky at Mass General.

"God, it sounds so sad. I'm almost glad I missed it," said Harry after hearing how the service and interment went. "I wouldn't have wanted to have gone through that, the guy was so young and full of life."

We both were silent for a moment, and Harry—his voice sounding brighter—resumed, "Hey, I was doing head math stunts for the nurses, too. Cube roots, even threw in some fourth and fifth roots. Know what? They didn't have any tables or a calculator to check out what I was saying, so they just assumed I wasn't really doing them. You know, just babbling from the blow on the head. So, the upshot's they're keeping me here for observation."

I decided to let Harry handle his own credibility with the medical staff. "How is the elbow?" I asked.

"Hurts like hell. But I can still type. Poon Sung dropped off my laptop here last night. He's a great guy to have around, but he's still into broken English. Can't you guys tutor him or something?"

Poon Sung was a new grad student Harry and I shared, each of us putting up half the funds for his research assistantship. From Malaysia, Poon was driven to succeed in math and science. His grades on English language mastery in the TOEFL exams, though, were just borderline; otherwise, he was way ahead of the game.

"I'll encourage him to work out at the language lab," I said. "Good luck with the code cracking."

We hung up, and I'd just started to rummage through the pile of mail on my desk when the phone rang. It was Lieutenant Haggerty.

"How's things going, Rundle?"

"Fine, Lieutenant. How about yourself?"

No answer. A pause. Then, "Anything you'd like to tell me?"

"Actually, there's something I'd like to ask you. Was Justin murdered? Is this a murder case?"

"Rundle, all I can tell you is it's under investigation."

"Don't you have any hunches?"

"It's officially listed as an accident. Like he fell in. The other possibilities are suicide, homicide. Right now it's carried as accidental, pending further investigation."

"And your leaning on me is part of that investigation?"

"You got it. And you're not helping very much with that investigation."

He enunciated that last sentence slowly, his voice falling in pitch with each syllable. I was reminded of the phrase "Slow *spondee* stalks…" invoked by my senior year high school English teacher to help us remember the name of the poetic meter where the syllables were like heavy footfalls closing in behind you—like Haggerty was seeming to do.

"I'm cooperating as best I can," I said.

Pause.

"I'll be in touch, Rundle. Something is going on, and you and Mirsky know something about it. Maybe not everything about it, but something." Another pause. Haggerty was deep into the pregnant pause. "I'll be in touch," he said, and hung up.

I riffled quickly through my stack of mail. Nothing too urgent, so I set it all aside for later. I logged onto my desktop Mac, and after checking a few routine emails that could wait or I could delegate, I saw one that brought me up short.

TO: rundle@ccl.cognition.mit.edu
FROM: poon@cogito_cognition.mit.edu
sent Thurs 22 December 09.36.04

received Thurs 22 December 09.36.18
message id <936921128-71.1>
status: R

Dr. Rundle:

Bad thing happen. Two man grab me outside
Walker building last night after I come from hospital
and professor Mirsky. Very strong, wear stocking on
face. have very funny voices like talking in barrel.
They push me in car, drive pretty fast. No turns, a
few bends maybe. Go kilometer, maybe more. they
punch me, I get dizzy. But I know for sure I see sign
pointing to monument for your famous Doctor East.
That is for sure.
I see moon on water. they go round big circle then
stay right then go to right. We stop at three floor
red house, next door is two floor gray house. They
take me in kitchen of low floor of gray house and
try make me tell how get to messages in professor
Mirsky's or in your machine. i not tell. They hit me
more, real bad. Knock me out. When wake up I
on side steps of Walker. I go to medical center on
Carleton Street where they fix jaw.
I am at my house now. I am ok. I rest. You must be
careful because they are very hard guys.
I tell you this, but I do not tell professor Mirsky yet,
as he just got too hurt.

-Poon.

  I printed out Poon's message, took the MTA over to Mass General,
and reached Harry's room. He was propped up, his laptop set up on a

tray that straddled his bed. "That laptop of yours cost Poon something to deliver," I said as I handed him the email note. "Take a look."

Harry scanned the page. "Oh, shit. Probably the same bastards that worked me over. Poor Poon." He crumpled the note in a wad and tossed it back to me.

"I tried to figure out on the way over where the hell they took him," I said. "But the description is not very helpful. Just some things he saw on the way. Pretty much garbled—the town's all new to him. What he says doesn't match up with anything I can think of."

"Let's have it back," Harry said. He held out his hand, wincing at the twinge he'd just given himself in his right shoulder. I watched Harry's eyes whisk over the crumpled printout.

Harry bit his lip. I could sense the wheels turning. He began, "Well, I don't know about any 'Doctor East.' There's Dr. West toothbrushes, but I don't think there's a monument around these parts to him or them. So it's probably not a doctor."

He looked at the ceiling, then at me. He continued, "Not a doctor. OK. 'East' is a direction. 'Dr.' can stand for 'drive.' East Drive? Haven't heard of that around here, and he says he didn't go far."

Harry paused a millisecond, then raced on, "A monument can be a memorial and vice versa. Let's say he got the words a bit screwed up. How about 'Memorial Drive'? You can drive fast on that OK. So, we got Memorial Drive East."

Another look at the ceiling. "Lessee, there's a sign that says just that at the traffic circle near the Cambridge Boat House. I pass it every day coming in." He cleared his throat. "Ok. The water's gotta be the Charles River. The moon? They said on TV that last night was overcast, but it could have been a street lamp reflection. Ok—so, you swing around right, go a bit, then another right and you're on Mount Auburn Street." He paused. "Yeah. Mount Auburn Hospital on the right, bunch of houses on the left. Check them out for a red and gray, but remember the colors could be off since it was at night."

He smiled his "gotcha" smile. But I guess he sensed my chagrin at missing what was now so obvious, because he continued, "Look, sometime back I saw this TV program on PBS about Linus Pauling. You remember Pauling. He got two Nobel prizes, one for chemistry, the other the peace prize. Anyway, they had some footage of him solving a little puzzle. Guessing the shape of some gizmo rattling around in a box. They wanted to show a smart guy thinking out loud.

"He'd rock the box one way, the gizmo wouldn't roll. Rock it the opposite way, it rolled. So, he says it's some kind of cylinder. But it's a "clunky" roll, so he says it's not a cylinder but a prism. How many sides? Well, it *does* roll, so he says not three or four. Eight sides? Not that smooth a roll. Five or seven? He says, well, the puzzle is not that sophisticated, so he concludes no, it's gotta be six sides. They tell him to open the box, and there it is, a hexagonal prism, like he says. I paid attention all through. Logic, zing, zing, zing. Now, whenever I'm stuck, I ask myself, 'What would you do if you were Linus Pauling?'"

"Thanks. Really," I said, but I guess my tone of voice smacked of my hurt pride.

"You think it's unfair to be across the board smart, right?" he said. He paused, and wet his lips. "You know, my father always said, 'You got a choice between smart and lucky? Pick lucky.'" He cocked his head. "Shit, I'd give ten IQ points for some of your looks. Fifteen, maybe. Look at you, for chrissakes, a red-haired Cary Grant."

"Harry, you do fine." The last few times I'd spotted Harry at his Thursday after-class coffee klatches at Au Bon Pain he was invariably ringed by young women grad assistants palpably enthralled by his brilliance and hanging on his every word. It was hard to feel sorry for him on that score.

I took back Poon's crumpled note, stuffed it in my pocket, and headed for the door.

"Thanks for zeroing in on where they took Poon. But call me right away, you solve *that* puzzle, Harry." I gestured toward his laptop. I went out the door.

I heard a yell behind me. "Oh Rundle!" A couple of nurses walking toward me cringed at the sound.

I popped back in Harry's room.

"What the hell was that about?"

"You said to call if I solved Justin's code. So. I just called."

One of the nurses burst in the door behind me. Harry smiled and nodded. She checked Harry's chart, got him to reassure her he was OK, and went out down the corridor.

"You cracked it?" I asked.

"Yeah. Final touches. Between when you phoned earlier and when you showed up here now."

"Good God, Harry! Why didn't you say so! Come on, what is it?"

"Well, it's an expert system, like I said. But damn unusual in that it's about controlling something moving about in space."

"Like flying around?"

"Nah. I tried 3-D space, but it all looked crazy. Then I collapsed the actions to two dimensions, like some kind of autonomous robot vehicle going about on land."

"So it's a program that drives some kind of car. A tank, maybe."

"Hold on, I didn't say that. I thought it might be. But the land in the model was pretty weird because it would shift about all the time."

"Like going over sand dunes?"

"Yeah, like that. Except they were pretty unstable sand dunes."

"Ok—then what?"

"So then, I said to myself maybe it's not land, maybe it's water."

"And?"

"And it all fell into place."

"Yes," I said.

He paused.

"Well, come on, Harry."

"It's how to sail a boat."

I sat down on the edge of the bed.

"What do you mean?"

"What I mean is it's how to sail a boat."

"Like pushing the tiller around? Trimming the sails?"

"Yeah, like that. But listen. It's not just an instruction program that shows you how to sail in ten easy lessons. The program can actually sail the boat."

"Sail the boat?"

"Yeah. It can sail the boat. It can be rigged up either to send commands to actuators, like electric winches, or it can send out verbal orders to live sailors to tell them to haul on that line, trim that sail, or whatever. Or both. Oh, and it takes wind speed and direction into account. Current and tide. It figures out what kind of sea you got, like it's a 'following sea,' maybe, that's taking your boat along with it."

I started to interrupt, but Harry held up his hand.

"Hold on. There's more. It knows strategy. It's got all the competitive sailing smarts you'd ever want. Like, when to tack, when to come about, how to overtake another boat so you steal their wind and leave their sails flapping limp. And not just for some little dinghy in the Charles. Even if you…"

This time I interrupted him. "Even if you wanted it to sail an ocean yacht?"

"Yeah, like one of those."

"Like an America's Cup racer."

"Yeah." An impish look came over his face. "Yeah, even one of those babies. Hey, I modeled it on the screen. Take a look." Harry punched a few keys on his laptop and swung the screen around so I could see it better.

Harry was a lousy artist. But there it was, a crude ship's hull of glowing green light with a couple of triangles tacked above it to portray mainsail and jib. The glowing green boat scudded slowly across Harry's screen, tracking closely behind a similar boat image done in red.

"Root for the green one. That's us."

The two boat shapes headed for a pulsating "X" in the middle of the screen, the green boat slightly behind the red one, but veering dead on the X marker.

"Watch them swing around that little 'X' marker—that's one of the course buoys." The little colored boats cut around the X and crossed paths, the green vessel now taking the lead.

"That's a pretty smart racing jibe there," said Harry. "See how it stole the air from red's sails. There's a damn good skipper aboard that green boat."

"Yeah, and a damn good hacker behind that keyboard. I owe you, Harry, and I don't know where to begin to pay you back for this one."

"You can pay me back by not going to where you may be thinking of going. I'm such a smartass figuring out where Poon probably got worked over that I forgot what you might do about it."

"Harry, I..."

"Give it all to the cops, Bill! We know what Justin's code is about now. It's just about sailing boats, not a scheme to spread anthrax in the New York subway system. Let them take it from here."

"I don't know. Justin most likely got killed for it. Then there's what happened to you, and now Poon."

"Yeah. All the more reason to hand it off to the cops."

"Justin entrusted me with his program. There may be some good explanation why he didn't call the cops himself if he had some fears about what might happen to it."

"Just stay away from that gray house."

I said thanks again to Harry, and headed home.

Chapter 12

I don't have much of a track record in breaking and entering, but I decided not to let that stop me.

It's amazing how quickly you get some of the basics down. Dark clothes. No belts or shoulder-loops to snag on anything. Nothing in pockets to jingle and signal your presence. No fluorescent dial watches. I was having subliminal recollections of old WWII late night movies with David Niven or Errol Flynn parachuting behind enemy lines in Burma or wherever.

In any case, I found myself at 5:25 that evening on Mount Auburn Street. The weather was clear, the snow having let up, leaving maybe six inches or so on the ground, all freshly plowed.

There was only one house in the area that fit Poon's description—a gray double-decker next to a red triple-decker. I crossed the street and approached the house. A streetlamp illuminated my path as I crossed, one of those halogen types that make everything look a sickly off-yellow. My stealth persona cautioned me that I should have skirted the lamp's cone of light, but once I started across I thought that I'd just draw more attention to myself if I abruptly changed direction. However, except for a car to my left pulling out from the Mount Auburn Hospital parking facility, and a bent-over figure some distance away to my right hauling shopping bags, there was no one about to witness whatever way I veered.

Poon said they dragged him into the "low" floor; I took that to be the first. I slowed my steps as I neared the gateway, glancing up at the porch. It was set back about fifteen feet from the street.

Except for a first floor hall lamp, there were no lights on in the house. Pausing at the gateway, I looked left, then right. No one about, if you discounted an MBTA trolley bus lumbering by headed for Harvard Square.

I surveyed the unshoveled path to the porch. There was a single set of footprints in the snow, going up to the house and back out to the gate. The depressions were mostly filled back in by snow, suggesting they'd been made much earlier in the afternoon. Stepping carefully in the forward facing prints, I made my way toward the house.

I reached the porch and went up its three stairs. Hanging on the door was a mail basket of woven rattan holding a couple flyers— one from Circuit City, the other from Shaw's Market. Both were addressed to "Occupant." Could someone be inside, having already picked up their mail and left these behind? Maybe. On balance, it looked like no one was at home either up or down. This time was as good as any. And I'd better do it now before someone did arrive.

I tried the front door. Locked.

The window to the left of the door had aluminum storms. I pushed at the edge of the lower pane to test its fit. Snugged tight. I tried the window to the right of the door, which like its mate, had aluminum storms. Again, snugged up tight. I considered using the screwdriver I'd brought to pry it up, but decided it was too much to hope that I'd just look to any passers-by like someone who had lost his keys. Instead, I'd try the back of the house.

I went down the snowed-over path at the right of the house to the back yard. I passed on my left what I guessed to be parlor windows, a smaller bathroom one, and then a pair of windows that were probably kitchen. There were no lights on the first or the second floor.

I mounted the steps of the back porch. It was roofed over, and its floor was only partially covered by blown snow. A bare bulb in a wire mesh cage was mounted on the jamb of the rear door and illumined a sector of the otherwise murky back yard, a space maybe twenty feet by thirty feet.

The yard was empty except for a Y-shaped swivel clothesline. A snaggle of loose rope trailed from the clothesline's outstretched arms onto the ground. The yard's snow cover was pristine except for some tracks and rifts made by a small animal trying to plough its way through.

A sudden movement on the porch floor caught my eye, something low and shadowy, slinking along. More movement. A cat.

A calico, it emerged from the shadows into the dim circle of light and came toward me in a sinuous walk. It began to meow. I started to shush it, but thought better. Its yowl was part of the local sound ecology, while my shush was not.

The cat rubbed up against my legs. I reached down and gave it a few pats. It had double paws in front, toes like a bunch of grapes. I'd read somewhere that all New England cats who had double front paws were descended from a single ancestor who lived in Salem, Massachusetts, sometime around the Civil War. Or was it earlier, around 1840? I made a mental note to check it out, plus a mental note to research whether aspiring break-in artists let themselves get distracted about such things as cats' feet.

Time was passing. If I pushed the cat away, would it break out into a loud caterwaul? This was his territory, not mine. I waited until the cat became uninfatuated with my leg, which was a good long minute, and watched him slink off around the corner of the house.

I surveyed the porch. A pair of windows to the right of the door featured the same aluminum storms that had stymied me out front. I decided to test the door.

I turned the knob and pushed. Locked. The striker behind the bolt, though, seemed mushy to my touch. Maybe would give way with enough force. I braced myself and gave a firm push.

The wood on the jamb gave way and the striker plate fell to the floor behind the door. No clatter from its fall. Must be a rug behind there. I pushed the door open.

I was in a small, square-shaped entry. A door opposite the one I'd just forced led, I surmised, into the kitchen. An identical door to my right probably led to the cellar.

It was a small sheaf of folded newspapers, not a rug, that had let the striker plate to fall without clatter. The papers framed a water bowl and an open, half-devoured can of Frisky Fancy Treat or whatever. I stepped over the setup of bowl and can and tried the door opposite the entryway. Unlocked.

Some small amount of light came into the room from the back porch bulb and, distantly, from the lampposts on Mount Auburn Street. I could make out a double sink to my left, under the windows. The bulk of a refrigerator loomed just beyond, festooned with notepapers held by plastic magnets. To the right of the refrigerator was a door, then a large poster of the young Marlon Brando slouching next to a motorcycle. Farther to the right, beyond the opposite corner of the kitchen, was another door.

I stepped cautiously into the room. The knuckles of my right hand rapped into the edge of a table. In the half-light I could make out an oil-cloth covering, salt and pepper shakers, an oval sugar bowl with a spoon stuck in it, and, next to a stack of cereal dishes, a crumpled box of Special K. Mentally, I tossed a coin. Heads, the door across by the fridge; tails, the door to the right. Tails. I cut across the kitchen to the door opposite, opened it and went through.

Damn. I'd crashed my right knee into some contraption just beyond the door. I groped about. I could feel a set of handlebars and a seat mounted on a rigid frame—an exercise bike. I'd made a bit of noise in the bump, though I hoped not loud enough for anyone to hear if they were, say, napping upstairs.

I listened intently for a moment or two. I could dash out the back door, if I had to. Except for the hum of the refrigerator behind me, I heard nothing. I decided all was clear to go ahead.

I was in a hallway. I put my hands out to either side and groped along the walls. Ahead and to my left, I could discern a faint, grayish patch. A doorway. I worked my way to it, and entered.

A pair of windows set in the wall opposite let in enough light for me to see I was in what was probably the dining room. A long table filled the center of the room, an elaborate, multi-armed light fixture suspended over it. There was some kind of credenza (is that what you called those things you put flatware in?) against the wall to my right. I wasn't sure exactly what I was looking for, but this didn't look to be it. I turned to go back through the door into the hall.

A soft creak sounded—like a floorboard easing back into place when a foot lifted from it. I froze.

Had it come down the hall toward the front of the house? Or off to my right from whatever rooms lay in that direction? Or had I imagined it?

I shrugged it off as old house noise. I hadn't heard the front door open. Surely, if anyone were coming home now and entering by that way, they wouldn't know I was here, and wouldn't be tiptoeing in.

I turned left down the hall and stepped softly and slowly toward the front of the house. Another grayish rectangle came into focus— another door, ahead and to the right.

Dammit. I'd crashed my foot into something hard and heavy.

My heart pounded in my chest. Had I said "Dammit" out loud? I couldn't tell, couldn't remember. Anyway, the crash of my foot had been loud enough.

I strained my ears. Again, nothing. I waited a long minute. Still nothing. I put out my hand to feel what I had bumped into. Again, a bicycle seat, this time set vertical to the wall, and mounted on what felt like steel tubing—a rowing machine. Whoever lived here, they were in good shape. Or they had bought these things and, after some broken exercise resolutions, just stood them up against the walls. I took a couple of cautious steps around the rower, and went through the doorway on the right.

The space I'd entered was a large parlor, open at the far end, and connected to an equally large living room area. Several windows admitted a measure of dim light from the street. Along the wall to my left was a large fish tank, backlit with purplish light—maybe to grow algae to feed the fish, or to keep it from growing so as not to choke the fish. In any case, the purplish light helped illumine five tables aligned in a row down through the parlor and into the living room.

These weren't ordinary tables, but ones with drafting boards tilted at a slant and measuring maybe four feet by six. Mechanical

T-squares were built into their left edges, and large sheets of paper were attached to their surfaces. Each of the drafting tables had its associated computer workstation set alongside it, the screens glowing a dim green, prompt cursors pulsating faintly in the dark.

I walked deeper into the room. Beyond where the fish tank was situated, the entire wall to my left seemed to be one large bulletin board, covered with drawings and photographs of what looked like boats and parts of boats.

I had to have a closer look at what was on those drafting tables. I retrieved the small flashlight I'd slipped into my jacket pocket, along with a swatch of terrycloth, one quarter of an old bath towel. I folded the terrycloth on itself twice, wrapped it over the flashlight's lens, switched the beam on, and approached the nearest table.

Held in place by strips of masking tape was a meticulously detailed blueprint. It showed in profile the hull of a racing yacht, sleek and shark-like, with a bulbous fin-keel hanging below. Above and to the right of the central figure of the boat were several blow-up drawings of sub-regions of the hull.

I needed a bit more light. I peeled away a layer of the terrycloth.

One of the blow-ups depicted an electric motor embedded in the hull and linked via fiber-optic circuitry to a microprocessor. The motor, in turn, appeared to be linked via a concealed mechanical connection to one of the boat's "coffee grinders"—the two-handled winches crew members use to trim the sails during tacking and jibing maneuvers.

As best I could tell from the drawing, the coffee-grinder could be cranked in the usual way by hand, but could be operated just as well by the hidden computer-controlled motor.

Again, I heard a sound, ever so soft, like that of a floorboard creaking under a foot tread. I switched off the flashlight and stuffed it and the toweling back in my pocket.

My instincts told me it was high time to get out—maybe even too late to make a clean exit. I stepped as quietly as I could back out into the hall.

A breeze caught my face. A silent swish of fabric touched my elbow. Someone had just knifed past me and down the hall toward the front of the house.

I strained to see down the hall. Recalling the old night fighter's trick of using peripheral vision, I scanned my eyes back and forth. A bit of light coming in from the street helped define the edges of the front door frame. I could make out nothing else.

I heard a soft sound that seemed to be coming from the hall toward the rear of the house, a subtle rustle not unlike someone turning the pages of a book. The sound stopped.

There had to be at least two of them, one ahead of me down the hall by the front door, the other behind me—both of them silently awaiting my slightest movement.

I could make a run. At either end of hall there'd be—for a moment anyway—only one of them to cope with before the other could come to his aid.

I considered sprinting to the back door, the way I'd come in. But if I made it, I'd be out in the backyard and maybe get pinned in there. Not so good. If I could instead make it out through the front door, there'd at least be Mount Auburn Street with its pedestrians and cars going by.

The front door looked like the way to go. I took a deep breath and began to sprint down the hall.

I didn't get far.

A blow like that of an iron fist crashed into my chest. Followed by another one across my right ear. I staggered back. I couldn't see a blessed thing. I clutched to my left at what felt like the frame of a doorway, and plunged through. Whoever had that iron hand plunged in after me.

Light—not a lot—but enough to see on a table to my left some kind of brass figurine. In a panic, and with a move I would have never thought was in me, I spun about, snatched the figurine, and, following through, caught whoever was after me on the side of his head. He crashed at my feet, an arm flailing across my ankle.

He lay there, rock still.

There was still someone else out there. Had he come down the hall and was waiting just outside?

The door to the room—set up as a kind of home office—was hung so as to swing inward from the hall. In the dim light, I saw a ladder-back chair standing in front of a small desk. I grabbed the chair, and with my free hand swung the door closed.

I propped the chair, back to, up and under the doorknob, and kicked at the bottom of the legs to wedge it in tight. As I gave it a final kick, I could see the doorknob twist. Someone was trying to open the door.

I raced to the window, yanked off the curtains and shade, and tossed them aside.

A crash like a gunshot assaulted my ears. There was another crash at the door, and the splintering of wood. Someone out there knew how to use his feet.

I pushed the window lock free and pulled up the sash. I shoved the storm window in its frame out onto the snow, just as a third thunderous kick behind me split the door down the middle and sent the ladder-back chair flying across the room.

Praying for a reasonably soft landing, I dove out the window headfirst, my legs trailing behind me. My right foot didn't clear, but caught on the sill. I landed head and arms first on the snowy ground, my trunk and legs rearing up behind me at a crazy angle.

Whoever had broken through the door now gave out a loud grunt as he wrapped his arms around the ankle of my snagged leg and held me fast.

With great effort, I twisted about and looked up and back over my shoulder. In the pale light from the street I could faintly make out his face. Large round head with coarse black hair. A glint of wire-frame spectacles made him look scholarly, like a crazily zealous librarian determined I wouldn't leave the premises without properly checking out my books.

I cocked my free leg back and sent it into the head with the coarse black hair. Contact. The eyeglasses went sailing. He uttered a soft "aaaargh." His grip on my ankle loosened enough for me to pull away, leaving my shoe behind.

I scrambled to my feet and loped down the walk to Mount Auburn

Street. An MBTA bus, headed for Watertown, was paused at the corner. I flagged the bus and jumped on. My shoeless foot caught the driver's eye. As she pulled the bus away and I groped for fare change, I started to mutter an explanation, but decided to hell with it.

The bus was about half full. Ignoring the curious stares at my feet, I took a seat down in back, and tried to calm myself with long slow breaths. Maybe that Greek restaurant in Watertown Square would be open, and not mind serving a semi-shod customer whose hands were shaking because he was wondering whether he might have just killed a man by a blow to the head with a brass figurine.

Chapter 13

The next day was to be a busy one.

I was grateful for that. Maybe the activity would keep my mind off the previous night's mayhem—and the nagging thought of what I might have done.

I was in my office at a quarter to nine. I checked my email and found a stack of messages: some requests for article reprints, Calls for Papers for several computer conferences, a note from my secretary that a prospective grad student had phoned, was to be in town next week, and was there some chance I could interview her?

There were also emailed requests from SRO—the lab's Sponsor Relations Office—for half-hour visits from this or that corporation, some of whom were footing our bills. These were always time sinks, but necessary. Sometimes SRO said, OK, a grad student can do this, but often they noted that only a faculty member would do. There was such a visit already scheduled for 9:30 this morning when a group from KWA Electronics of Kyoto would arrive, eleven engineers plus a managing director. They were all interested in "human interface," which, of the various research groups in the lab, most directly involved mine. I would have them for a full two hours.

Yesterday, I'd alerted a couple of grad students to help with the KWA demos. Without them on hand to run things, I'd just be standing in the middle of my lab area all by myself without the foggiest notion of how to set things in motion.

But unless you alerted them beforehand, you couldn't necessarily count on any grad students to be available to assist. Computer "hackers" are essentially nocturnal creatures; if you ask one to be on hand for a morning demo, chances are he or she is not rising early, but staying up late.

I plugged in the small electric pot on the side table, boiled some water, made tea, and settled in to knock off some email replies. At 9:30 sharp, there was a knock on the door.

Gail Everett from SRO stood in the doorway. An oriental languages major at Princeton, she had spent four years in Japan with the Tokyo office of IBM before coming to work with us. A tall, waspy brunette in a becomingly cut business suit, she towered over the contingent of Japanese in their business suits who were milling about in the hall behind her. Whatever intimidation her height might cause them was offset by her command of their language.

I rose quickly from my desk and went forward to greet the group. There was a flurry of trading of business cards, with the obligatory lingering over them. The leader of their group, Mr. Takeshi Ono, managing director, seemed impatient with the process, though the others were deferential to it, seemingly torn between tradition and the more "Western" outlook of their boss.

The ritual of savoring business cards completed, I led the group down the hallway to my lab area. Gail brought up the rear, talking animatedly in Japanese to some of the stragglers. I rapped loudly on the closed door to alert my crew to our arrival, then opened the door and led the group in.

While my students conducted the demos, I stood off to one side with Mr. Ono, who divided his attention between our conversation and the flashing graphics displays.

"I very much admire the American ways of research," he said in his nearly perfect English. "I would like to get our board to approve the establishment of—well, a lab like this." He gestured about. "You know, I got my doctorate at MIT. In electrical engineering."

"Have you ever spoken with Dr. Etherington about some kind of closer collaboration?"

"Yes, I have indeed. He says he could help us copy the Cognitive Computer Lab, but that it probably would be a superficial copy only.

He maintains that our whole educational system in Japan trains people differently than in America. 'You beat all the creativity and curiosity out of them,' he says, or something like that."

"Maybe a new lab in Japan, with students trained here—or elsewhere at the Institute—could help." To not sound like an MIT chauvinist, I added, "Or trained at Stanford or maybe Carnegie-Mellon."

Mr. Ono smiled. "Yes, yes. There is so much rivalry in the world, is there not? Did you know..." he leaned forward as he spoke, "... that officially Russia is still at war with Japan? I read on the plane flying over that their Foreign Minister and our Prime Minister had some talks recently, but our countries are still at war, technically, after more than fifty-five years."

I smiled and nodded. Technologically as well as technically, I added to myself, recalling Sergei's vehemence. And, in his case, more like ninety-five years, not just fifty-five.

After the demo sessions and a short break, we all headed for a formal lunch set up in the lab's main conference room. Gail helped whenever the language channel failed to connect. Then, after an elaborate round of parting formalities, the KWA Electronics group docilely followed her to the elevator and to their afternoon agenda of visits with other groups within the lab.

That duty done, what I felt the need to do was to find out, if possible, any dire consequences of the previous night's misadventure. With not a little trepidation, I went downstairs to the lab's main reception desk and retrieved a copy of the *Boston Globe* from the stack of dailies on the counter. Back in my office, I tore in to the "City & Region" section, where accounts of the last twenty-four hours of stabbings, drive-by shootings, and miscellaneous break-ins would be posted.

I could find nothing about any MIT faculty breaking into a house on Mount Auburn Street and killing an occupant with a blow from a blunt instrument.

I folded the paper up and tossed it aside. I riffled through the pile of mail my secretary had put on my desk. A small envelope with the return address of John Creedon on it caught my eye. I tore it open. Inside was a handwritten note over Creedon's signature inviting me—given, he said, my interest in classic guitars—to view some he had in his collection of rare instruments. RSVP by phone at the following number.

Why he'd—out of the blue—be asking me to his home was as puzzling as how he knew of my interest in guitars. But just as I was reaching for my phone to call and accept Creedon's invitation, a figure leaned in at the doorway.

"Hello, American! How you doing?"

It was Kenichi Tsukamoto.

He held up a sheaf of papers in his left hand to shield his eyes from the low early-afternoon winter sun that streamed in the window at my back. His right hand held a crumpled brown paper bag.

"Crazy town, your Cambridge. Crazy town."

I waved him in. "What happened, Kenichi?" As if I didn't know.

Tsukamoto came in and stood across from my desk. As he lowered his left hand holding the papers, I could see a large purple welt across his cheek. One bow of his eyeglasses was wound with a swatch of what looked like black electrician's tape.

"Some guy broke in our house early last night, just after dark. He went all around inside. We jumped him, and had a big fight."

"Did he get away?"

Tsukamoto smiled playfully. "Yes. He slipped out. He was a pretty wily guy."

I asked my real question. "Anyone get hurt? I mean, beyond that bruise of yours?" I gestured toward the left side of his face.

Tsukamoto answered with a question of his own.

"What do you think, Professor Rundle? What would anyone want in our house?"

"To steal something. Maybe looking for drug money, or something they could sell."

"No. I think not. This was different. This guy was searching our place. Looking for something." Tsukamoto's voice took on a steely tone. "Someone wanted to see what we were doing in our house."

I leant back in my chair and tucked my hands behind my head. "Oh, what *are* you doing?"

His tone even harder, Tsukamoto replied, "We are students. We are trying to learn about oceanographics and ship design. We are studying, and we are minding our own business."

The air between us was cold and edgy. After a moment, I said, "You and your friends have every right to do that. Without being harassed by break-ins."

Tsukamoto fixed me in an icy stare, his look made all the more chilling by the angry welt on his cheek. Again, I fished for what I wanted so desperately to know. "Anyway, you guys are all ok?"

Tsukamoto smirked.

"You're really worried about our welfare in this town, Professor Rundle? We appreciate your concern."

He turned and headed for the door.

"Yes," I said, "I hope everything is all right."

Tsukamoto paused in the doorway, and turned back to face me.

"We have a clue about our intruder. Maybe even a suspect."

Tucking the sheaf of papers under his arm, he opened the brown paper bag and held up its contents.

It was my right shoe, the one I'd left behind.

"From our Cinderella," he said, his mouth breaking into a sardonic smile.

"You have a clue, then?"

"Yes, a clue. Maybe not a good clue, though. So many feet in Cambridge about this size." He held the shoe up higher. "Maybe even your size, too? No?"

He dangled the shoe a moment by its laces. It pivoted slowly about like a magnetic compass, its toe coming to rest pointing at me.

"What was it that Johnnie Cochran said in the O. J. Simpson case? Oh, yeah. 'If the glove don't fit, you must acquit.' What would he say here, I wonder? Let's see. Maybe 'The shoe in the bundle, it points to—whoever.'"

He dropped the shoe back into the paper bag and, with something between a smile and a sneer, tossed it onto the floor beside my desk.

101

"Got to go. Have a good day, Professor Rundle." With that, he turned and walked out the door and into the hall.

Goddammit, Kenichi, I yelled inside myself. What about the guy I clubbed?

As if hearing my thoughts, Tsukamoto wheeled about and stuck his head back in the doorway. "Oh yeah," he said. "Everyone's ok. Just a few bruises. Thought you'd like to know."

"Good. Good to hear that," I said, repressing my sigh of relief.

Tsukamoto gave me another of his sardonic smiles. "Thank you for your solicitous nature. You are kind to inquire after our health."

With that, he again disappeared into the hallway.

I rose, went to my office door, closed it, and went back to slump in my chair. My heart was racing with the elation of relief. I hadn't killed whomever it was. He was OK.

I picked up Creedon's note and dialed the RSVP number. An androgynous voice answered, "Oakhill. The Creedon residence." Upon identifying myself, I was told my call was expected, and that if convenient I could come out to visit Mr. Creedon this afternoon. I said fine, I'd be there at 3:00 p.m. The androgynous voice then proceeded to issue very precise directions on how to get to Creedon's home.

I put the phone down, and stared over at the paper bag that held my shoe. Thank God, I said to myself over and over, thank God I hadn't killed him.

Chapter 14

As I drove west from Cambridge on the Mass Pike, I pondered the invitation from Creedon. His invitation both flattered and puzzled. Flattered, because a man with a billion-dollar enterprise like ZIDEX was asking me to his home to look over his collection of classic guitars. False modesty aside, though, people in his position just don't invite MIT researchers of my middling rank and repute out on a social basis unless there is something behind it. I was curious what that something might be.

Turning off the Pike, I drove a couple of miles into the very upscale suburb of Weston, and, just where I was told I would see it, spotted the small weathered sign saying "Oakhill - Private Way."

I turned right onto a deeply rutted road that eventually transformed itself into an immaculately groomed gravel drive. As I approached the brick gatehouse, a fiftyish, powerfully built man in a green ski parka stepped quickly out and signaled me to pull up. I showed him my invitation note from Creedon, which he perused impassively. He squinted at my car, consulted a small notebook, then, breaking into a broad smile, waved me on, pointing to where the drive widened in a semi-circle in front of a grand Georgian-style manor house.

As I got out of my car, a slim young man with slicked-down brown hair greeted me warmly from the steps in that same androgynous voice I'd heard over the phone. A kind of junior majordomo or whatever in his lemon-hued blazer, he led me inside and, after taking my coat, escorted me through the foyer and down a central hall, at the end of which French doors opened onto a brick-paved indoor patio.

Opposite me, across the patio floor, a double staircase descended to a vast orangery lined with sculptured yew hedges framing flowerbeds that could have graced Monet's wondrous gardens at Giverny. The patio itself extended left and right perhaps seventy feet on either side. On the left side, toward the end, John Creedon rose from a wicker chair.

"Good afternoon, Professor Rundle," he called out as he approached. "Hope you didn't have trouble finding the right lane. They insist on unobtrusive signs in this town, and sometimes one can barely read them."

"No trouble," I said.

"Something to drink before we head up to the gallery?"

Creedon spoke in a pleasing voice, his enunciation precise and clipped. The quality of his speech triggered some memory association—something someone had said—but I couldn't zero in on what exactly it was.

"Scotch neat would be perfect," I replied.

He ordered it from the yellow-jacketed young man, and the same for himself. He sat me down in a wicker chair opposite his, and for maybe ten minutes Creedon made small talk. How did I like MIT? Was I up for tenure? He muttered something about knowing some people on Academic Council. Then he said, "But what you really are here for is to see some of my guitars. How do I know of your interest, you might wonder? Well, I saw your *New American Physicist* article on the acoustics of stringed instruments. Don't be surprised at that—I skim a lot of technical journals. And you play classical guitar yourself, don't you? At least the bio blurb at the end of the article said you did."

"I was junior author on that article. It's Alec Hudson in our physics department who really knows his sound waves. I just helped with some simulations. Yes, I do play. Some friends and I have a guitar group that meets every two weeks or so—just to keep ourselves up on our practice."

"Come, let me show you some guitars, part of my instrument collection. Bring your drink along."

He led me from the patio, through the central hall, then upstairs to a long library-like room where the walls were lined, not with books, but with antique stringed instruments. My eye quickly found the corner devoted to guitars.

"You may take any of them down," Creedon said. "By all means play them, if you like. I have someone who comes by every month or so to tune them, oil the wood, and play them a bit, but I'm afraid they're not used nearly as much as they ought to be."

He was right. Wooden instruments need to be played to keep their "voice."

I took down a Panormo, dating, so the nearby placard said, from 1832. I checked the tuning and launched into a study by Sor. Even with its great age and its seldom-played state, the guitar had a beautifully sonorous tone.

Creedon relaxed in a corner chair, listening attentively while I tried in turn a Lacôte, a Pernas, a Ramiriz, and last—and, to my ear, best of all—a Torres dating from 1864, made during the master's prime. It was all wonderful, a rare treat, but after maybe twenty minutes of indulging myself I had to turn to business.

"I really appreciate seeing these guitars," I said. "They're legendary, and you're very kind to let me try them. But, if I may be so bold, I think there's more than guitars behind your invitation."

Creedon shifted in his chair. "You're right. There's something more." He fixed me steadily in the eye. "Do you believe in ghosts, Rundle?"

I returned his gaze. What was he driving at?

"I'm asking," he went on, "because your student Justin Marsh came into my plant in Waltham at 2:04 a.m. on the Monday after you reportedly found him in the Charles. That's a rather remarkable twenty-four hour new lease on life."

I froze in my chair. Good God, I thought. I had gotten a message from Justin after he was dead. Here was Creedon claiming now that he had had a bodily visitation from Justin. I tried to keep the expression on my face immobile, not to give anything in my mind away. My thoughts raced, but I didn't speak.

"I have a security system at Bear Hill Road," Creedon said. "That's where my Waltham plant is. The system is one we make and sell. It's called I-Lok. It identifies people by scanning the iris of their eye with a laser. Iris patterns are as individual as fingerprints. It was Justin Marsh who stood in that spot early Tuesday morning, looked up at the laser, and got himself into my plant."

Creedon swished the cubes in his glass about and gulped down the remnants of his drink.

"The man was dead, Rundle. You found him. At least, that's what you told us all at Hale's gathering. Can you explain it?"

"Perhaps your system—what is it? I-Lok?—made a…"

Creedon cut me off, his tone testy in contrast to his up-till-now affability. "It doesn't make mistakes. Justin was there at my plant. But how could that be? You found him dead. How could it possibly be?"

I looked down and studied the inlaid purling around the top edge of the Torres. My instincts told me not to say anything about Justin's missing eye, bizarre as that connection might be. "I have no idea," I said. "It's just not possible."

Creedon's voice softened, but his eyes remained intently on mine. "Rundle, he sent something to you. The system communication records at my plant show that his computer sent you a message hours after he must have died—a long message. Was it also a ghost doing that? Do you deny getting a message from him?"

My mind raced. What should I tell him? I had to assume he knew a lot about what happened electronically at his plant, so it would be no use denying it.

"Yes. I got an email message from Justin after he died. It appeared to originate from his computer at our lab, but I suppose it could have been forwarded from somewhere else."

"That somewhere was ZIDEX. May I ask what the message was? It seems it was a very long one—not just a note, but a program, perhaps."

I decided to tell Creedon something, though not everything.

"Actually," I said, "I couldn't make out what it was. Because of its length, I assumed it was a draft of his thesis that he wanted me to look at, but it was all garbled. Probably some glitch in transmission."

"In any event, I'd like to get that message back, garbled or not," Creedon said with icy cordiality. "It may have been a copy of this thesis, as you say. But it may also have been some program material he was creating here. It was volunteer work, something he was doing with us—for a charity, if you will—so he wasn't breaking any of your lab's rules on having outside jobs. In any case, it's the property of ZIDEX. Can you send it to me?"

"Well, because it was unintelligible," I said, "I may have just deleted it. I'll check anyhow to see if I still have it, and if it's there I'll send it along."

That sounded weak. It was implausible that I or any faculty would throw away *any* message from a student who had just died under mysterious circumstances. I'd just let him think whatever he wanted to think.

"Thanks," Creedon said. "I'd be much obliged." He scribbled something on the back of a business card, and handed it to me. "Here's where to send it. And may I ask that you delete your copy afterwards? Trouble with email, copies of everything just proliferate all over."

His demeanor had relaxed and the edge had gone from his voice. Creedon pointed to my empty whisky glass and, in an artful mix of hospitality and dismissal, added, "One for the road?"

As I drove back to Cambridge, my mind buzzed with Creedon's claim of Justin being at his plant early Monday morning. No, it hadn't been a ghost, nor could it have been Justin himself. I was repelled by the thought, but it could only have been Justin's eye— borne by someone who had killed him to obtain it because they were desperate to get into ZIDEX.

But how could a human eye be taken out and a day later be— well, fresh enough—to pass muster under the exacting scrutiny of a computer-driven, iris-scanning security system? It didn't make sense.

I did, though, make the connection between the sound of

Creedon's voice and what it was that someone had said. It was Karen Hewitt, and it was how she'd described the voice of the occasional telephone caller of last summer—the one who'd been asking to speak with Justin…

Chapter 15

Christmas weekend came and went pleasantly enough. Irina and I made another trip out to South Hadley, where we got to cross-country ski with her parents, ride on an old-fashioned sleigh around the Mount Holyoke College campus, and go caroling with some of her parents' neighbors.

By the time Irina and I returned to Cambridge late Monday evening, life had almost restored itself to a semblance of normality—but not for very long.

Early Tuesday morning, as I was walking down Irving Street toward my car to go to the lab, a pale blue Chevrolet Silverado began to tag along abreast of me. A heavy-duty suspension raised the truck's body high over outsized all-terrain tires that bore the legend "Baja Widetracker." A strip of spotlights stretched across the top of the cab.

The driver, a heavy-featured man with a walrus moustache, leaned out his window and said softly, "Rundle?" My head jerked ever so slightly in response to my name. I answered, "Pardon?" He said nothing. If his purpose was to identify me, he already had.

He gunned his engine, pulled a bit ahead, and stopped. He leaned over to the passenger side and swung open the door. I heard him say crisply, "Go, Sam!" A dark shape clambered out.

The shape turned into a large, short-haired dog that stood rock still on the sidewalk. It had patches of white on its chest and face and white "booties" on each foot. Pointed ears gave it a jaunty look, and its panting mouth looked almost smiling. Powerfully muscled legs and a deep chest bespoke the born fighter. A chill went through me as I realized what it was: a pit bull.

The door of the Silverado slammed shut and the driver whooped through the open window, "Get 'im, Sam!" As the truck pulled away, the dog came at me like a cannon shot.

Panicked, I looked for some way to fight him off.

A worn-out push broom, the heavy kind for sweeping patios, stuck handle down in a barrel nearby at sidewalk's edge. Thank God for trash day. I snatched it up, and leveled the brush head in the path of the charging dog.

What must have been at least eighty pounds of fury crashed collar-high against the head of the broom. I staggered back from the impact. The handle was nearly wrenched from my grip, but I managed to hold on.

The broom head must have hit the dog on the windpipe. He spun back and his bark turned to a low sputter. But only for a second. He snarled and plunged at me again. Once more, I held the broom out in front of me. My feet slid back as he rammed against it, his teeth slashing up and over the bristles.

I was terrified. I couldn't keep fending him off. I was going to be mauled. Maybe killed, if he got to my throat. There was no one to help me. My arms trembled as I pressed back on the broom.

The broom handle broke and clattered to the sidewalk.

In a flash the dog clamped his muzzle on my left forearm. I felt his teeth rip through my jacket, sink down through my flesh and into the bone. He shook his head back and forth, a great furrow of muscle and fur rising above his neck. Oddly, I felt no pain—just the incredible force of his jaws.

A Doberman or a German Shepherd would just bite and hold. But a pit bull bites, holds, and tears. Rising up on his hind legs for a better grip, his forepaws clawing my face, he wrenched me about, and with a chewing action began working his way up my arm.

In my right hand I still held the yard-long remnant of the broom handle. The splintered end tapered sharply. In desperation, I set the point over the dog's collarbone and, falling to my knees to give the thrust my full weight, jammed it down into his chest. Over a foot of broom handle went into him.

To my horror, the thrust barely slowed him. He dropped my forearm, but with a deep growl immediately grabbed me in his jaws again, now up about my elbow. Blood was spilling from my sleeve. He yanked me forward savagely. I lost balance and pitched forward onto him as we both crashed to the ground.

In the fall, he'd rolled onto his back, his head cradled between roadway and curb. I lay partly on top of him, my elbow still clamped in his jaw. Our faces were inches apart, the breath from his nostrils hot on my cheek. His eyes rolled about furiously.

Trying to pull my elbow away only set his teeth in tighter. Instead, I drove my elbow deeper into his mouth, folding my forearm close to my upper arm to make the joint angle as sharp as possible. With my right hand I clutched the hilt of the broom handle and churned it about, hoping the point deep in his chest would hit something vital.

Thankfully, I felt his grip begin to relax. Blood was now flooding from his nostrils, staining the white patch on his chest. His eyes took on a dreamy, imploring look, as if asking why I was doing this to him. But I didn't dare let him up.

We lay locked together, our blood pooling together on the black asphalt of the street. Then a strangely gentle shudder went through him. His grip softened, then let completely go. His breath had stopped. I lay on top of him in shock and exhaustion.

I staggered to my feet. My jacket sleeve had gaping rents and was sopped to the cuff in blood. My arm inside hung limp and throbbing.

Down the street, maybe thirty yards away, two young women carrying attaché cases stared at me and the dog in bewilderment. An elderly man standing near them was pointing toward the dog and then at me and saying something to the women. They hadn't tried to help, and I couldn't blame them. They could have done nothing against such an animal, and could themselves have been badly hurt.

I turned and stumbled back up Irving Street toward my apartment. Up ahead, the pale blue Silverado made a left turn from Cambridge Street onto Irving and headed toward me. The truck slowed, and the heavy-featured driver with the walrus moustache stared at me blankly. He gunned the motor and rolled down to where the dog lay, pulled up, and jumped out.

Ignoring the women and the old man, he knelt in the gutter beside the dog. His hand stroked its body tenderly. Then he looked down the street at me. "Bastarrrrrrrrd!!" he screamed. He stood up, straddling the dog, his fists clenched in the air. "Bastarrrrrrrrrrrd!!"

I hurried down the stairs to my door, got it open with my good hand, and locked myself inside. I could still hear his screaming from the street as I dialed 911.

Chapter 16

The police had come quickly in response to my call, but the mustached guy had scooped up the dog's body and made off before they arrived. Taking down my story en route, they drove me to the emergency room at Cambridge City Hospital.

I was pretty lucky, the doctor said. Tendons intact, minimal nerve damage—if indeed any. She gave me an initial rabies shot; there could be more if tests on the dog show it was rabid. She bandaged me up, telling me the stiffness and numbness might stay around for a while, but that the arm ought to recover OK.

I didn't tell the doctor I was a serious—albeit amateur—guitarist. But therein lay my biggest fear about my arm. No concert career was at stake, but the thought of not being able to play, or being able to play only poorly, was depressing enough.

Though my left arm was numb and trussed up in a sling, I could still drive a car with my right, and my plan for the afternoon was a visit to Justin's uncle, Bennett Eames. Eames may have had his own questions in mind when he invited me, but I had some of my own that I wanted to ask him.

I set out a bit after one o'clock under clear skies, though the weather reports promised rain for later. Eames lived, so Karen Hewitt had told me, in Marblehead on the ocean side of Ocean Avenue in a section of town known as Marblehead Neck. I recalled Karen saying I couldn't miss the house, it resembling a small castle, complete with crenellated turrets on each of four corners.

Karen was right. Though not quite as large as the houses before

113

and after, it was easily the most distinctive. The turrets were there, one topped with a flagpole bearing a tattered yachting ensign that flapped defiantly in the blustery wind off the ocean. A semi-circular driveway led off the street, down to the house, and then back out to the road. I followed the drive and parked in front of the entrance.

The house grounds looked untended. Sizeable sections of downed tree limbs lay strewn about the lawn, casualties of the unusually strong hurricane we'd had in late September. A particularly large maple branch rested across the basin of an octagonal stone fountain, having in its fall sheered the arm from a bronze nymph atop the fountain's central pedestal. To my left, beyond the castle's wall and half hidden by a row of tall pines, was a large boat set in a wooden cradle. A faded tarpaulin covered its superstructure. The hull below the tarp showed sleek lines, though its paint was scaled and flaked like some rampant skin condition.

It had begun to rain. I ducked out of the Cherokee, ran to the cover of the portico, shook myself off, and pushed the doorbell. As I waited, I carefully adjusted the sling on my left forearm, trying to ignore the constant throbbing.

Some moments went by. Was Eames at home? I'd been unable to phone ahead because Karen didn't have a number to give me, nor did information have a listing. I pressed the bell again.

Someone was home. I heard a scuffing sound on the other side of the door, then a voice through the intercom asking, "Who is it?"

I replied, "Is that you, Mr. Eames? It's Bill Rundle. I was your nephew Justin's advisor at MIT. We met briefly at the funeral."

"Yes, I remember."

"You wanted to have a talk? Is this a good time for me to have come by?"

"Yes, yes, of course. Just a moment."

A few more scuffling sounds, and the door swung wide open. There was Bennett Eames, as I remembered him, in his electric powered wheelchair. In contrast to his castle's disheveled grounds, he was immaculately groomed, in navy blazer, silk ascot, sharply creased gray trousers, and white deck shoes. He waved me in, bade me hang my jacket on a bent oak coat rack, and, deftly steering his powered chair, led the way into his living room.

There was a small fire going in his fireplace. Above the mantle, two finely crafted clipper ship models flanked a framed diploma from the United States Naval Academy. More ship models—from lateen-rigged feluccas to WWII Liberty ships—were situated about the room, while the walls were replete with sailing prints and wooden plaques bearing half-hull models of racing yachts.

Eames maneuvered his chair to an open spot in front of, and a bit to the right of, the fireplace. "Please sit down," he said, waving a gnarled, weathered hand toward a chair opposite him. "If you like sherry, try that." His voice, now unamplified by the front door's microphone, was soft and barely audible. He pointed to a decanter and set of small-stemmed glasses on a table next to the chair. "And pour me one, too, if you please."

With my free arm, I set out two of the glasses side by side. I took the stopper out of the decanter and poured. The decanter, of the finest Waterford crystal, was proverbially as heavy as lead.

Eames watched solicitously my one-armed bartending efforts. "I beg your pardon," he said. "I hadn't noticed that empty sleeve—the sling under your jacket. Didn't mean to put you through all those gyrations."

I was touched that someone with his affliction should show concern about such minor stuff as my temporarily out-of-commission arm.

"No problem—just takes a moment or two longer," I said. I raised my slung arm a bit more out from its cover under my jacket. "Ran into a nasty dog in the neighborhood yesterday. We had an altercation about who owned the sidewalk in front of my house. Despite the look of my arm, he lost."

I passed Eames his glass, took mine, and settled into the chair across from him.

"I heard a lot about you from Justin," Eames said. "He liked you very much. And I could see that you cared, too, coming to his burial."

Eames shifted in his chair and straightened up. The effort made him breathy, his eyes taking on a strained look. It must have been sheer pride that made him sit sternly erect in my presence.

I asked, "How can I help you, sir? You wanted me to…"

"Oh, for God's sake, don't call me 'sir'! It's Bennett. Call me Bennett."

"Yes…" I said, almost calling him "sir" again. He looked like one of those people who could be addressed only in that way. "Yes—Bennett—and please call me Bill. In any case, how might I help you?"

Eames looked away for a moment, then turned back to me and said, "Justin is gone. But I can't understand *why* he's gone. The police tell us nothing, really. They say it was most likely some muggers grabbed him. They say he must have fought back. His attackers, they say, probably clubbed him—maybe hard enough to kill him—and then threw his body into the Charles."

I could see Eames becoming agitated. He was having difficulty breathing. I raised my hand to encourage him to slow down, but he waved it away and went on, "But you see, Bill, his wallet wasn't taken. It wasn't robbery. The whole thing doesn't make sense, unless…

"I've asked myself if Justin took his own life. There's been so much of that at MIT in recent years, as you must know. His mother is asking herself that same question, too, though I don't dare to talk with her about that possibility. Or with his friend Karen either, for that matter."

Eames paused to catch his breath, then went on. "Look, Bill, how well was Justin really doing at the Institute this last fall? You were his advisor. You must have known how he was doing. He was doing good work, wasn't he? On multi-modal something or other, I recall. Talking to computers, with gestures and so forth. Tracking eyes, too—the computer would know where you were looking. Like having a conversation with the machine."

Justin had evidently told him about the thesis work he was doing with me. But that was not the kind of thing that might have got him killed, except figuratively, perhaps, by his thesis committee.

I answered, "Yes, it was good work; some of the very best, in my view. We were breaking through the last real frontier in human/

computer dialogue. The machine would listen to you talk, watch your hand motions, follow where your eyes were looking. And Justin was leading the way. It's all a great loss to computer science, but a greater personal loss."

I paused. Eames looked steadily at me, his frame ramrod straight in his chair. As a midshipman at Annapolis they'd had him "brace," and the lesson still held.

"But there may have been other work he was doing," I said. "Work I didn't know about."

Eames' face took on a puzzled look.

"I don't mean things he shouldn't have been doing," I went on, "just things I didn't know about—like a project with someone else at the lab. Or maybe something he was doing on the side somewhere else. For instance, wasn't he working last summer at some place out on route 128—in Waltham, maybe?"

I deliberately didn't name Creedon's company, to see whether Eames would confirm it. He did.

"Yes, he was," Eames said. "At ZIDEX Corporation. In Waltham, Bear Hill Road."

"Do you know what he was doing there?"

"Yes. He was programming."

"Do you know what kind of programming? Did he ever tell you?"

"It was something special he was doing. He didn't want me to talk with anyone about it. I have to respect that wish. I may already have said too much."

The firm line of his mouth told me as much as his words that he was not going to share anything about what the program was unless it was of overriding importance to do so.

I went on, "There may have been something about that program that—well, he just may have been killed for that program."

"'Killed for that program'! What do you mean 'killed for that program'?" Eames' voice was strained and rasping. With great effort, he pulled himself forward in his chair.

"I'm afraid I mean just that," I said. "The police aren't saying much, and I know I can't prove it to them, or to you now for that matter, but I think Justin was murdered, and because of a computer program."

Eames composed himself. He said, "You'll have to tell me what you mean by all of this."

I told him how I had found Justin's body—omitting mention of the missing eye as maybe too much to bring up, at least for the moment. I told him about the mark on the side of Justin's head and how, while he could have hit something as he fell, it could as well have been caused by a sharp blow. Eames listened intently.

I told him, too, of the long coded message I had received from Justin's computer, how I'd passed it to a colleague to decipher, and how he'd been beaten badly enough to land him in the hospital. Lastly, I told him of how I had been attacked by a pit bull.

"What can all that have to do with Justin's death?" Eames said. "The police didn't tell us anything about a message..."

"That program—the one Justin had his computer rigged up to send me if he didn't log in regularly—is about sailing a boat. It's about sailing an America's Cup racer, if you will. You've got to tell me what you know about that program because there are people who are after it who are attacking my associates and me, and who are probably the same people who killed Justin in the first place."

Eames pushed a switch on the arm of his wheelchair and swung about to face the bay window at the far end of the room. It was even more rainy and blustery outside than when I had arrived. I could see the ocean out through the panes, slate gray with whitecaps blown up by the wind.

Over his shoulder, Eames asked, "Bill, do you know what ALS is? What those letters stand for?"

"I think so," I said. "Lou Gehrig's disease."

He spoke over his shoulder, "Yeah, Lou Gehrig's disease. The long name is 'amyotrophic lateral sclerosis.' I have it. Almost two years, now. They say you have maybe three years, maybe five..."

He cleared his throat. "I used to walk without those," he said, pointing to a pair of aluminum crutches leaning against the wall next to the fireplace. "I can support myself on them for a little while. Most of the time now, though, I need this thing to get around." He tapped the arm of his electric wheelchair.

"I have trouble breathing," he went on. "My voice is going. I can't shout anymore." He paused, gazing far off out the window as if following the speck of a sail on the horizon. "I used to be a sailor, you know. Ocean racing. Like that." Eames swung his chair about and gestured toward a large oil painting on the side wall depicting a pair of twelve-meter yachts, heeled over, wakes tumbling behind them.

"Newport to Bermuda. Santa Catalina to Hawaii. Marblehead to Halifax. The Kerrwood Cup. The Transpacific. The Liberty Cup. Sydney to Auckland. I did 'em all. For nineteen years I was number one in the World Match Race rankings. America's Cup, too. Twice I defended it for the U.S.A. Nobody snatched it away from the U.S. on my trick at the helm."

He wheeled his chair about to face me and continued, "Now, I'm so weak my voice won't carry across the beam of a dory. I can't sail anymore, dammit! I can't even go out to teach anyone what I know!"

His voice cracked. I looked away.

After taking a moment to calm, he maneuvered himself back to his spot by the fire. He motioned for me to take more sherry, and to pour him some, too. I did, and handed him his glass.

"What I mean is, I couldn't have gone out to teach anyone until Justin fixed things. He made it possible for me to teach, to pass on to young sailors what I know. He said it was for me, that he did it for me."

"What was it? What did he do that let you teach?"

"Why, man, he let me go to sea again!" Eames exclaimed in what, for him, was a shout. He must have seen my puzzlement, for he continued, "No, no, not go to sea in a boat. Not a *real* boat, that is. Instead, it was a bloody computer rig. But it was some rig. Damnedest thing I ever saw. He made the whole ocean come up, there in that room."

"Make the ocean come up in a room? How do you mean?"

"You're in computers, aren't you? Don't you know about this 'artificial reality' stuff?"

119

"I do know about it. There's some of it going on in our lab. But how did Justin…"

"It wasn't *all* at your lab. Most of it was at ZIDEX. That's one of John Creedon's companies—ever hear of him?" I nodded. Eames continued, "He's a yachting buff and is even readying an America's Cup entry. Anyway, there was this setup there, a real yacht cockpit. We did most of it there, just some final touch-ups at your lab."

"Was there anyone there with Justin? Or was it just you and him?"

"There might have been a couple of people looking in now and then. Don't know who they were. Maybe ZIDEX people working late. Oh, there was this oriental guy came along with Justin a few times to help. Name like 'Pong.' Something like that."

"I guess you mean Poon Sung. He's a new person at our lab. So you're saying there was a mock-up of a yacht at ZIDEX…"

"Yeah. But not the whole boat—just the cockpit. It was in a warehouse out on their back lot. We'd go there at night. Everything was locked up, but Justin would get us in. He'd stare at this blinking red light over the warehouse door. The thing would scan his eye, and the door would come unlocked."

"Scan his eye?"

"Right. There was this gadget up over the door of the warehouse. It was a small black box with a blinking red light on it. I guess it was some kind of camera up over the doorway. Justin would stand in front of the door and this tinny voice would ask him to look up. There'd be a faint flash, the red light would stop blinking and stay on steady for maybe three or four seconds. Then the tinny voice would say, 'You may enter, Mr. Marsh.' The door would buzz a bit, and Justin would push it open."

I filed all that away.

"Go on, Bennett. Sorry I interrupted."

He drained his sherry glass and said, "Well, we'd go into this big open area. It was circular, oh, about sixty feet across, with these big curved walls like movie screens all around you. Bunch of cameras and projectors hanging from girders in the ceiling. Justin would help me up into this kind of platform, not very big, but shaped like a racing yacht's cockpit—wheel, binnacle, compass, anemometer, the whole thing. Then he'd wire me up."

"Wire you up?"

"Yeah, wire me up. He'd open my shirt, and he'd put these little electrodes on me, the kind the docs put on you when they take an electrocardiogram. You know, an EKG. Justin said, though, the electrodes were to measure my muscle responses. Then he'd get my shirt back on, and he'd go off to the side in this kind of—well, control booth, I guess you'd call it. He'd douse the lights and then—then..."

"What then?"

"Why, then the whole damn place would come alive! The projectors would throw up these wall-size images. Just like at the Omnimax at the Science Museum, only they'd be all around you, on all sides. Sky! Water! Waves! I tell you, I was on a boat! Right out on a boat! Jesus, it was wonderful! Jesus!"

Eames waved for me to refill his sherry. I poured some out and took a bit more for myself. He continued his story.

"Then there was the sound! Wind whistling through the shrouds! Halyard slapping the mast! Water rushing by! Gorgeous. And the way the whole thing would move. The cockpit setup was mounted on these hydraulic posts, one on each corner. Those posts were big sons-of-guns, maybe six feet tall, but they'd telescope in and out in a wink. Made my cockpit pitch, roll, and yaw just like the real thing."

Eames closed his eyes. Then he opened them and looked squarely into mine.

"OK. OK, I knew it wasn't real. But it was the next best thing. Real lovely. Damn lovely. And then we got to work."

"What was that?"

"I'd *sail* the blessed thing! That was what! We were *racing*! The scene he'd be projecting would have this other yacht alongside. There'd be a cannon report behind us, and off we'd go."

Eames leaned forward in his chair and fixed me with his eyes.

"You see, Justin created a miracle for me. I could sail again. I could take the wheel. There was even a mike clipped to my collar so I could bark orders to the crew."

Eames chuckled to himself.

"That crew!" he went on. "They were these animations. They looked real life-like, though. Mostly men, though he'd put in a woman or two, I guess just to be…what's the new thing…'politically correct.' You know, some guy a few years ago had this all-woman crew gimmick. That whole squabble's a lot of crap, anyway, I can tell you firsthand. My sister Lilian, Justin's mother—we called her 'Wunnel' because her name had only one 'l' in the middle—why, she could spin a coffee grinder—that's those two-handled cranks we use to haul the sheets and halyards—as good as any man. You just got to be in shape, that's all."

Eames paused. "Where the hell was I?"

"You were talking about how it felt in the cockpit," I said. "How it was so real."

"Oh, yeah. Yeah. Anyway, there'd be the crew in their slickers, and we'd be heeling and taking lots of spray. They'd scurry all around, cranking the grinders, setting the jib pole, unfurling the spinnaker if we needed it. Justin said the crew figures were done using 'inverse kinematics.' I got such a kick out of it, I learned that term. 'Inverse kinematics.' Justin'd be proud of me, I still remember that. The figures would not only look like they had real body weight, but the physics of the boat—the way the hull would yaw, pitch, and roll— and the wind, too, would act upon them. You'd swear to God you had real people with you.

"The simulation stuff, the 'artificial reality' and all, Justin said was just copies of what he and all you guys were doing at your lab. The big thing he added on, he told me, was this program that would be learning to sail by watching me! He said it was an 'expert system.' Well, not expert at first, because I had to teach it."

"Just how did you teach it?" I asked. "Did you tell it what to do?"

"No, I didn't tell it anything, except now and then. I just sailed the boat like I would if we were really racing." Eames smiled, and wagged his head in remembered delight. "Well, we *were* racing. I'd just act like I would then, just be myself. I'd man the wheel. I'd yell out orders. Point to this thing or that, look at the crew, tell 'em to do this or that." Eames paused. "Hey, sounds like some of your stuff was in there, too."

"Yes," I said, "I did some things on looking, pointing, speaking to displays. But I didn't know it all had gone to sea."

Eames went on, "Well, this system, so Justin said, would be learning from me just as if I had told it all I knew. He said it did even more." His voice became lower. "He said that, as a sailor, it *became* me. It was my apprentice, and it *became* me.

"Don't you see what he did, Bill? He took the best part of me, that part that could sail, and he put it in that machine. He said that it was a part of me that could go on and teach new sailors what I'd learned all these years—tactics, strategy, when to jibe, when to come about, how to tack on a turn to steal the lead.

"He even had these—he called them 'scenarios'—playing on the computer. They were setups of classic situations: you and another boat close-in and dueling for the wind, the other boat trying to cut you off at the buoy, maneuvering in tight. I'd have to sail my boat through these, and that computer would be taking in all my moves and orders."

"How—how were you able to…"

"Able to move, you mean? Man the wheel? Yell out, you mean? All the things I can barely do—can't do—now?"

"Yes."

"That's what those electrodes were for. I'd be at the wheel, but of course I couldn't move like before. But those electrodes would pick up whatever it was that I *could* do. I didn't have to reach out or turn all that far, Justin said, or even be all that quick. The computer would sense the muscle impulse through the electrodes and amplify it. It would pick up my intention, even though I couldn't really turn the wheel that far or fast. 'Computer-augmented,' Justin called it. And my voice! I'd be speaking in this whispery voice like you hear now, but that little mike he clipped on me would pick it up and make me sound like Captain Bligh."

"What was he going to do with this program, once it had your sailing knowledge in it?"

Eames relaxed and sat back in his cart. He fingered his sherry glass, then took a small sip.

"He had this dream about it. He'd said he'd try to design some low-cost simulator rig to go with the expert part of the program, and make the whole thing interactive so it could talk, teach, and demo all at once. Then he'd make it available to kids to tutor in sailing techniques, you know, for schools that had sailing teams, or community boating clubs like we have on the Charles River there. Or for kids' sailing programs. I guess that was…"

Eames averted his face. He didn't want me to see the tears that were welling up.

"You know, Justin's father died when he was six. Cancer. Wunnel—his mother, my sister—and I were always very close, and they didn't live all that far away. I was a bachelor, with no one at home. So I guess I became his second father. Wunnel never married again, so he had just me.

"When he was younger, before he went off to Dartmouth, we used to sail, Justin and I. Yeah, I took him out a lot. Even began to teach him some of the tough competition stuff. Then, when he came back up here to the Boston area, I told him I'd teach him some more. But then I came down with—*this*. I couldn't take him out…"

Eames' voice cracked. With great effort he added, "So I guess you could say he took *me* out. Justin said there'd always be that part of me that's going out to sea. And I would be teaching not just him, but lots of kids."

Eames picked up a small napkin from beside his sherry glass and daubed his eyes. I looked out the window toward the darkening sea. After a long minute, Eames said, "So, where are we now? Why do you say he was killed for it?"

"I can't *prove* he was killed for that program. I can't even prove he was *killed*. But from what I saw when I found Justin and what's happening now to me and to others, there's no other explanation."

"What about the police? Aren't they doing anything?"

"What they're doing is suspecting me because I found Justin's body. Beyond leaning on me now and then, they won't tell me much of anything."

"Haven't you told them about Justin setting up his computer to send his program to you? That shows he was expecting some kind of trouble, doesn't it?"

"But why didn't Justin go directly to the police if he felt he was in danger? It seems it was the program more than himself he was trying to protect. I've held it back until we deciphered what it was, but now I guess I have to give it over to the police." Even though it makes me guilty of withholding evidence, I added silently to myself.

"Yes," Eames said, his voice taking on a stern tone. "You've got to tell the police about the program and Justin's note. I insist you do. Maybe then they'll be able to track down whoever killed Justin, if that's in fact what happened." He added, "It may even lift some of the threat from you and your colleagues."

I promised Eames I would give the program over to the police. We emptied our sherry glasses, and he escorted me to the foyer. As we reached the outside door, I decided to tell Eames one more thing in the hope that he could shed some light upon it

"I realize this is grisly, and I don't mean to upset you, but when I found Justin's body that morning his left eye was missing."

Eames gave a start, then stared blankly back at me.

"I'm sorry," I said. "I wouldn't have mentioned this except I keep thinking how you said the warehouse at ZIDEX opened up after checking Justin's eye."

"It's OK. Justin's left eye was a prosthesis. He'd been working on a woodturning lathe in high school shop class when he lost his grip on the chisel and it flew up and hit him."

"I worked with him nearly every day. I never could tell he had a false eye."

"Nobody could. The docs preserved enough of the eye globe and the muscles behind it so the prosthesis just sat on top and moved along with the other eye. Justin got a kick that it even fooled the eye checker at ZIDEX." Eames paused and swallowed hard. "Maybe it just became dislodged when he was in the water."

"Maybe."

I could see that Eames was becoming exhausted, so I excused myself. "Bennett, I've got to be getting back. I'm glad you invited me here and we had this talk."

"Bill, thank you for coming. Though I can't say that all you told me is very comforting. It was bad enough thinking Justin might have ended his own life. But now, to think he was murdered for something—for something he was trying to do for me."

I knew all too well from my memory of Valerie how desolate and gnawing the feeling could be that you somehow brought about another's death—especially that of a loved one.

"You didn't cause his death, Bennett," I told him with as firm a voice as I could muster. "If my hunch is right that Justin was killed for that program, it's whoever did that who's responsible."

I thanked Eames for his time. We shook hands, and I headed out the door into the rain.

Later, back home, I looked at my calendar and winced. In the next dozen or so days I was scheduled to travel, in two gigantic hops, around the globe.

The first hop would take me to Sydney, Australia, where I'd be delivering a paper at a computer conference and touching base with my peripatetic boss, Jean-Paul, concerning the proposal I'd been putting together. It also was where I'd be taking up Irina's cousin Sergei on his invitation to get a look at *Orel*, Team St. Petersburg's cup entry.

The second leap would take me from Sydney to Venice. There, I was to attend a by-invitation-only conference on interactive computer interfaces sponsored by AESDR—the All-Europe Society for Digital Research—to be held at the Cini Foundation, an ancient monastery complex on Isola di San Giorgio, across the *bacino* from Piazza San Marco.

I'd been almost too preoccupied to prepare the "position paper" each invitee to the AESDR meeting was required to present, and had thought of canceling. But when I learned from Irina that a paper she'd submitted to the Russian/European Market Conference in Rome had been accepted, and following that she could join me in Venice, all was sealed. Yes, our schedules meant we'd miss having New Year's together—but we'd make up for that in Venice.

Chapter 17

I hate long air trips. And Los Angeles to Sydney, Australia, is a big reach, especially coming on top of the flight from Boston to the West Coast. Indigestion. Insomnia. Leg cramps. At least I'd no need to plan for additional rabies shots, the test on the dog proving negative.

There'd still be the odd effect of losing a calendar day. I'd be taking off from L.A. on Saturday, December thirtieth and arriving in Sydney on Monday, January second, having had Sunday—New Year's Day—zapped by crossing the International Dateline somewhere over the Pacific.

The Qantas 747 landed at 6:05 a.m. at Sydney's Kingsford Smith Airport. I retrieved my bags and went by cab the five or so miles to the Hotel Inter-Continental near the Royal Botanic Gardens.

After catching up on some sleep, I took in a few of the city's sights—Sydney Harbour Bridge, the historic Rocks section, the Opera House with its dramatic cluster of clamshell roofs—doing it the easy way, by tour bus. At four, I phoned Irina in Rome to wish her luck with her talk. It was almost a wake-up call, really, it being seven a.m. in her part of the world. That evening, I got in a bit of pub crawling, ending with a couple of pints of Three Sheets Ale at the storied Lord Nelson Brewery Hotel in the Rocks.

Next morning, rising surprisingly refreshed and invigorated, I headed to the mezzanine lobby and the registration desk of the Fourth Annual Meeting of the International Society for Intelligent Interactive Computer Interfaces. While picking up my conferee's packet, I spotted some familiar faces and launched into re-acquaintance chats with colleagues, some of whom I hadn't seen for several years. Then, toting coffee and danish, we all went into Victoria Ballroom A and took our seats for the morning's keynote talk.

The speaker—Conference Chair Roger Latham of University of Sydney's Computer Science & Engineering Section—was witty and engaging. But my mind was elsewhere.

First, there was the invitation from Irina's cousin Sergei to go for a sail in Sydney Harbour and maybe get a sail-by peek at the Team St. Petersburg's America's Cup challenger, *Orel*. More to the point, perhaps I could get a clue as to what Sergei may have had in mind when, back in South Hadley, he'd seemed to hint at some secret weapon or other Team St. Petersburg had in the offing.

Second, I had an evening dinner date with Jean-Paul Etherington. He'd be flying in today from Singapore to give an invited talk at the conference tomorrow morning. Perhaps I'd learn from him more about the fate of the proposal I'd been working on the day I found Justin in the Charles, and maybe why—as Jean-Paul was well-connected with Sydney's upper-crust ocean racing circles— the crack Australian yachtsman who'd been hired as skipper by Team Nippon for their entry *Chrysanthemum* had finally decided, according to the weekend papers, to opt out.

I checked my watch. Sergei had said to phone him at 10:30 am, or a little after. It was time. I excused myself to a row of attendees as I sidled by them, and headed for a lobby phone.

"Sergei, it's Bill Rundle. Hope I'm not disturbing."

"Not at all, Professor. You had a good flight?"

"As good as fourteen and a half hours on any plane can be. Anyway, I hope your offer of a sail is still on."

"Most certainly. May I pick you up early this afternoon? Say, 1:30?"

"Fine," I said, and gave him the name of my hotel. "I'll be out front."

"See you then, Professor. I'll bring a slicker for you. For the spray, not the cold. It should be about 26, maybe 28, Celsius. That's about 80 degrees in Fahrenheit."

Right, I thought, as we hung up. Sydney's January is Cambridge's June.

"You need to take more luff out of the jib, Professor!" Sergei shouted over the whistling of the wind. I pulled harder on the port jib sheet until the jib smoothed out, and made fast the sheet to its cleat.

"Sergei, please stop calling me 'Professor.' Doesn't fit out here. 'Bill' is just fine."

"OK, Pro...I mean OK, Bill."

Sergei handled the tiller and main sheet gracefully and easily, though the wind was strong and gusting. We were in a Star Class sloop that Sergei had rented at a marina in Rushcutters Bay, a keel boat with a planked hull, twenty-three feet long. Sydney Harbour stretched before us, blue water below, cloudless blue sky above.

Sergei took us through some tacking and jibing exercises, a useful refresher course for me since my total boating experience amounted to two weeks as a teenager in a sailing camp at Brewster on Cape Cod.

Tacking is the easier maneuver. Sergei would yell "Ready about..." to alert the crew—in this case, me—that a tack was coming up. He'd follow that by "Hard-a-lee," and swing the tiller so we'd face into the wind. My job was to release the jib sheet to free up the jib sail, which would flutter freely as we came about. As the wind crossed our bow, the mainsail and boom would swing over, forcing us both to duck. I'd then haul on the opposite jib sheet to set the jib for our new course.

Jibing is trickier. It's when you swing the mainsail to the opposite side of the boat when sailing "downwind," that is, with the wind at your back. Do the jibe wrong, and you can go into a "knockdown"—a perilous lean—or even capsize the boat.

To signal me, Sergei would call out, "Ready to jibe." Then he'd call "Jibe-oh," and swing the tiller to windward. As the wind caught the other side of the mainsail, the boom would swing across the cockpit—but much faster than when we'd tack, because the boom would be swinging through a far wider arc. My job was simple—let loose the jib sheet and let the jib flap whichever way, and remember to duck.

We'd come maybe three miles from Rushcutters Bay when Sergei pointed and cried out, "There she is."

The waterfront area off our port side was a clutter of wharves and warehouses. Next to a low red building, pulled up and out of the water on a marine railway, was a long white shape. *Orel.*

"She's having her keel checked, Bill. We'll go in closer," Sergei added, as he eased the tiller over a bit.

"I thought Cup contender crews hid their boat's keels out of sight to keep the competition in the dark. There was a 1992 Cup entry— Dennis Conner's *Stars & Stripes,* I think—where they put a skirt around the keel so no one could see its shape when they hauled it out of the water."

"Yes," replied Sergei, laughing. "There were even some scuba divers—some think they were a group of your U.S. Navy Seals hired by the competition—who were trying to photograph the keel by coming up to it underwater."

We drew close to the shoreline near *Orel.* Up on dry land, and supported by rough timbers, she nonetheless gave an impression of great speed.

"So Team St. Petersburg is not afraid of anyone checking out the design of the hull and keel?"

"No. We are not afraid. The shape of the boat is a big factor, and how the keel is suspended. But these are not the only things that matter."

"What's the biggest factor?"

"How she is sailed. The skill of the crew." Sergei paused, and looked off in the direction of Sydney Harbour Bridge and the famed Opera House with its sail-like roofs. "We may have an edge there," he added. "Maybe a decisive edge."

Sergei called out, "Ready to jibe...Jibe, oh!" and we brought the

Star about and headed out deeper into the harbor, leaving *Orel* behind us. The wind had picked up a great deal, and was gusting strongly. I studied Sergei's face, solemn and sternly set as it had been that evening back in South Hadley at Irina's parents' gathering.

"Sergei, you were saying Orel would have a decisive edge—what would that be?" I asked.

"Yes, a better way to sail."

"You mean you are training hard? That *Orel*'s crew is getting pretty good?"

"Yes, that. And we also may have new skills for handling the boat."

"You mean you all are learning new tactics?"

Sergei's voice became icy. "Yes, learning is one way to acquire new tactics."

I looked Sergei directly in the eye. "Are there other ways to acquire new tactics?" I asked.

Sergei was silent. Suddenly, he shouted something unintelligible and, with a second shout, shoved the tiller away from him and yanked in the main sheet.

A jibe. I wasn't prepared. As the boat swung about, the heavy boom swept across the cockpit and crashed into the side of my head.

When I came to, I was lying on my back on the floor of the cockpit. My head throbbed, and pinpoints of light stabbed across my vision. My ears seemed muffled as I heard a voice calling, "Professor Rundle! Professor Rundle! Are you all right?"

It took some moments to focus, but gradually I could make out Sergei standing over me, the slackened mainsail whipping and thrashing about behind him in the stiff wind. He reached down and helped me up to a sitting position on the starboard gunwale.

"I am so sorry," Sergei began. "I meant to tell you we were going to jibe, but it came out in Russian. It's how I talk all day with *Orel*'s crew. It was a slip. I am so sorry. Are you OK?"

Gingerly, I touched the side of my head. I could feel a large welt rising. My hand, when I took it away, ran with rivulets of blood. I took out my handkerchief and motioned for Sergei to dip it alongside in the cold water. He wrung it out and passed it back. I folded it, pressing it to my head as a compress.

"Sergei," I managed to say, "let's go back to the dock. You do the sailing. I don't think I can handle the jib."

"Oh, my God, Professor Rundle. I am so sorry this has happened."

I stared at Sergei, forcing my eyes to focus. His words of apology sounded sincere, but I could see in his face no expression whatsoever.

"It's OK," I said. "It was an accident. Let's just get back to the dock."

Sergei sat still, returning my gaze. The boat's hull, pushed by the wind, drifted slowly backwards. He got up, lowered the jib, and, grasping the tiller and hauling on the main sheet, brought us back past the tip of Garden Island to Rushcutters Bay and dockside.

X-rays taken later at Sydney Hospital revealed no skull fracture. Like most scalp wounds, the volume of bleeding had been out of all proportion to the size of the cut on my head, and it took only a couple of stitches to close things up. Sergei again was profoundly apologetic as he drove me back to my hotel, but otherwise was grim and silent. I thanked him for the lift back and the afternoon sail—despite the mishap—and waved goodbye to him curbside at the entrance of my hotel.

I took the elevator to the fourth floor, got to my door, and reached into my pocket for the key—a flat plastic card with code holes punched in one end.

Missing.

I searched my other pocket, the pockets of my windbreaker. Not there, either. I went back to the lobby for a duplicate, took the elevator back up, and opened my door.

The room was awash in clutter. The surge of adrenaline made my head pound with alarm, reviving in full the trauma of the clout from the boom.

The contents of my bags and briefcase were strewn about. I checked to see if anything was missing. Some cash I had stuffed in my camera case was still there, along with a very expensive reflex.

The Mont Blanc pen Irina had given me for Christmas was still tucked in my writing folder.

My laptop, though, was gone.

I took some deep breaths to restore focus to my spinning thoughts. The loss of the laptop would be an inconvenience, not a disaster; I had backups of everything on my home computer. In particular, Justin's code wasn't on it, so if that was the thief's target, he would be disappointed.

A call to the front desk shed no light on what might have happened. There had been no report of a break-in from any of the staff. Nor had the staff seen anyone suspicious lurking about the fourth floor.

It took me all of a half hour to restore order. I stretched out on the bed. I was tempted to phone Jean-Paul and beg off our dinner engagement, but decided to tough it out. At the very least there was the item about Team Nippon and their erstwhile Australian skipper that I wanted to check out with him, and I decided that, throbbing skull or no, I'd better go.

Chapter 18

Eight o'clock that evening found me at the Royal Sydney Yacht Club, Jean-Paul Etherington having sent a cab for me at my hotel. I had just told the attendant at the Chief Steward's desk that I was a guest of Jean-Paul's when there he was, striding across the foyer toward me.

Australian by birth, though with a French mother, he, at forty-two, projected a striking image. With his thick shock of sun-bleached hair, longish tan face and lean jaw, his six-foot-three frame in the safari clothes he favored, he exuded the 1930s glamour of the open-cockpit aviator.

"Good to see you, Bill," Jean-Paul said. He looked at me intently. "You look a little peaked, though. Feeling ok?"

"I was out sailing this afternoon. Didn't duck the boom fast enough." Omitting names and particulars, I gave a brief account of what had happened on the boat.

"Are you sure you're up for dinner?" Jean-Paul asked. "That must have been a nasty hit."

"Yes, no problem. I feel fine," I lied. I felt like hell, and I was still seething inwardly at Sergei, his clumsiness—or his intent.

"Are you sure you're all right?"

"Yes—yes, I'll be fine."

"OK, then. We'll go right to the dining room."

We strode on through the club, the way cushioned with deep pile carpets, and redolent of aged leather and fine cigars. The dining room proved to be a private one, spacious, with mahogany paneling, polished brass sconces, paintings and prints of sailing ships, and, through a picture window at the far end, a dazzling view of Sydney Harbour. As we entered, I noted an engraved plate on the door to the effect that the room had been presented to the club by one Allan Etherington.

"Your father?" I asked, indicating the plate.

"The same," Jean-Paul replied. "He loved the view from here, but hated the furnishings. So he gave the club a gift to do it over."

As two waiters in black trousers and white jackets with nautical piping ushered us into our respective chairs, I recalled what, in a *Fortune* magazine profile, I'd read about Jean-Paul's father.

Allan Etherington, in his heyday, could easily have afforded to refurbish clubrooms on a whim. A financial legend in the '70s, he had parlayed a modest stake in cattle and mining in New South Wales into an international fortune embracing oil refineries, electronics, publishing, and much else. With sumptuous homes in New York, London, Paris, Antibes, Geneva, and Rome, he had pretty much left his native Australia behind.

By the end of the decade, though, rumors had spread of over-extension and risky investments gone sour. When Allan Etherington, alone in his classic Isotta-Fraschini roadster and going well over 100 miles per hour, slammed into a tunnel buttress near Switzerland's Simplon Pass, no one really knew—perhaps not even Jean-Paul, then doing graduate work at Oxford—whether the crash was accidental or intended.

After courts and creditors, little was left to Allan's widow and John-Paul beyond the original holdings in New South Wales, now long since sold. Jean-Paul's real legacy from his father, however, had been *entrée*—first-name access to many of the world's movers and shakers in industry, finance, and politics—plus an air of urbane assurance with which to exploit that access.

We sat down. Plates laden with blue swimmer crab and prawns appeared, accompanied by a chilled 1990 Rosemount Estate Semillon Chardonnay.

Jean-Paul and I talked first about my proposal. He opened a

leather folio at his right hand and took out a sheaf of papers—which I recognized as a print-out of the text I had previously sent—and set it down between us.

"Bill, you never cease to amaze me with so many innovative ideas. Like that strategy you came up with last September for gaze-sensitive displays. Really great. And it complemented so nicely what Greg Evans was doing..."

Jean-Paul was a master of the "old one-two"—high praise to pump you up, then the zinger to deflate you. I could see it coming.

"...And that's why, Bill, I can't understand how, in this proposal draft you sent me, you could completely lose the point of it all and produce something so lame and unconvincing."

Good God, I thought to myself, how bad can a day get? A boom to the head, maybe deliberate. A break-in and theft. Now, a lambasting from Jean-Paul. And I'd come halfway around the globe for it all.

"I'm sorry, Jean-Paul," I said. "I'd thought this was on target—the linking of speech input to virtual semantics. Maybe it's too nutty..."

"No, it's not nutty. It's novel. Over the edge. Exactly where we want Cognitive Computing Lab stuff to be. It's just that, the way you present it, the punch is lost."

He pushed the draft, marked up in blue pencil, over to me.

"Look, it's simple," he continued. "First, you need to state how, in the graphics world, everything is virtual. Next, show how classical semiotics *could* apply to graphical objects, but not necessarily. Then, as a solution, you propose your system of 'virtual semantics' to do the linkage."

Between mouthfuls of seafood and sips of wine, he cut through the issues in a way that I, being too close to my own ideas, hadn't managed to. As he commented on this or that passage, I made quick notes at the margins.

"Those are suggestions," Jean-Paul concluded, "not set in concrete. You're free to elaborate all and everything. In any case, it would be nice to see a final draft in two, three days at most? Can you do it?"

I winced. I'd have to buy a new laptop, dial-up my computer at the lab, and retrieve the text of my draft. That would be the easy part.

Then I'd have to pull apart and redo the whole thing to work in Jean-Paul's suggestions. That would be the hard part. Maybe I could use the long flight time to Venice to clean it all up.

Or, maybe I could stab Jean-Paul in the jugular with my dessert fork then and there.

I thought better of the latter, and instead said, "Yeah, I'll handle it. I'll get it to you."

"Great. We need to submit this fast. Our funding situation's become critical. The lab's in the red—been there for the last six months. I'll be telling everyone next faculty meeting, but, FYI, we're down by $2.8 million. At least that—maybe more, even as we speak. Everything costs. Equipment, major and minor. Revamping the acoustics lab area. Graduate fellowship stipends. Travel—like coming here. The works. It's all gotten out of control."

"I'll get this out," I said, tapping the draft with my finger. "And let me know what else I can do."

"Getting that proposal out the door will be plenty," Jean-Paul replied.

The waiters cleared the appetizer plates and brought on the main course: seared beef steak wrapped in paper, the accompanying wine a 1990 Penfolds Grange Hermitage Shiraz. Indeed, there were certain compensations for working at the Cognitive Computing Lab...

"Jean-Paul," I asked as we dug into the rich steak and the even richer flavors of the wine, "it was in the papers—oh, sometime in November, I think—that Ian Halsey was considering dropping out as skipper for Team Nippon in the America's Cup trials. There'd been so much publicity, an Australian sailing for the Japanese. The Cup is nothing if not nationalistic. Still, it's kind of a surprise, isn't it—him just cutting out and no explanation?"

"Not a surprise to me. I'm the one who talked him out of it."

"Oh? Why was that?"

I followed Jean-Paul's gaze as he looked out at the imposing Sydney Harbour Bridge.

"A sense of 'homeland,' I suppose," he said. "Though I've spent most of my life elsewhere. Anyway, I reminded him he was Australian, and it just didn't figure for him to skipper for the Japanese, or anyone else, for that matter. Besides, I've got a one-twelfth interest in the Australian entry, and I wanted to protect my investment. Ian will be where he should be, skippering for us."

"Where does that leave the Japanese?"

"In a desperate situation, I would think. They haven't had the time to develop an ocean racing tradition. Their yachting ranks just don't have depth. On the other hand, maybe they'll come up with something."

"Such as?"

"I couldn't guess. But you know the saying, 'Damned clever, those Japanese.'"

I pressed on, all too aware that I might be sailing into dangerous conversational waters. "But if they don't have a first-rate skipper, Jean-Paul, how could they possibly win?"

Jean-Paul paused. "Like I said, they can be damned clever when they put their minds to it." He broke eye contact with me—a signal that he was done with that topic—and fixed his eyes on the approaching waiters.

The main course was cleared away and followed by a platter of crackers, dried fruit, and cheese—Meredith Roquefort and King Island Brie from Tasmania. A fresh wine bottle came with it, another chardonnay, this time Penfields Koonunga Hill 1995.

The rest of our dinner talk focused on departmental matters: what specialties the next faculty hires should have, whom to invite to the lab as guest lecturers, the new format for the doctoral proseminar. Then, after some strong coffee—by then badly needed, at least by me—Jean-Paul excused himself.

"I don't mean to be rushing things," he said as we made for the foyer, "but there's a few calls I have to make. Hope you don't mind."

"Not at all," I said.

"Just one last thing, Bill. There're a couple of European companies I know that just might leap at the thing that your grad student Justin Marsh was working on before his death. Could mean big funding."

"You mean the interactive shading algorithms?"

"No. Good stuff, though. But not that. I mean the expert system. The one that does sailing."

I could not have been more stunned had Jean-Paul torn one of the half-hull yacht models from the foyer wall and clubbed me on the same spot the boom had struck.

How in the world did Jean-Paul know about Justin's program? My shock must have shown, as he said, "What's wrong, Bill? Your head feeling…"

"No, I'm fine," I managed. "Just dizzy for a second. I'm fine."

"You're positive?"

"Yes, yes. I'm OK."

"Anyway, I mean the sailing program that Marsh was doing. Might be a big winner."

I didn't know what to say to him. I needed somehow to stall, to not say too much before I could comprehend just what was happening. "Jean-Paul, I'm not sure I know of…"

"Bill, don't look so surprised. Maybe you didn't know. But it's my business to know what's going on around the lab, not just official projects but *sub rosa* stuff as well."

"He wasn't supposed to be…"

"I know. He wasn't supposed to be doing things on the side. But any program or part thereof written on a lab machine by someone holding down a research assistantship is automatically lab property. In any event, can you track down the expert sailing system he was doing and get a copy to me so I can see whether or not it's worth doing anything with? OK?"

I nodded. "OK, I'll see what I can do." The doorman pushed the door open for me, whistled a cab over, and I went back to my room at the Hotel Inter-Continental.

The rest of the conference sped by. Jean-Paul's speech the next morning provoked the usual polar reactions—cogent and challenging to some, to others an outrage—after which, true to form, he fled the auditorium for the airport. My paper, given later in the afternoon, was—judging from audience reaction—a middling success. I got to hear some interesting presentations, though, on interactive holography and interface "agents."

Later that evening, I was comfortably stretched out in business class on a Qantas flight to Bangkok International Airport, the first leg of a two-leg journey to Rome; there I'd rendezvous with Irina, and we'd go by train to Venice.

The trip from Sydney to Rome would take all of twenty-two hours, ten minutes, so I could reassure myself I'd have plenty of time to work Jean-Paul's critiques and suggestions into the text of my revised proposal.

Except that my thoughts kept wandering...

That blow from the boom in Sydney Harbour could well have killed me. I felt the side of my head; the swelling by now had mostly subsided. Had Sergei meant to hit me? Or was it, as he insisted so profusely, an accident?

And what of my missing hotel key? Accident or not, had Sergei taken it from my pocket while I was knocked out? It couldn't have been Sergei himself who entered my room, as he went with me to the hospital. But he could have passed the key on to someone while I was being stitched up.

I recalled my shock at Jean-Paul's asking for Justin's code. Was there any connection between his request for the code and the lab's $2.8 million shortfall?

Whatever that shortfall meant for Jean-Paul, it certainly didn't inhibit his penchant for the finer things. From a copy of *Wine Enthusiast* the Qantas flight attendant had handed me, I'd tallied that in that one meal we'd gone through—just the two of us—nearly $500 worth of wine. Surely, it being a "working dinner," its cost would be charged to the lab. But could dining like that be something someone really worried about budgets would do?

And why ask me for Justin's code? Maybe Jean-Paul had some ace-in-the-hole in mind, not just my chancy research proposal, that would relieve the financial plight of the Lab.

I could only imagine it was connected with Jean-Paul's talking Ian Halsey off of the Japanese Cup team. Was there more to it than a "sense of homeland," as he put it? Was it in fact a ploy to make the Japanese desperate, and then offer them—at a suitably steep price— Justin's program, either as a coaching aid or even to actually sail the boat? Was that what Jean-Paul meant by his remark that the Japanese might have a good chance anyway? Meaning not that they'd cook up some new sailing strategies on their own, but that they'd have— thanks to him—a new secret weapon in the form of Justin's program?

I thought back to the yacht blueprints I'd spied at Kenichi's house on Mount Auburn Street the night I'd broken in. The plans showed a boat outfitted with a motorized rudder and winches that could be computer controlled by a program such as Justin's. Kenichi had motive and means: his trumpeting at Provost Hale's party that Japan could well take the America's Cup, coupled with his family's wealth—reputed to be in the hundreds of millions. Could Jean-Paul be thinking of setting up a swap with him—Justin's code for new funds to rescue the lab?

My thoughts returned to Sergei. What did he—or others on Team St. Petersburg—know of all of this? Did they know of Justin's code? Did they fear it could go to a rival team? Did they want it for themselves? Had they, along with Sergei, concluded that the link to that code, now that Justin was dead, was me?

I pushed my seat back, closed my eyes, and, doing some deep breathing, tried to sooth my agitated reverie. I'd just dozed off to the muted roar of the air stream on the fuselage, when something surged up from my unconscious and woke me with a start.

A memory of something I'd read. Read some years ago, while seated on a plane, as I was now. Maybe the similar circumstance was what made it come back.

It was an article in the *International Herald Tribune,* one profiling the Russian Mafia. In between paragraphs about extortion, drug dealing, money laundering, and the like, there was mention of how certain Russian gangsters had a superstition that the eye of a murder victim yet held in death the image of their slayer. The only way, they claimed, to remove such damning evidence was to gouge out and destroy the tell-tale eye.

Chapter 19

Venice in winter. A good time to go. No sweltering heat, no pushing through tourist crowds. Just the sights of that lovely, melancholy city veiled in mist.

My conference meetings at the Cini Foundation were from nine until three. Irina would spend the morning and early afternoon taking photographs and ducking into churches to view the Titians, Tintorettos, and Bellinis that seemed to be everywhere. At three, I'd take the foundation's mahogany launch back to Piazza San Marco and join her for coffee at Florian's. From there, we'd roam the city and get lost in a magical labyrinth of little bridges, side canals, and lantern-lit *vias*, finally to have dinner at some half-hidden *trattoria* where—hearing only Italian or Venetian dialect spoken inside—we'd order what the locals ate.

It was late evening on our second full day in Venice, when, as we picked up our keys at the desk of the Hotel Bellini, we were handed a folded note. It was addressed to both of us:

> Allow me to introduce myself. My name is Igor Menshikov. Mr. Sergei Tatarinoff is a friend and colleague of mine, and told me you would be coming to Venice and staying at the Hotel Bellini in the Cannaregio.
>
> Would you do me the honor of having dinner with me tomorrow evening? The Taverna San Trovaso nearby Ponte dell'Accademia at, say, 8:30? Ask the

headwaiter for my table as you come in.
I hope to see you both then.

Cordially,
—I. M.

"No, I have no idea who he is," said Irina as we ascended in the tiny elevator. "I did mention to Sergei when I last spoke with him on the phone that I'd be going to Rome and Venice, but I don't think I told him you'd be here, or that we'd be at the *Bellini.*"

"Maybe they have their sources. Anyway, shall we take him up on it?"

"I don't know. What do you think?"

"He seems sure we'll accept. What would you rather do?"

We decided to sleep on it, but we both knew inside where and with whom we would be dining next evening.

From the Hotel Bellini, it was just a few steps to the waterbus landing at Ferrovia, where we boarded *vaporetto* number 1 and took seats near the bow. Both on its fore and aft open decks and within its covered center cabin, the boat was nearly empty of passengers.

It was early evening, about a quarter to seven, and the lights in the *palazzos* were just coming on. Number 1 began to weave its way down the Grand Canal, crossing from side to side as it visited the waterbus stops one after the other along its mile-and-one-half length.

"We're going to be early," I said. "Let's go all the way down to the Salute and walk back." Irina nodded agreement.

The air was cool, and we pulled our trench coat lapels up about our necks. Billows of fog wafted along and across the canal, refracting the lamplights along the *fondamente* on either side into multi-colored auras.

As the *palazzi* slipped by, we peeked in beyond the Gothic colonnades and trefoil windows to spy upon great paneled rooms alight with fanciful Murano glass candelabra. Some held the beginnings of a dinner party, men and women milling about in formal evening dress; others disclosed walls hung with antique portraits and vast shelves of leather-backed books, but otherwise appearing utterly empty. All, though, seemed steeped in exotic tales and deep mysteries.

Our *vaporetto* pushed along the length of the canal, under the Rialto Bridge, the Accademia Bridge, and—last stop before Piazza San Marco—sidled up to the landing by the massive baroque cathedral of Santa Maria della Salute, Venice's tribute to the Virgin for halting a plague of the Black Death which had, in 1630, taken more than a third of the population of the city.

It was a night made for walking. Heading toward the Accademia Bridge, we cut behind the Abbey of San Gregorio and then up Calle Bastion. The narrow lamp-lit path led us by the service entrance of the Ca' Dario, a fourteenth century palazzo famous for its canal façade of Moorish archways, rosette windows, inverted-cone shaped chimney pots—and for its sinister curse.

"Aren't most of the owners who lived here supposed to have died violent deaths?" Irina whispered, clutching my elbow.

"So I've read. The latest to go was the industrialist, Raul Gardini. His servants found him dead in bed one morning. He had put a bullet in his head."

"I remember reading about that. Didn't he have yachts in the America's Cup?"

"Indeed, he did. In '88, and again in '92. Five boats in all, all of them named *Il Moro di Venezia.*"

"Why did he kill himself?"

"Big political scandal. Bribes. Over 140 million dollars' worth. His life was coming apart, so he decided to take leave of it."

It was by now 8:20, and we walked a bit faster, not wanting to be late.

At the Taverna San Trovaso we gave our host's name at the door, as our invitation had said we should, and were ushered into a quiet corner where a thick-set man rose ceremoniously to greet us.

His large head was topped by dark, flattened-down hair. Any hint of irresolution given off by his watery blue eyes was offset by a jaw both jutting and determined. His blue blazer, though well-cut and obviously expensive, seemed a size too small for his bull-like chest; below, his legs were encased in impeccably creased gray trousers.

"Good evening, Professor Rundle and Signorina Tatarinoff. So good of you to come. I am Menshikov. But please call me Igor."

We greeted him in turn, and insisted he call us Bill and Irina.

"I trust you are enjoying the city," Menshikov said, while our waiter poured us each a glass of red wine from a bottle he had just presented for our host's inspection and approval. "I don't come here often—that is, to Venice—but there were some business matters that needed tending. And now, pleasure as well. Your company." He raised his glass to us across the table.

"For that pleasure I have to thank your cousin Sergei," he continued, smiling broadly at Irina. "You see, I have an interest in—a connection with—Team St. Petersburg. And your Sergei, he is a valued member of the crew of *Orel*.

"Bill, I don't suppose you know—well, Irina, you may know this—that the world's oldest yachting club is Russian? Did you know that?"

We both shook our heads.

"You would think it would be British, no? Or Dutch, perhaps? But, no, it is Russian—the 'Flotilla of the Neva.' Founded in 1718, by Piotr Veliki—excuse me, Peter the Great—who founded so many things. He would have all these nobles in their boats going by sail all about the Gulf of Finland. Not that they all loved it; most of them surely did not. They had, in anything where Peter was involved, not much choice."

As we placed our orders—Irina trying *spaghetti alle sepple,* Menshikov asking for *fegato alla veneziana,* a liver dish, and I tempting fate with baked eel with laurel—Menshikov poured out more wine.

Throughout dinner, he regaled us with anecdote and gossip about the varied businesses he and his associates were trying to start. Right now, he said, he was trying to set up a consortium to import hand-worked leather goods from Florence, and blown glass from Venice and Murano for sale in Russia, mostly in the upscale shops of Moscow and St. Petersburg.

"There is a lot of money about," he informed us in a discreetly lowered voice. "It is not in Russia all like the sad story you may be reading in the Western papers. There are many people—mostly they are young, in their thirties and forties—who are doing well. Quite well."

It was not until dessert—Tiramisu and coffee all around—that the other shoe fell.

"You know, I try never to mix business with pleasure," Menshikov said as he leaned forward to us with an air of confidentiality. "But there is a little bit of that, that I must bring up."

"How to begin…" He studied his coffee cup. "Well, there is this rumor—more than a rumor, I would say—that a certain young man at MIT, a student of yours, in fact, Bill, has created a unique program. It is a program that knows how to sail an ocean racing yacht." He paused. "You know of this remarkable program, Bill, do you not?"

I returned his gaze, but said nothing. After a moment, he went on:

"Well, it turns out that this young man is now dead. By drowning in the river near MIT. An accident, some say. A suicide, others say. Who knows? In any case, he may have left that program behind. Maybe on a computer hard drive. Maybe on a computer at your Cognitive Computing Laboratory, Professor Rundle."

Again, I said nothing, but kept looking back into his watery gaze.

"Would you know of this, Professor Rundle?"

His shift from first name to formal address underscored the chill that had come over our conversation.

"I don't have any such program sitting in my computers," I answered. My reply was simultaneously a lie and the truth. I had the program in a sense, but it resided in Harry Mirsky's laptop and on the pair of floppies in the wire basket in my office, and not in any of my machines.

Menshikov stirred his coffee.

"It's a pity you do not," he resumed. "That it is somehow missing. I would give much to have it." He raised his cup and took a sip. "In fact, I would give, say, a half-million dollars American—that is, if somehow it turned up."

He paused, as if to let the amount of his offer sink in.

"Sergei, you know," Menshikov went on, "has been very helpful to the crew of *Orel*. To our syndicate. And, to me. In return, I promised to help him to regain a place called 'Krasnoe.' You surely know," he said as he fixed his watery eyes on Irina, "Miss Tatarinoff, what Krasnoe is. But, so far, I'm afraid Sergei has not been able to have success."

"The estate at Krasnoe was lost to our family in the Bolshevik Revolution," said Irina. "Sergei should let it go, and not try to bring back what is dead and gone."

"Perhaps you are right. But sometimes 'people of family' perhaps think differently, as does Sergei. You know, my namesake, Prince Menshikov—the favorite of Peter the Great—was supposed to have had ninety thousand serfs. Not to mention his palaces and treasures. Before Peter took them all away from him. But that is another story. Suffice it to say my forebears were nothing like the famous Menshikov in wealth. In fact, they were themselves serfs. Serfs"— he winced and pursed his lips as if the word gave off a bad taste in his mouth—"as far back as anyone can remember. Not owned by the famous Menshikov, but by—the Tatarinoff."

I could see Irina stiffen at his words.

"How the times do change," Menshikov continued. "You see, it is now *I* who own Krasnoe. I bought it just over a year ago. From an acquaintance who was a party head in Tula province, and preserved it as a *dacha* for himself and his family. It is all intact: the main house, the allées of ancient elms, even the little church. It is all very lovely. And it is mine."

He looked intently at Irina.

"Does that repulse you, gentle lady? Well, Sergei's dream— foolish or not, that is his affair—is to regain Krasnoe for the Tatarinoffs. And he might be able to do so if he can help persuade

148

somehow that mysterious program to re-appear, and be handed over to me…"

Beyond the cordial modulation he managed to maintain in his voice, Menshikov did little to mask the venom in his message. I felt stifled, and I sensed Irina did as well. Menshikov waved to the waiter, called out "*Il conto, per favore*," paid up, and we all left the Taverna San Trovaso.

Outside on the *fondamenta*, he offered me a business card. "This is where I am for the next three days." The five-star Hotel Gritti Palace. Yes, certain people were doing very well.

"And," he said as he handed me another card, "you can always reach me through email here." Under the lamplight, I could see it had, in Russian/English on either side, a business address in St. Petersburg. "Just in case a certain program shows up. A half-million for your trouble. An estate, maybe, for Sergei."

He slipped his arms into his trench coat and wrapped the ends of his belt together in a loose knot.

"Well, it was a pleasure. Signorina Tatarinoff…Professor Rundle."

He extended his hand. Neither Irina nor I was of a mind to grasp it. An awkward moment later, Menshikov turned on his heel and stalked down the *fondamenta* in the direction of the Accademia Bridge. We stood and watched his figure fade into the dark.

The baked eel was resting lightly on my stomach, but other matters were not.

"Irina, do you think that is true, that his family were owned by your family? Or would he be making that up? He seems so spiteful…"

Irina shook her head. "Oh, I don't know. It could be true. But it would be way back. Alexander II emancipated the serfs in 1861. And our branch of Tatarinoffs had freed theirs much earlier, around 1830—my father would know when—and contracted with them to work the fields."

We walked up the *fondamenta* in the direction opposite from that taken by Menshikov, breathing deeply of the night air as if to clear away some acrid residue from the dinner conversation.

The mists had parted somewhat, and the renewed visibility brought out a few gondoliers in their be-ribboned straw hats, with dark jackets over their striped jerseys to ward off the chill. To give ourselves some better memories of the evening, we engaged one, agreeing up front for a fifty-minute gondola ride for the equivalent of sixty-five American dollars. Steep, but where else but in Venice can you buy such a memory?

As the gondolier sculled us across the Grand Canal away from Santa Maria della Salute and toward a very grand and brilliantly illumined *palazzo*, I turned and said to him over my shoulder, "That palace ahead with all the lights? Can you tell us about it?"

"*Si,*" he replied, as he leaned on his oar. "That *palazzo* all lit up is sixteenth century. It belong to the Contarini."

"To the Contarini...What do they do, the Contarini?" I asked innocently, wondering what occupations a family might engage in to afford such splendor.

He shrugged. "They...they are *Contarini,*" he said simply, with a hint of indignation at the presumption of my question.

Or, if this were old Russia, I thought, "...they are *Tatarinoff.*"

I pondered Sergei's dream—no, *obsession*—to restore something of what his family had lost in the Revolution of 1917 and was now in the possession of someone, possibly a gangster. To what lengths would Sergei go? Possibly has already gone?

Our gondolier steered us into a small side canal and headed toward the Church of San Moisè. We glided beneath tiny, artfully arched bridges, and alongside ancient brick walls set on slabs of Istrian marble. All was stillness, the only sound the dip of the oar and the lapping of the gondola's wake on stone and wood.

Irina lay her head on my shoulder. Like me, she could not seem to shake the image of Menshikov from her mind.

"What a strange man," she said. "First so charming, but then he turned sinister. And his clothes. All so elegant, except his blazer fit badly, all stretched and pulling at the buttons."

"That, Irina, was due not to a bad tailor, but to his wearing a bullet-proof vest."

Probably one made of Kevlar fabric, I added to myself as we passed San Moisè and floated dreamlike toward La Fenice opera house. It's a small world. Kevlar is what they use nowadays to make sails for Cup racers...

Chapter 20

The choir intoned the Second Antiphon: "Put not your trust in princes, in sons of men in whom there is no salvation…" Good advice, I thought.

We were back in Boston, and I was standing beside Irina through the liturgy at the Russian Orthodox Cathedral in The Fenway. The service was almost two hours long; and the custom was to stand throughout. Lapsed Catholic that I was, I found the Orthodox ritual deeply compelling, perhaps because, not unlike the pre-Vatican II Tridentine Mass, it was replete with a dignity and solemnity lost in folk masses and gratuitous, Jesus-as-your-pal homilies.

The words of the Antiphon felt especially apt as I turned my thoughts to the dinner meeting I'd had with Jean-Paul Etherington in Sydney. He *was* a prince in a way: imperious, beholden to no one, used to calling his own shots, moneyed enough through his wife's family fortune to say "no" to the call of others. And I was beginning to convince myself, since the trip to Sydney, that I ought not trust him. I told Irina so, as we drove from the onion-domed cathedral to brunch at Donato's in the Charles Hotel complex off Harvard Square.

"What are you thinking, Bill? That Jean-Paul wants to sell Justin's program to the Japanese?"

"Exactly. What else could it be? The Cognitive Computing Lab's focus is on human-computer interaction, not on racing sailboats. If anyone had suggested a student should spend his time on such a thing, Jean-Paul'd squelch it right away. He'd never have backed up anyone spending their time—*his* lab's time—like that. But if he

152

somehow got wind of Justin's program, and it'd clicked with him that he had something to dangle for big cash before Team Nippon, then he'd not only look the other way but goad the student on to finish it."

"But sell it to the Japanese Cup racing team? That's so unethical. I mean, wouldn't he believe that it's cheating?"

We stopped for a red light on Memorial Drive where it crossed Western Avenue. "Yeah. It's cheating. It's sneaky. He'd be right down there with Team Nippon, if in fact the Japanese syndicate wants to use that program now that they've lost that Australian guy—Ian Halsey, I think his name is—who was going to skipper their boat."

The light changed and we started up.

"So you suspect Jean-Paul pressured the Australian to quit so the Japanese would feel desperate? That they needed something like Justin's program to have a chance at all at the Cup?"

"I can't prove it, but it sure looks that way to me," I said as we turned from Memorial Drive onto JFK Street. "And the Japanese connection could just be Kenichi Tsukamoto. Jean-Paul's known Kenichi's family for years. Part of his boardroom networking." I paused, and added, "But it's not only the program, Irina. It's the rest of it, too."

"What do you mean? That Jean-Paul might be involved in Justin's death?"

"Exactly."

We turned left onto Eliot Street, parked in the garage under the Charles Hotel, and went upstairs and across the plaza to Donato's.

Brunch was silent. I could see that my deepening mood was bringing Irina down. We picked at our food.

Finally, Irina said, "Bill, I think you just may have it all wrong. Yes, maybe Jean-Paul's an opportunist, a wheeler-dealer. I guess you have to be that to fund a research lab these days. But selling a program to help the Japanese cheat at sailing? You don't even know whether the Japanese team is looking to cheat…"

"Good God, Irina!" I interrupted. "I told you about all that yacht design paraphernalia Kenichi had at his house. Blueprints showing motors and computers hidden away in the innards of a sailing yacht.

What do you think he is trying to do with all that?" I waved off in the direction of Mount Auburn Street, where Kenichi had tried to tackle me and I'd kicked him in the head. "And those belligerent remarks he made at Provost Hale's party about 'how would you Americans like it if Japan snatched away the America's Cup.' Isn't that proof?"

"No, it isn't proof. It is not proof enough," Irina replied, her speech getting more formal and her accent thickening as she became more insistent. "It *could* be the way you say. But it does not *have* to be."

"All the pieces are there. What else could it be?"

I was nearly yelling. People at nearby tables were looking at us. Irina took my hand, in a gesture to calm me. "Maybe it all fits," she said. "But do you actually *know* if Kenichi is after Justin's program? If he's fronting for the Japanese Cup team?"

"He could be fronting for them," I said, managing to lower my voice. "Or maybe he's in it for himself? Who knows? Maybe he somehow found out what Justin had been doing, and saw an opportunity to get the program and sell it to his own people."

"But isn't his family rich? Why would he need money?"

"Maybe his family is shutting him off. Families do that with spendthrift kids."

"Are you thinking Kenichi may have killed Justin? And that now he's after you? That he was the one leaving that note to put the floppy disks at those places around the MIT campus?"

"Yes, he could have done that. Greg said the phony UPS guy who was in the hall outside our offices looked Asian. The people who attacked Harry in the parking lot were into martial arts. Just like the ones who beat up Poon Song, and we know for sure it was Kenichi and his housemates who did that."

Irina let my hand go and lapsed back in her seat. Her eggs Benedict and my French toast lay cooling on our plates.

"But what about John Creedon?" Irina asked. "You said he wants Justin's program, and he thinks you might have it."

"Maybe Creedon just wants the program because it was partly created at his place, and thinks maybe it's super valuable. Or, maybe he thought of using it to sail the Cup entry his consortium—the

Weston Group—is putting up. He asks Justin for it, and, for whatever reason, Justin refuses. Creedon's used to having his way, so he hires some strong arm types who spin out of control and do Justin in. But the program's disappeared from any of ZIDEX's computers, and Creedon figures Justin may have sent the program to me."

"But it's hard to suppose that he could be behind Justin's death. He is a respected businessman. Rich. To win a race, he doesn't have to kill a student for a program. He can afford to hire all kinds of good sailors and yacht captains."

Irina lowered her voice as the waiter approached and cleared our plates. We both ordered cappuccinos. The waiter left, and Irina went on, "Bill, I know you are trying to get to the bottom of this, but maybe it is all too much. You have three people now—Jean-Paul, Kenichi, and John Creedon—that you think may have killed Justin because he wouldn't give them his program. And now whoever it is may be after you."

"And maybe after you, too, to get at me."

Irina flinched, then straightened up in her seat. She eyed me sternly.

"I can watch out for me. It is you who are making too much of all this. You are accusing all these people. Maybe Kenichi is an aggressive person, and all that, but we are talking about murder. And, about Jean-Paul and Creedon killing Justin, or having him killed somehow. It is all too much…"

"How do you think I feel?" I said testily. "To be filled with suspicions about this one, that one. Sometimes I'm even suspicious of Greg."

"You can't mean that! He's your oldest friend!"

"I know—I know. But if anyone knew that Justin was working on some secret project or whatever, it would have to be Greg. Sure, I was Justin's advisor, but on a day-to-day basis it was Greg who worked most closely with him."

"But you can't think he killed Justin, can you?"

I shook my head. "No. No, I don't think that. But he could be involved in some way I cannot even imagine right now."

"Bill, that is what the trouble is! You are imagining too many things. Don't you see that..."

Irina paused as the waiter brought us our coffees. After he had set them down and withdrawn, Irina collected her thoughts and continued, "You know, Bill, maybe Justin did kill himself that morning. He idolized his uncle, who had become incapacitated, and sadly, will probably be dying before too long. He wanted to immortalize him in a way by putting his uncle's skills into that program. But maybe it was too difficult, and he could not do it. Maybe the program did not work, can never work. He could not face himself that he had failed his uncle, the man who had brought him up and given him so much."

"Irina, when I visited Harry at Mass General, it looked like that program ran pretty good. But, even if you believe Justin jumped in the Charles by himself, still there are people who are after that program. What about that?"

"Yes, someone is after it, because they know the program exists, and they want it badly. But that same person need not have killed Justin." She took a sip of coffee. "I do not like the way you are going after this. Maybe it is time to give it all to that Lieutenant Haggerty."

For the first time in our relationship, I felt Irina becoming cold and distant. I badly wanted her moral support, not just her help in thinking things through. But this business of Justin, and my brewing incessantly about it, was driving a wedge between us.

I guess I resented what was happening to us, and what I was beginning to regard as her lack of faith in me and how I was handling it all. In my chagrin, I felt like striking out at her, and—though I believed in what I was about to say—I knew it was risky to say it.

"My suspect list doesn't stop with Greg, Irina. There's someone else who might be deeply involved in this. And who may have taken part in Justin's death as well."

"And who is that?" Irina asked, her voice stern.

I paused. I could see her face darken, her lip line stiffen, in sudden realization of what I was implying.

"Oh, no. No, you cannot think that," Irina said, her face drawn, her speech even more formal. "I know he is young, and that he has bad judgment about lots of things. But, no, he cannot be part of what you are saying."

I began to wish I had not said what I had just said, but I went on.

"I'm sorry. But Sergei is just as much a possibility as all the others. It figures he hates the Japanese with a passion. They killed his great-grandfather—that picture I saw in the hall at your parents' house—in the naval battle in the Tsushima Straits. They captured his ship—the *Orel*—and put it in the Japanese navy. It figures, too, that he'd love nothing more than to beat them out of the Cup, humiliate them, and in a yacht named *Orel,* no less. But with the *Orel's* so-so skipper and crew, Team St. Petersburg's the one likely to be humiliated. However, with Justin's program piloting the *Orel*..."

Irina interrupted, "I cannot believe what you are saying! You cannot be saying this! Yes, he is a very young man, and a hothead, but what you are saying is impossible."

I reached out for Irina's hand, to try to calm her, but she pulled away.

"Irina, I'm sorry. But I have to say this about Sergei. He has all the motives. And he may not be all that squeamish about...well, you know, the clout I got on the head in Sydney."

"So. I see. You think now that Sergei may have killed Justin. You had an accident on the boat with him—all because of a misunderstanding—and now you think he was trying to kill you!"

Irina rose to her feet and snatched up her coat. I could see her face harden, fighting back tears.

"I cannot listen to this, Bill! You have become a different person since all this started. You are suspicious of this one, of that one. Of everyone! It is not good for me to be around you!"

She wheeled about and strode toward the door. Again, patrons at nearby tables looked at us as I got up out of my chair and plunged after her.

"Irina! Wait...please let me..."

She stopped at the door, turning to face me. Her cheeks were wet.

"Please, I have to go. Don't call me. Not for now, anyway. I cannot listen to this. Something has happened to you, and it is not good." She turned and went out the door.

I went back to our table, threw some money down, gathered my coat and scarf, and left Donato's. The plaza outside was cold, windy, empty. I went across and cut through the Charles Hotel lobby, reaching the street just in time to see Irina stepping into a cab. She spied me, and quickly turned her head away. The cab pulled away from the curb, and Irina did not look back.

Chapter 21

I stood on the curb for some moments after Irina had pulled away, cursing myself and full of agitation.

How could I have been so out of control and accusatory?

Easy, when you're me and plagued by questions and doubts about how to deal with the whole Justin business.

Maybe I should have—should even now—give the whole mess to the police, to Lieutenant Haggerty. What was I doing hanging on to it all, anyway?

I quickly answered my own question: Justin had entrusted me to do the right thing with what he'd sent me—and I was busy trying to discover what that right thing might be. But did I have enough trust in myself to hold on and do that?

The trust I once had in myself had been badly shattered that night Valerie was driving me back from my birthday party—the trust one ought to have in oneself that one would and could do the 'right thing.'

The memory of that terrible night was keeping me, too, from having the courage to ask Irina fully to commit herself to me. She surely was the best thing now in my life, but—despite the strength of my feelings for her—I was filled with self-doubt that I could ask her to tie her fate to mine.

No, I needed to see this Justin thing through, no matter where it led. Whatever the outcome, as long as I could manage to be faithful to that trust, perhaps I could begin again truly to trust myself and maybe feel I could ask others—Irina—to place their full trust in me.

What were the police doing? Nothing I could see. Sure, I could give the code over, but that would be the last I'd ever hear of it, and I'd probably never learn what it was that had really happened to Justin.

Someone was convinced I had his code, and though they—for whatever reason—seemed to have let up the pressure on me for a while, I was sure it was just a lull, and they'd be after me again in renewed earnest. There was a risk in being a target like that, but I felt it was the only way that whoever it was would step out and reveal themselves, and I'd finally know who it was and why they were doing what they were doing.

I left my car in the hotel garage and walked over to Brattle Street with its brick sidewalks, ancient trees, and stately houses—a calm and calming place to stroll and reflect. I had lots to think about and many questions to ask myself.

Menshikov…

I didn't doubt he could have had Justin killed. But why kill someone you're trying to get something from? Wouldn't it be in your interest to keep him alive so you could at least put pressure on him to hand over what you wanted?

But maybe it had gone wrong. Heavy-handed subordinates could have overplayed things, rattled Justin, maybe made him react in a way that those directly applying the pressure got rattled themselves and ended up killing him…

I paused by the gate of the Craigie-Longfellow House and looked up the walkway to the grand yellow and white pile. It had served briefly as Washington's headquarters early on in the Revolutionary War, and later was the home of the celebrated poet. I wondered, would Longfellow's poems be the same if, instead of a nubby ink pen, he had tapped them out on a computer keyboard? If Longfellow had had a houseful of computers—like Kenichi Tsukamoto.

Yes, Kenichi had a household full of computers and computer-aided design equipment. But why not? He had plenty of money to stock up his house like a university lab. And he *was* studying ship design. Those drawings could have been about automating a sailing craft, but using some other program—not Justin's—to run the whole thing.

What about Tsukamoto's habitual air of belligerence?

OK, he wasn't reticent, humble—the stereotype of the visiting Japanese. Far from it. But that didn't make him Justin's killer.

I resumed my slow walk up Brattle Street. The clouds had lifted a bit, revealing a pale blue sky. The low afternoon sun glinted through ice crystals on the tree branches, on a wooden trellis, on a rusty iron-gate arbor. I crossed the intersection where Craigie Street runs into Brattle, a large Italianate villa on one corner, the ornate St. James Armenian Apostolic Church on the other.

My thoughts turned to my boss at the lab, Jean-Paul Etherington.

Jean-Paul had every right to Justin's work, I supposed, at least to whatever extent it had been done on the lab's computers and using the lab's equipment.

But had he asked me for Justin's program because he was planning to sell it to the Japanese? Surely Etherington was adept enough at raising money not to have to resort to that. And was it credible that he had coerced and threatened Justin—then killed him or had him killed?

Etherington had every right, too, to talk crack Australian yachtsman Ian Halsey out of skippering for the Japanese. It needn't have been part of a scheme to apply pressure to the Japanese to buy a program he'd murdered for. Just because circumstances 'fit,' doesn't mean there's only one fit...

A three-story house with white pillars across the street caught my eye. I'd read in some book on 'Old Cambridge' that that particular house had once been jacked up, turned about, and plunked down on a new foundation to face away from the street. Couldn't have been an easy task, given the size of the place.

John Creedon, and his more than ample house in Weston, came into mind. He was another one who, like Etherington, had asked me to hand back *their* program. Like Etherington, Creedon surely had some justification for thinking he 'owned' Justin's program—if in fact it had been developed, as he claimed, at his company.

But to *kill* for it? Or order that Justin be threatened to the point of death to hand it over? That was a bit of a reach.

I paced onward, past the imposing Hooper-Lee-Nichols House with its off-white balustrade set above a dark gray façade, then past the three-story Ruggles-Fayerweather House with its arched wrought-iron gate complete with pendant lantern. All these spacious and venerable houses made me wonder what the Krasnoe estate of Irina's family must have been like, and how it exerted its pull on Irina's cousin Sergei. What might he have been willing to do to restore it to his family?

Reaching the corner where Fayerweather Street comes into Brattle, I crossed the street and began to wend my way back toward Harvard Square.

Sergei—what if he, too, were innocent, and I was unjustly maligning him?

Suspicions about Sergei's involvement, though, were harder to dismiss than such thoughts concerning Tsukamoto, Etherington, and Creedon. Of all my accusations at Donato's, the one implicating Sergei—naturally enough—most distressed Irina. Perhaps she had had thoughts along those lines, too.

I continued to muse on Sergei and his namesake from the Russo-Japanese War. "What's in a name?" Shakespeare had asked. Maybe much, if you have the same name as an ancestor who died at sea in mortal struggle with the people who were now the main rivals of your sailing team. And if your boat bears the same name as the warship your forebear sailed on...

"Irina," I mumbled half aloud, "can't you see how it all fits with Sergei?" Maybe she saw it all too well.

Back nearly at my starting point on Brattle Street, my mind churning over and over, I found myself abreast of the little park opposite the Craigie-Longfellow House. The poet had preserved the park free of structures so he could watch the sailing barges pass by on the Charles. I paused and took a few deep breaths. Maybe the walk had helped me shake off the worst of my paranoia, of my runaway suspicions.

I walked back to the parking garage under the Charles Hotel, retrieved my car, and drove home to Irving Street.

I had a small pile of reading to do, starting with an excruciatingly badly written thesis draft that kept me reaching for my red pencil to jot comments and corrections. I tried my best to keep focused on it, but just before five o'clock, the sky already turned dark, I decided to chance it and phone Irina.

It did not go well.

"Look," I began, "I was wrong to..."

"You needn't apologize. I thought about it all after I left you."

"I still want to tell you how sorry..."

"Bill, you don't have to. I can see all the reasons that make you think the things you do. Even about Sergei." She paused. "I have been thinking them, too—and I find it very hard."

"I'm sorry anyway, Irina. It's one thing to have real proof, and another..."

"But, Bill, it's just that. You have no *real* proof of any of the things you said. It's just a lot of things that you've seen or heard that could just be innocent, but which you make into suspicions. You begin to have wild hunches and mistrust everything and everyone."

"But, Irina, some of these things do add up and make sense. I mean, all those blueprints in Kenichi's apartment, the way they had set up their boat to..."

"I know. You said that before," Irina said testily. "Kenichi and his people could be planning all kinds of things for their boat that you have no idea of. It needn't have anything to do with killing Justin."

I could feel the conversation slipping away into a re-run of the blow-up we'd just had. I needed to convince Irina, though, that it all was serious business, and that—as I told her at Donato's—her life might be in danger as well.

"Irina, you don't seem to want to believe that any of these hunches might be true. Look, Justin was murdered. And it wasn't any random mugging. It had to do with the program that he sent me. It cost him his life. And whoever did him in went after me with that bloody dog. And sent Harry to the hospital. It isn't someone from outer space who's doing these things. It's someone close by."

"Close by, like you think Sergei might be?"

"Irina, please let…"

"Answer me! Do you think Sergei might have killed Justin?"

I wanted to say no, but I couldn't. I couldn't let Irina drop her guard—if she were willing to have any guard up at all, given her disposition to want to think well of everyone.

"Yes!" I said, almost shouting into the phone. "Yes! I don't mean that he's a murderer himself, but the people he's involved with are capable of anything. You've got to realize that, Irina!"

She was silent a moment, and then said, "Maybe you think I'm defending him, that I know something about all this and how Sergei may be deeply involved and I am just protecting him. Maybe you think that is what *I* am doing."

"You *are* defending him. Not because you're hiding any crime of his, but because you are loyal to him. You want him to be innocent, and that's kind and wonderful of you, Irina. But those feelings of yours are betraying you now. They're putting you in real danger. They're…"

"Oh, God! Enough! Enough! Bill, I cannot—I really cannot listen to this any more. You say you are concerned about me, but you do not respect my convictions. I know Sergei would not kill anyone. He would not keep company with murderers."

"Irina…"

"I have to go, Bill. I am sorry we are like this, you and I. But, as I told you at the restaurant, you have changed in ways which are very hard to understand." Her voice broke, and she added, "I have to go. Goodbye."

I must have sat there some while, the receiver in my hand, until the phone's insistent I'm-off-the-hook buzzing jarred me from my reverie. I hung up. That reverie was far from pleasant, as it was filled with imaginations of how Irina might become the object of nameless dangers, all due to me, and the realization that I'd been unable to convince her of my suspicions.

Chapter 22

The sight of them together was like a slap in the face. Two days after the blowup at Donato's, shortly after noon, I was in Harvard Square walking down Holyoke Street when I saw—across the way and seated at a window table at Delphine's—Irina and Greg.

From the way they were leaning toward each other, their conversation seemed earnest indeed.

Had Irina decided to take up with Greg? Having known him all these years, I guess I just took him for granted as a buddy and never had given a thought to how he might appear to women. In a way, he was an attractive guy—his golden retriever eyes gave him a soft, trusting look that Irina might find restful and reassuring after the *sturm und drang* she'd been enduring with me.

Hoping not to be spotted, I ducked into the corner doorway of a health food shop across the way, from where I could glance over at Delphine's and try to size up what was going on. I could see Greg reach across the table and take hold of Irina's hand. She let it be held.

I pretended to scan the array of homeopathic remedies featured in the window display. Regret and jealousy resonated through me. The dull ache of a memory sent my mind back to a hot July afternoon in Charlestown when I was eleven and forlornly, inarticulately in love with a classmate named Connie, and how I'd circled endlessly on my bike around the block where she lived hoping to catch a glimpse of her—yet fearing that I would—only to see her coming down the street with Greg, both struggling to manage dripping ice cream cones…

I couldn't stay where I was, half-hidden in this doorway. It had been by a store doorway in Harvard Square I'd first met Irina. Was I seeing her slip away from me from another Harvard Square doorway? I glanced both ways. The best escape route looked to be back up Holyoke Street. I pulled my hat down, flipped the lapels of my raincoat up, and set off.

Having gone a few paces, I wheeled about, stepped back, and—cursing my curiosity—again stole a glance across to the window at Delphine's. What was I looking for? Confirmation that I was losing—had lost—Irina?

Her hand was still in his, their faces conspiratorial in their closeness.

I wheeled about and plunged determinedly back up the street. If she's had enough of me, I told myself, well, so be it.

But I couldn't believe a word I was telling myself...

Chapter 23

Another two days had passed, two more days in which to ponder what had gone wrong, where I was going wrong.

The late afternoon sun streamed across my desk at the lab. I watched the highlighted dust motes swirl about, mimicking the way thoughts were churning through my mind about Justin's death, Irina and Greg. I tried—though only with partial success—to repress my thoughts about whatever might have begun between the two of them. But, concerning Justin, there was one thought in particular I couldn't shake. It had to do with that moment in December when I'd found Justin's body—when I'd pulled his head back and found his eye was missing.

Why would anyone take that eye? More to the point, how would anyone—beyond his family, that is—even know that Justin had a false eye?

The old saying goes that two heads are better than one. As I had with so many problems with computers and research issues, I decided to share my musings with Greg—despite my queasiness about what I'd seen in the window at Delphine's.

I took the few steps down the hall to his office. His door was open, and Greg was—as usual—bent over his desk and peering into his color monitor. I softly rapped on the doorjamb.

"Yeah, come in," Greg muttered without turning around. "Bill, right? I can tell by the sound of the knuckles. Everyone's got a different resonance."

"You got it right, Greg. Uncanny. Anyway, I think I'm

onto something about Justin's death that I think the police are overlooking."

"What's that?" Greg called over his shoulder.

"The eye. Justin's missing eye."

"What about the eye? Didn't you say it was missing when you found his body?"

"Yeah. I learned from talking with Justin's uncle that it was a prosthesis—a false eye."

Still clutching his computer mouse, Greg pushed himself away from the monitor and sat straight up in his chair. "A false eye? Then couldn't it just have fallen out?"

"Yeah. It could have. But I don't think so. I think it was taken out."

"Hah! Why would anyone want to take a glass eye from anyone? First, they'd have to know it was there…"

"Exactly," I interrupted. "They'd have to know Justin's right eye was a…"

As I spoke I was jostled by a rough hand grabbing my shoulder and a brusque voice bursting in my ear, "Rundle! I've got to talk with you!"

It was Lieutenant Haggerty.

"I see you make house calls, Lieutenant," I said, making no attempt to temper the pique in my voice.

"More than doctors do nowadays, Rundle."

I turned to Greg, who was glancing back and forth between Haggerty and me, a look of puzzlement on his face. Haggerty had 'cop' written all over, so I'm sure Greg sensed I was having a visit from headquarters. Also, Haggerty most likely had quizzed him during the initial investigation.

"Let's go to my office, Lieutenant," I said. "It's just a couple of doors up."

"I know where it is," snapped Haggerty. "First place I looked for you."

"Greg, my apologies for the—interruption. I'll be back in a bit."

"No problem," Greg said as he swung back to face his computer screen. "Take your time."

168

I nodded in the direction of Greg, then led Haggerty up the hallway, he trailing behind me with a great flapping of his raincoat's tails and lapels as if he were trying to make himself more visible to the students and visitors passing in the hall than he already was.

I started to close my office door to create some privacy.

"Leave it open," Haggerty said.

"Do we have to..."

"Leave it open."

"Maybe I should..."

"Should what?"

"Have a lawyer here with me."

Pause. A heavy stare from Haggerty.

"Feel you need one?"

"I don't know. Is this the way police detectives operate?"

"What do you mean?"

"I mean the barging in, the big show."

"I just do what I need to, Rundle. Call it what you want. And call a lawyer, if you feel you need one."

I'd hold off on that for now. I'd nothing to hide. Except for not telling about Justin's email and the program he'd sent me.

I left the door open, as Haggerty directed. A knot of curious students passing by looked in at us.

Haggerty began, "You and Marsh had an argument the night before his body showed up. Late. Around eleven-thirty, or maybe closer to twelve. You were in his office."

"I already told you I was in his office."

"And you were arguing with him..."

"Arguing? Is that a statement or a question?"

Haggerty's face reddened even beyond his usual glow. "It's a bit of both," he growled.

"Yeah. I suppose you could say we were arguing," I said, trying to soften my voice so as to not provoke him any more than I seemed to be doing already.

"Why didn't you tell me about that when you were making your statement at headquarters?"

"I did tell you."

"I don't mean about being in his office. I mean about the argument. We've been talking again with some of your students, going over exactly what they saw and heard late that night or early morning. Maybe they felt they might be unfairly fingering you the first time we talked with them, but on re-questioning not a few of them allowed as how Marsh's voice and yours—particularly yours—were pretty loud at times."

"OK, an argument, then. Let's say it was an argument."

"What were you arguing about?"

"I told you. I was there at the lab trying to finish up a research proposal. The main sections were mine, but I needed his help with some of the boilerplate. He'd…"

"Boilerplate? What's 'boilerplate'?"

"That's a section in the proposal describing the hardware setup, underlying systems programs—that kind of stuff. Routine, but tricky to get right."

"OK. Go on."

"Well, he'd had since late November to pull his part together. But what he'd handed me thus far was all in bits and pieces. Some parts were really confusing, unusable. To tell the truth, I was pretty pissed off. And under a lot of pressure to get the thing together."

"So you had a fight with him?"

"Not a *fight*. An argument, maybe. I told you I was pissed off. He was way behind on stuff I needed. I guess our voices got pretty loud. Mostly mine, I suppose."

"What was his story on why he was late with your stuff?"

"He said he was sorry. He said he'd been distracted."

"Distracted? You used that word before about Marsh when I first quizzed you at the station—'distracted.' What was he distracted about?"

"He didn't say what. Just that he'd had a lot on his mind. I didn't press him on it."

"Why not? Weren't you his advisor?"

"Yeah, I was his advisor. But I thought it might be something personal—trouble with his girlfriend—something like that. I didn't want to butt in on his life."

"But you were mad at him?"

"Yeah. Mad enough to chew him out. But not mad…"

"Not mad enough to kill him—right?"

"Right. Not mad enough to kill him."

Haggerty gazed at me stonily. Then, glancing down at his watch, he said, "I'll be wanting to talk more about this, Rundle. All of the leads we have are beginning to converge. You're just about the last person anyone saw Marsh with. And your chat with him wasn't just an amicable discussion."

With that, Haggerty and his billowing raincoat swept out of my office and down the hall to the elevator.

I went out my door to go back to Greg's office to wind up our chat, and nearly crashed into Alec Hudson.

In addition to being a crack physicist and co-author with me on our articles on stringed instrument acoustics, every couple of weeks Alec hosted a classical guitar circle at his Dana Street apartment. There, amidst slices of pizza and mugs of Heineken, a half-dozen of us reasonably accomplished amateur players would gather to perform for each other whatever piece we were currently working on, trading critiques and encouragement.

"Bill, you're coming this evening to circle, aren't you?"

He glanced down at my left arm. He knew about the dog attack, and was concerned whether I'd be able to play at all, or even ever again.

"Of course I'm coming," I said. "I can still listen and critique." I flexed the fingers of my left hand into a few chord patterns. "Maybe play something—something simple. Anyway, I'll come a bit early and help you set up."

Alec could see that my control of my fingers was none too good. "Do what you can, Bill. It will come back." He paused, a sympathetic look on his face. "Maybe it will all come back, OK?"

"Are you in a hurry?" I asked. "Wait just a second."

I ducked back into my office, retrieved a packet bound in faded brown paper and tied with several loops of coarse string, and returned to Alec in the hall.

"Alec, take this with you. It's some stuff I picked up in Venice—a set of duets for guitar by Vivaldi. Printed in 1748. These scores may not have been played from in over a century. We—or, you and someone—can try them out at guitar circle tonight."

Alec's eyes widened as I handed him the packet. "Vivaldi! Bill, this is fantastic!"

"Guard them well," I said. "They may be worth a lot of money, if nothing else."

He stuffed the packet into his briefcase and started down the hall. "Bill," he called back to me, "I'll guard them with my life!"

I waved back to Alec. As I turned about to go back into my office, I saw Greg standing outside his door. His face was expressionless, but I could see his eyes fixed past me and down the hall, following the receding figure of Alec Hudson. After a long moment, Greg gave me a nod of recognition, crumpled a paper he had in his hand, and ducked back into his office.

I went down to Greg's office, paused at the door, and knocked. "Where were we?" I asked.

Greg was standing over by his coat rack, retrieving his loden coat.

"Bill, I'm not feeling all that great. Going to do an early getaway. Maybe lie down for a while. Sorry I can't continue our chat about—what was it?—Justin's eye?"

Greg did look a little pale.

"No problem," I said. "Another time. It'll keep."

"Yes, another time. Good night."

"Good night. Take care of yourself."

Greg disappeared down the hall, while I went back to my office. I slumped down in my chair and tried to work through the eerie sense of disquiet that had arisen in my mind.

Had I seen what I thought I had seen?

In that split second between my asking Greg how anyone might know about Justin's right eye and Haggerty's interruption—had I seen Greg's hand twitch as he rested it upon his computer mouse?

I was so familiar with that tic of Greg's—triggered by anything he felt was wrong—that I could readily spot it happening, subtle as it was. Yet I couldn't be sure, and it troubled me.

For it wasn't Justin's *right* eye I had meant to ask about. I'd made a slip of the tongue. I'd meant to say Justin's *left* eye.

And Greg's hand had twitched when he heard me say the wrong eye...

There hadn't been any mention of a missing eye in the newspaper reports, only that the body may have been mutilated. And, while I'd told Greg about the missing eye on the trip back from the Hales' party in Concord, as best I could recall I hadn't said *which* eye.

Sure, Justin's family, his girlfriend Karen, maybe a few others, would know he had a false eye, and which one it was. Now, here was Greg's hand unconsciously signaling that *he,* too, knew.

But how could he have known? And, had he been the one who...

I pushed the thought from my mind.

There were many ways Greg could have known about the eye. After all, he'd been working closely with Justin for almost two years. I'd never myself noticed anything amiss with Justin's eyes, but someone like Greg—who was a keen observer and who'd even designed an eye-tracking apparatus—would surely have spotted the false eye. And as for being the one who'd killed Justin and taken the eye...

Good God, Bill, I told myself, this is Greg you're wondering about. Your best friend since you both were five. Growing up on the same street in Charlestown, playing stickball and tag rush together. Double-dating in high school. Even when his dad had struck it rich with a chain of laundromats and he and his folks upgraded their home to suburban Lexington, he'd kept in touch. His attending high-tuition MIT and your going to low-cost University of Massachusetts didn't part you. He was the one who had introduced you to Jean-Paul Etherington, and persuaded him to take a chance and hire you—a PhD in psychology amidst the 'techies'—when, to the rest of the lab faculty, your hire might well have been a no-go...

I closed my eyes and tried to project myself back in time. Had I really seen Greg's hand twitch? Or was it the jostle from Haggerty that made me think I'd seen it?

And even if I'd seen it, I told myself it didn't prove anything. Greg could have known about that eye in a hundred different ways.

I pushed all such thoughts from my mind. Just a few more things to wind up at my office and I'd be heading for Alec Hudson's guitar circle—where I'd see just how much the nerves in my left arm had or had not healed.

Chapter 24

The work day over, I stopped by home on my way to Alec's to pick up my guitar. It's a del Pilar, constructed in 1963. With its easy action, crisp treble, and sonorous bass, it's a lovely 'axe,' as my old guitar teacher used to term guitars. He'd found it for me—well-used but in pristine condition—through a dealer in Manhattan. I'd wanted to play classical guitar ever since, while studying late one winter night in my sophomore college year and listening to public radio, I heard a recording of a guitarist with the wonderful name of Sanchez Granada playing *Recuerdos de La Alhambra*—*Memories of the Alhambra*—by Francisco Tárrega. *Recuerdos* is a tremolo study, its fluttering notes like the beating of a bird's wings. Lush and haunting, it begins in E-minor, shifts to G-major, reaches a grace-note climax, then trails off softly to its final bar.

That lovely song had fed a fantasy. A few weeks of lessons—of course, I'd have made amazing progress—and I'd quit school and be a café player somewhere on the coast of Spain. Málaga, maybe. I'd be slouching in a chair amidst a ring of tables on a lantern-lit terrace. Bougainvillea all about, the scent of orange blossom hanging in the air. The proprietor would nod. I'd stub out my smoldering Gauloise, take a sip of Rioja, and launch into *Recuerdos*. All talk would hush as I wove my spell. The last note trailing off, the patrons would shake off their reverie and break into wild applause and "*Olés*." Coins and bills showering my table. Dark-eyed women hurling roses…

Alas, I stuck with college instead, and ended up in computers at

MIT. Guitar evening was the closest I'd ever gotten to that terrace in Málaga.

I decided to take a chance and phone Irina, pledging to myself absolutely no more talk—no matter what—about my suspicions.

"How about a beer tonight after I get out of guitar?"

She replied, "Depends on how many you've had at Alec's beforehand." Her voice sounded relaxed. Maybe time—even a few days—does cure all things.

"I'll try to keep count," I replied.

"How is your arm? You'll be able to play OK?"

"It still goes numb on me. I'll stick with some easy stuff. Anyway, about eight-thirty?"

"I should be clear by then. Greg Evans phoned just before you called. He wanted me to join him for early dinner. He's still pretty down over Justin's death. He said he needed to talk a bit. I'd asked him to lunch at Delphine's a few days ago where he let *me* cry on *his* shoulder, so I owe it to him. He said he knew you'd be at your guitar group, so he decided to ring me. He wants me to meet him at the lab, and we'll go over to Legal Seafood."

I froze at Irina's words. All the uncertainties that had been torturing me raged again through my mind.

Had I really seen Greg's hand twitch?

I fought to dismiss my fears. Yet that—imagined?—sighting of Greg's twitch haunted me, like a sentinel who hears a twig snap in the darkness and *knows* something is out there, however deep the ensuing silence. And why that stony expression on Greg's face as he looked down the hall toward me after Haggerty's visit? My mind spun about with indecision and apprehension. Irina alone with Greg...

"Irina, I think it might be..."

I cut myself off mid-sentence. Hadn't I done enough damage with my suspicions? Worse, despite the innocence of Irina's lunch with Greg at Delphine's, could it be sheer jealousy on my part that was behind my feelings?

"You think what might be?" asked Irina.

"I think it might be great for you to go for dinner with Greg," I said, swallowing my misgivings. "Good of you to do that. He just may be going into real depression. Look—I'll ring your cell phone when I leave guitar circle. If Greg still needs to talk some, then maybe we can all go for a beer. OK?"

"OK. I'll take the cell with me. Bye."

"Bye."

It was a bit after 6:15 when I knocked on the door of Alec Hudson's Dana Street apartment. My rapping set his unlatched door swinging slowly inward.

Alec's living room looked the same as it always did for guitar night: sofa pushed back, folding chairs and music racks stacked in the corner, ready to be set out.

"Alec," I called out.

No answer.

I went out to the kitchen. Empty. I called his name out again. Still no answer. Probably ducked out for more beer.

I headed back into the living room. I decided I'd just set up the chairs, music racks, and footrests, and wait.

Then I saw what the sofa had blocked from my view as I'd come in—a rivulet of blood glistening and caking on the hardwood floor.

The track of blood widened to a dark crimson pool three feet beyond, where Alec's guitar stand lay overturned, his body sprawled beside it. A bronze letter-opener lay by the foot of the sofa. Its serrated blade, maybe ten inches long, was mottled with red stains.

Alec lay on his back, the front of his pale blue shirt soaked in blood. His eyes, wide open, gazed emptily at the ceiling, while his hands—spattered with blood—cradled his guitar.

I quickly knelt and checked his breath and pulse. He had neither.

I called 911 and told them what I'd found. They said not to touch anything and that a car would be right over.

I sat on the arm of the sofa and stared in disbelief at Alec's body. What kind of maniac would have done this? The apartment door was open, but not forced. Had Alec let someone in? Someone he knew? I lowered my gaze to the guitar clenched in his hands. Blood smeared all over the blond wood top. Blood, too, way up on the ivory tuning keys. Why there? Had Alec been twisting them even while he was dying?

I reached down with my forefinger and brushed the bass strings of Alec's guitar. They were out of tune. The sixth string, usually an E, was tuned up to G. Odd. Sometimes you dropped the sixth down to a D for lute transcriptions, or a piece like Albeniz's *Tango*. Though I certainly didn't know the whole guitar literature, I'd never come across anything where you brought the sixth string up to G.

I plucked the fourth string, ordinarily a D. Relative to the fifth string it was up a whole tone to an E. Even odder.

The fifth string, the A, was like home base; you tuned it first, and then the other strings to it. Maybe it was off. I picked up the little brass pitch pipe lying on Alec's music rack, sounded an A, then plucked the fifth string. The string was a perfect A. The fourth and sixth strings had been tuned up to give not the usual E-A-D tuning, but instead G-A-E.

This is crazy, I thought, reflecting on what I was doing—plucking the strings of an instrument grasped by a corpse with a ghastly wound showing forth. I felt nauseated, ghoulish. Yet, if there were something hidden here…

I sounded the three treble strings. From lowest to highest, they should be G-B-E. Almost, but not quite. The B string had been tuned down to A.

Strings can stretch or slacken by themselves, the notes going lower. But strings don't tune higher on their own, and there were those two bass strings sounding higher than they should.

Alec must have done it. To tell me something? He knew I was heading to his place.

I swept my finger across all six strings. They said G-A-E-G-A-E. The G-A-E pattern, twice. Twice so there'd be no mistake. GAE. Gregory Arthur Evans.

I leapt to my feet and rushed from the apartment.

Chapter 25

Hurtling across town toward Kendall Square, I rang Irina's cell phone from mine. *Answer, dammit,* I yelled to myself. At the third ring, Irina's voice came on the line, tense and strained.

"Bill, you're phoning early. Was your guitar group called off?"

"Irina, are you with Greg? Are you still at Legal's?"

"No. We decided we'd go after..."

Irina's voice cut off, as if she'd turned to someone and was holding her hand over the phone. She came back on, saying, "We're at the Cognitive Computing Lab. In The Block in the new annex." She sounded hesitant, uncertain. "Greg wants to show me—show us—his new laser display."

"Irina? Are you OK?"

"Yes...I mean no, Bill! Don't..."

I heard a muffled thud. Silence. Then Greg's voice barking, "Rundle. Get over here. The Block. Fifteen minutes."

"Irina!" I yelled into the phone.

"She's fine," Greg answered. "Just *you* get here."

"Greg, what are you...?"

"Fifteen minutes."

The phone went dead.

The traffic on Massachusetts Avenue just before Central Square was maddening—a glut of cars all trying to get home, delivery trucks, pedestrians cutting every which way. I inched excruciatingly through the melee, as in a dream sequence where you're striving to run fast but your limbs are like lead.

179

I sounded the horn and cursed the lumbering mail van in front of me. Inwardly, I cursed Greg.

I could see now why Greg had gone after poor Alec Hudson. I sickened as I recalled Alec exclaiming, "I'll guard it with my life!" Greg must have heard it, too. He'd thought I'd handed Alec not something of indifferent value to him like some music by Vivaldi, but a copy of Justin's code.

I winced as I pictured what must have happened. Greg confronting Alec, cajoling him to give him the packet, maybe claiming it was all a mistake, that I'd given away some material that was really his. Alec hesitant, bewildered, claiming that what I'd given him held sheet music, and that there'd been no mistake. Greg getting impatient, belligerent, as was his wont—maybe even his right hand giving that telltale twitch—then stridently demanding that Alec hand it over. Alec steadfastly refusing to be bullied, as was *his* wont, saying "Greg, you have no right…" Then Greg, in a fury born of frustration and desperation, snatching up the bronze letter opener…

I finally managed to push through Central Square and make the left turn onto Main Street toward MIT's East Campus. Thankfully, the traffic pace picked up, and things rolled smoothly for several blocks—then stopped dead.

Damn! What was the holdup? I leaned out the window and squinted into the distance. A freight train with a seemingly endless string of boxcars and tank cars was rolling arthritically through the grade crossing just before Vassar Street. My Jeep Cherokee was no helicopter. I had to wait it out and pray Greg would have patience.

He'd certainly had duplicity, faking a car breakdown to get a lift home from the Hales' party—all to check on what Irina and I were thinking about my finding Justin's body. Then, begging a lift to Justin's funeral, saying his car was still out of commission, again to listen in on what we might be thinking, what the students might be saying, about Justin's death.

And I hadn't caught on, hadn't suspected his sudden need for emergency transportation when he'd never asked for that kind of help before.

My heart pounded with anxiety as I counted the rail cars rumbling through the crossing. I was certain now—not merely suspicious from spying a hand twitch—that it was Greg who'd killed Justin, just because, as did Alec, Justin had refused to give him the program.

A murderous desperation had grown up, was festering, in Greg. I could only think that it had something to do with the ill will he had voiced about John Creedon—labeling him a "slick operator"—as we'd walked together down the Institute's 'infinite corridor' the day before Justin's funeral. Greg had passed off what he'd said as poor boy resentment, but the bitter tone he'd had in his voice hinted it ran much deeper.

The freight train's caboose rolled by and the crossing gates swung away. Motors revved up, and the line of cars and trucks blocking my way to the lab began to move. Twenty minutes had passed since Greg had demanded I get myself to The Block. My heart continued to pound. God give him patience, I muttered to myself.

Reaching the lab, I raced to the lower level, pulled open the door of The Block and stepped in. Two spotlights mounted on opposite corners of the ceiling drew my eyes upward. They were the only illumination, and, being all of fifty feet above me, they barely dispelled the darkness down where I stood.

The Block's door swung closed behind me as I groped for the switches to turn up the room's main floodlights. The napped fabric on the wall panels felt like the fur of some huge rodent. I found the switches and slid them upward. Nothing. The circuits had been killed.

"Irina!" I called out, the expanse of the room swallowing the sound of my voice.

No answer.

I called again. Still no answer.

My eyes were getting used to the darkness. I quickly scanned the sixty-foot-square floor. Several shapes huddled against the wall opposite me.

One shape I made out to be the room's Bosendorfer grand piano, its lid propped up like the wing of a bat. Other shapes I took to be the computers and racks of electronics that controlled the Bosendorfer's automatic playing, plus cabinets holding some of the piano's high-wattage speakers. On the floor to the right of the piano was a clutter of boxes holding odds and ends of equipment. Lastly, I could make out two rows of folding chairs arranged in a half-circle before the piano, probably set there for a noon hour brown-bag lunch concert.

A muffled click came from behind me. I stepped back to the door and pushed the handle. Locked. I turned and walked out toward the center of the floor.

Greg's voice, whispery soft, insinuating, spoke at my right shoulder, into my ear. "Rundle. Rundle."

I shuddered and pulled back.

My eyes were now fully dark-adapted. Above me, I could dimly make out the steel rafters that spanned the room, the gantry crane suspended from the central beam, the catwalk forty feet up and bordering all four sides of the space. My eyes strained against the half-light above, the blackness below. No movement. No sound. Nothing.

"Rundle. Rundle," the voice came again, placed directly at my ear. I reached up and tried to brush it away like a foul cobweb. With the banks of phased-array loudspeakers deployed about The Block's wall, Greg could put his voice anywhere in the room, like a high-tech ventriloquist.

I retreated from the room's center and got up close to the wall, not far from the door I had come in. I figured the 3-D voice effect would work less well if I were on The Block's periphery.

I was right. The mocking "Rundle…Rundle…" came again, but off and away from me, not perched at my collarbone. Though I knew there'd be nothing there for me to see, I stared toward the source of the voice, a point in mid-air somewhere between room center and the chairs surrounding the Bosendorfer.

"You sure took your time, Rundle," Greg's voice said. "Or should I call you 'Bill' for old times' sake? Anyway, I wish to hell all this never had to happen."

"What have you done with Irina, Greg? Where is she?"

"She's with you. Check the corner to the right of the Bosendorfer. It's dark, but you'll find her."

I ran to the corner, fell to my knees, and groped about. A limp body—Irina.

"Hasn't she come to yet?" Greg said, a gentleness in his voice in eerie contrast to the hard edge it had over the cell phone just after he'd struck her.

Irina stirred. "Bill?" she asked shakily. "Where are we? Are we in the lab?"

"Yes, we're at the lab. In The Block. Take it slow."

She gave a start, and looked rapidly about. "Oh, God," she cried out. "Is he still here?"

"I'm afraid I'm still here, Irina," Greg said. "Sorry to cuff you like that. I guess it was a bit hard."

I helped Irina to her feet, steadying her. We turned and faced in the direction of Greg's disembodied voice.

"Bill," Greg continued, "I wish you hadn't got that program from Justin. I wish… But it's all gone too far. You couldn't just drop it and leave it alone. You're not that kind of guy. So…" His voice trailed off.

"You killed Alec Hudson!" I yelled, seething with anger. "You left him for dead, but he'd enough strength to twist your initials into the tuning of his guitar!"

"What the hell are you talking about? Initials in a guitar?"

"I found him clutching his guitar. He'd tuned the strings to G-A-E, G-A-E. His dying act! You went after him because you thought he had Justin's code, didn't you? You thought that I'd given it to him in that packet!"

"Yeah. You have it right. I saw you pass it to Alec. Guard it with his life, he said. What else could it have been? And right after you had the huddle with that cop Haggerty. What were you doing—fingering me to him? Irina told me at lunch the other day you were thinking I might've done in Justin."

"Greg, you killed Alec for nothing! For nothing! He never had any code of Justin's. That was a packet of sheet music I gave him."

183

Silence.

Then Greg said, "I thought he had the code, Bill. He denied it up and down. He showed me some old music sheets, and swore that's what you gave him. That was what he was guarding with his *life*? I took it he was lying, Bill. I lost my temper. I made a mistake."

"A mistake?" I cried out. "Your killing Justin—was that a mistake, too?"

"Yes, Justin's death *was* a mistake. Not like Alec's was, but a real mistake."

"A 'real mistake'? What in the name of God are you talking about?"

"I needed Justin's program. He'd made this expert system that would sail a racing yacht. You've heard of his uncle? Bennett Eames? The system was modeled on him. World-class sailor. Defended the America's Cup twice, and, if he hadn't got sick, could've done it again."

"Greg, I know all about the program. Harry Mirsky cracked the code. Eames told me about how he and Justin made it out at ZIDEX— John Creedon's company in Waltham."

"Well, I helped Justin get access to the virtual reality simulator at ZIDEX. Creedon's a yachtsman with this hero worship for Eames, so he was more than happy to offer it. I kibitzed Justin on how to work the simulator at first, but in no time he was off and running. By the time Justin started bringing his uncle in, I'd stepped back and just watched now and then from the sidelines. But the more I saw his program work, the clearer it was that the thing was absolutely brilliant. Justin's program could sail almost as well as Eames himself."

"So, you wanted to get the program?"

"*Wanted it?* Damn right. You know Kenichi Tsukamoto, don't you? That hothead exchange student over in Ocean Engineering who drops by the lab now and then to see what we're up to?"

"I know who you mean. He was at Hale's party, threatening Japan would be taking the America's Cup."

"Yeah, him. Anyway, I met him at the bar over at Legal Seafood, oh, late November. We had a few drinks. Boy, was he in a funk! He was moaning as how this Australian guy all of a sudden was thinking of copping out on being the skipper for Team Nippon. I told him about this program that would sail a Cup racer like a champ. Just mentioned it, like off-hand. Know what? That nationalistic son-of-a-bitch said he'd give me four hundred thousand dollars to deliver Justin's program containing his uncle's sailing smarts."

"You took him seriously? He was going to pay you that much?"

"No. I thought he was drunk, or—you know—on something. I must have said as much, because he took out his checkbook right there and then, and wrote one out for a hundred thousand dollars. Just like that. Can you believe it? 'It make you hot for three hundred thousand more,' he says as he hands it to me. Yeah, it did all right. I should have asked for double."

"Four hundred thousand? Was it Team Nippon syndicate money?"

"I don't think so. Kenichi's a member of the Team Nippon syndicate, but I think this was just his doing. His family's got billions. I'm talking dollars, not yen. Kenichi must get a few million a year just for walking-around money. Anyway, he told me—in confidence, he said—Team Nippon was in deep trouble and getting desperate. He wanted to help out. He said the crew could train with Justin's program until they located a replacement skipper. But I didn't put it past him to think that if the crew didn't shape up the program would do the actual sailing."

"So you were going to sell the program to Kenichi?"

"Yeah—that was the plan."

"But there was more to it than just money, wasn't there, Greg?"

Greg cleared his throat. "What do you mean 'more to it'?"

"I mean you saw giving Justin's program to the Japanese as a way to get at John Creedon."

"Yeah, you got it right, Bill. In a way, I couldn't give a damn about the money. What it really meant was I could screw over John Creedon. That bastard, Creedon. If I could give Justin's program to Kenichi, just maybe Team Nippon could outsail any yacht entry from his high-ass Weston Group."

"Just what is it you have against Creedon?"

"I guess you don't know any of this, do you?"

185

"I guess not."

"Creedon—the man with everything. I consulted for him at his company, ZIDEX. Even worked there part-time, starting maybe seven years back."

Greg paused and sighed deeply, as if to steel himself for some distasteful task.

He continued, "Anyway, I designed ZIDEX's I-Lok security system. It scans the iris of your eye to check your identity. But—shit-for-brains that I am—I signed this paper that says ZIDEX owns whatever research I did there. Oh, Creedon tells me, you can have fifteen percent of whatever profits ZIDEX makes on what you invent or develop."

"That's not bad," I said. "I don't know what the standard is for high-tech companies, but fifteen percent sounds pretty good."

"Hah! Sure, fifteen percent! *If* you can prove that *you* are the inventor. That fifteen percent evaporated down to three. Three percent of next to nothing!"

Greg paused. I could hear him swallow, then clear his throat. He continued, "OK. Why did Creedon stiff me like that on the percentage? Because, he claims, I didn't 'originate' a frigging bit of the iris scanner. There were five of us working on the I-Lok—even though it was me who had all the good ideas. Anyway, he says it was the *team* that did it, not me. The best I'll be getting, he says, is a three percent royalty, the fifteen percent split five ways, which he says would be 'sizeable' over the years.

"So, I wait six months to see what the first payout would be. Would you believe three-hundred eighty-nine dollars? Sizeable? Three-hundred eighty-nine dollars? The I-Lok was selling like hotcakes! Big breakthrough in security systems! I asked him how come I was getting peanuts. Well, he says, there were patent fees, legal fees, start-up costs, amortizing engineering expenses, capitalizing the manufacturing line—all kinds of shit. The three-hundred eighty-nine was my three percent *minus* all that stuff off the top. Can you believe it? That two-faced bastard with his thousand-dollar suits, his corporate planes, his platinum-plated whores."

"So you began leaning on Justin to give you his program?"

"Not leaning. *Asking.* I asked him for a copy of the program. Said I needed to check out some parts of the graphics generator. He said he'd consider it. But he stalled. Time went by. I asked him again and again. I began to wonder if maybe Justin was going to give Creedon the program as a kind of thank you, or maybe Creedon would just grab it, and his Weston Group would have a leg up on the Cup."

"Greg, didn't it occur to you that Justin didn't want to just hand his uncle's sailing legacy over to you? Or to Creedon? Or to anyone? Eames dreamed of passing on his sailing skill to young sailors. That program was a way he could do that, not just in a book, but in a computer program that could sail like he could."

"Maybe...maybe..."

"So you were leaning on—correction—'asking' Justin for his program while Kenichi was leaning on you. But things didn't get really serious, did they Greg, until the Russian Mafia stepped in? A gentleman by the name of Igor Menshikov?"

"Menshikov? How—how do you know about him?" Greg muttered.

"Irina and I had the pleasure when we were in Venice recently. He took us to dinner, and made a bid for Justin's program over dessert. Half a million. He thought I might have it, Justin being my student."

"Did you give...?"

"Of course not. He's still after you, isn't he? And a guy who goes around in a bullet-proof vest isn't someone to fool with."

"Ok. Yeah, the Russian Mafia got after Justin's program—after me, that is. They have this backdoor interest in Team St. Petersburg. They wanted it, too, to up their chances of winning the Cup."

"How did they even know it existed?"

"They told me how. There was this new guy at ZIDEX, Ivan Popovich, a physicist. I even met him. Recent émigré. Lives over in Brookline Village. Anyway, I never noticed anyone hanging around, but they say one night Popovich saw Justin working with Eames in the simulator, and me over on the sidelines watching it all. Popovich puts two and two together, and passes the word back to this guy Menshikov."

Greg muttered something I couldn't understand, then said, "Anyway, it's a real small world. Know who the go-between was with Menshikov and me?"

Irina and I stood silent.

"Come on. Three guesses."

I could feel Irina clutch my arm.

"Listen, Irina. I'll give you a hint," Greg said. "Think of it as being all in the family."

"Sergei!" exclaimed Irina. She grasped my arm even more tightly. "No! He's not involved with the Mafia! He's…"

"Think what you want, Irina," cooed Greg. "But I'm afraid he is. He's a good kid. Just got himself caught up with them. Doesn't realize what deadly bastards they are."

Irina turned her head and gave me a long look. I squeezed her hand. "I didn't want to believe it, either," I said softly.

"Anyway," said Greg, clearing his throat, "they were offering even more than Kenichi. Eight hundred thousand. Jesus, the money these guys have! Hell, I told myself, I'll sell it to *both* of them! They'll never compare notes and figure out what's going on." Greg let out a cackling laugh. "I mean, the Japs and the Russians aren't exactly kissing cousins, are they?"

"All that, and 'getting' Creedon, too," I said. "A hat trick."

"Sure. A hat trick. Only, they changed their tune. The Russians, that is. They got antsy, even more than Kenichi. They said it was simple—if I wanted to live, I'd better get them Justin's program. You've got to admire their frankness, right? Anyway, they'd toss in the eight hundred thousand as a bonus—though my life was the main incentive. They gave me forty-eight hours to come up with the program. I couldn't stall any longer."

"So you were up against it," I said. "You had to get that program from Justin no matter what. But to *kill* him for it. Why couldn't you have…"

Greg interrupted, his voice testy. "I didn't *kill* him. It just happened. We were both up pretty late at the lab. It must have been, oh, like one-thirty. I went to his office. I told him I needed the program. Just a copy, I said. He said he couldn't give it to me; it was his uncle's thing. They were going to distribute it to kids' sailing clubs, and Creedon was going to underwrite the costs. I pleaded. I told him certain people were after me—people who were going to kill me if I didn't give them the program. I was down on my goddamn knees! But I couldn't make him believe me. He must have thought I was drunk or out of my mind, or something. He wouldn't believe me!"

"Then what happened?"

"I lost it. I hit him with that swimming trophy—you know, the one he had sitting on his desk. He dropped and didn't move. I didn't mean to kill him. I just lost it."

"You lost it? Jesus, Greg, don't we all lose it at times? You just can't…"

My mind flashed back to my break-in at Tsukamoto's house, how I'd, in the dark and in a panic, grasped a brass figurine and clubbed someone across the head. Luckily, for him—and for me—it had been a glancing blow, and he was OK. But with Justin and Greg, it had turned out differently. There but for the grace of God…

"I lost it, Bill," Greg repeated, reverting to calling me by my first name. "That's all. That's what happened. It was crazy. I was scared to death—but it was like I could still think straight. You know what I mean?"

I didn't answer.

Greg continued, "I looked in the janitor's closet, the one next to Justin's office. There was this canvas cart in there, plus a pile of big trash bags. I put him in one of the bags, and wheeled him to the elevator, then down to the loading platform. Christ, Bill, you don't know how bizarre this all was!"

Greg struggled to keep his voice even. He went on, "I had to figure out what to do, and fast. I could only think of the river—you know, make it look like he'd drowned. So I—maybe you don't want to hear this…"

Irina and I looked at one another. Despite the drawn look on her face, she nodded acquiescence.

189

"No," I said. "Let's hear it all."

"I—I slung him head down into the big sink there by the freight door, turned on the faucets, and pumped water into his lungs. You know, like artificial respiration in reverse. Then, I took him in my car to the Charles…"

Greg's voice had choked off. Irina was grasping my hand, and I could sense her whole body trembling as Greg unfolded what he'd done.

"But first you took his eye," I said. "You needed that eye to get past security into ZIDEX and try to locate Justin's program in the machines he'd used there."

"Yeah, yeah—I had to take it. Justin'd had this shop accident in high school, and was fitted with a fake eye. Beautiful piece of work. The iris on it even widened or closed by itself, depending how bright the light was. It was kind of a gag between us that he used that eye—his left—as the one he'd present to the security camera.

"Anyway, I was too shaken up to go out to ZIDEX right off. I went home. Started hitting a bottle of Jack Daniels till I passed out. When I came to, it was late afternoon. Could barely think straight. Finally decided I'd go out to ZIDEX after Hale's party. It surprised the hell out of me, though, when you announced at Hale's it was you who found the body."

"So you faked your car's breakdown so you could bum a ride home from Irina and me to see what we were thinking about Justin's death."

"Yeah. I needed to see what you might be on to. Then I borrowed—maybe 'boosted' is more like it—a neighbor's car and drove out to ZIDEX in Waltham. I got past security with Justin's fake eye all right, but I couldn't find Justin's program to save me. I drove back home. By then, I'm really going out of my mind. Then, surprise number two. Next morning just before noon I spot you and Mirsky at Au Bon Pain fine-combing some printout. So I sidle up and, good Jesus, I recognize the header lines. It's Justin's stuff!"

"So it was you, not some UPS guy, who slipped the note under my door demanding those packets of disks."

"Yeah. It was me."

"Did you pass the disks on to Ser—to the Russians?"

"Sure I did. But they couldn't get the suckers to work. You'd put some glitches in them, right?"

"Yeah. I did that."

"Thanks a lot, Bill. You almost had me killed then and there. Anyway, Sergei gives me back the disks. Fix 'em, he tells me. I tried my damnedest. Got nowhere. I told Sergei I needed more time. He keeps asking me if I'd killed Justin to get them. He was nervous, scared shitless. No way I killed Justin, I told him. I said Justin was having girlfriend trouble, was getting depressed, the holidays coming and all, so he jumped in the Charles. Anyway, Sergei says Menshikov wants me to know my time is running out."

Irina called up to Greg. "You're saying Sergei was part of all that? Of the threat to kill you if you didn't hand over the program?"

"Irina," answered Greg, "if it's any consolation to you, I think Sergei was as scared as I was. He's not a killer, but he was letting himself become a tool for Menshikov."

"So you sent the goons after Harry in the parking garage?" I asked. "Plus the ones who jumped Poon Song?"

"I got Kenichi and his guys to do that. He was impatient for the program, too. I told him he'd have to help me, or we'd never get it."

"And the mustached guy with the pit bull who went after me?"

"Oh, yeah. Dave's a buddy from the old neighborhood in Charlestown. He breeds pits. Dave's not exactly a genteel type—not everyone from our part of town ended up with a PhD. Listen—that thing with the dog was stupid. It shouldn't have happened. I was panicked. I wanted to put pressure on you. It was dumb. I'm sorry."

"And Menshikov and company were letting you live through all these delays?"

"Yeah, they realized it might take me a while to get the program, and were willing to give me a bit longer. I could see them losing patience, but I kept pleading through Sergei for more time." Greg paused. "You know, I could have just told Menshikov his discreet approach wouldn't work and my threat approach wasn't going to do it either, and he'd just have to sic some really bad boys on you. You have something to be grateful for—that I didn't do that."

"Why didn't you?"

"I guess to spare your hide, for old times' sake. But there was the eight hundred thou, too. Put that with Kenichi's, I'd have 1.2 million, and I could get the hell out..."

"So what is it you want now? Now that you've killed Alec, too—and for nothing?"

"Simple. I still need that code of Justin's. I've been given all the leases on life Menshikov and company are going to give me."

"Look, Greg. I'll give you the damn program. At least let Irina go."

"Don't trouble yourself. I'll get it myself. Before you came, I persuaded Irina to tell if she knew where you might be keeping the program. On a pair of floppy disks with a knotted rubber band around them and in a wire tray by your desk—sound right? Listen, Rundle! Before you chew her out for telling, realize her doing that is the only reason you're still standing there and able to talk. Anyway, I have your office door to jimmy open, and a plane to catch."

Greg's voice became oddly hesitant.

"You understand that...you realize that I can't let the both of you live. I mean, after all I've told you. You'll think it's funny, the way I have to do this. It's that I don't think I can do it myself. I mean..."

Greg became silent. Then, in a voice suddenly shrill, he cried out, "Don't be calling out for me! I'm going to be busy. For chrissake, I won't hear you, anyway!"

The door above by the third floor west entry—nearby Greg's office—opened, sending a shaft of light out through the criss-cross wire railing of The Block's catwalk. There was a muffled scraping as a large, shadowy shape crossed over the threshold. Then the door closed.

Chapter 26

Irina and I stood frozen in place.

"It's true, Bill. I told Greg where the disks were. I hoped it would keep him from going after you. I'm sorry I didn't believe you when you were telling me your suspicions."

"It's OK," I said. "I didn't want to believe it about Greg either. I should have just handed over the code from the beginning without trying to be smart and putting those glitches in it. I put Harry in danger. You. Everyone. Now, Alec Hudson is dead…"

"It's not your fault. You blame yourself too much. You were being loyal to the trust Justin put in you."

"Damn that trust! Look what it's done!"

"Bill, you are a good person. You are loyal. It's Greg who is disloyal and murderous."

I looked into Irina's eyes. We clung to each other tightly.

"He's planning to kill us, isn't he?" Irina whispered. "That's why he was talking over the sound system, so he wouldn't have to look at us, isn't it? And calling you by your last name to put you at a distance and make it easier for him to do it?"

"Yes. I'm afraid he's decided to kill us."

But not without a fight, I added to myself.

I pushed Irina away gently, and gestured to her to help scan the room. "Let's try to spot that thing Greg sent in here," I called to her. "Do you see where it…"

Karrah-rammm! The Bosendorfer came to life, pouring out ear-rending cadenzas. Crashing up and down the scale, the notes sounded

193

the 'diabolus' interval: the raucous, hee-hawing siren sound given off by ambulances and emergency vehicles, the tones that Anne Frank had heard as Nazi trucks rounded up victims for the gas ovens.

The chords from the great instrument cut like sabers through my skull. I could see Irina wince with pain. So this was how Greg would not hear us if we yelled to him—the piano would drown us out.

We plugged our fingers in our ears, but it did little good, as the sound simply pried right through them. Then, as suddenly as it had begun, the Bosendorfer fell silent. I peered into the dark. I could see nothing. My ears were ringing from the piano chords, but it seemed I could hear something making a soft whirring sound.

I heard it again, a bit louder. It sounded high and to our right, gradually approaching.

Then, we both saw it: a profile silhouetted against one of the ceiling spotlights like a cloud across the moon. Greg's helium mini-blimp! The whirring was from the small motors driving the blimp's twin propellers.

Above the constant whir of the motors, I could make out an intermittent whir of higher pitch. I'd heard it before, in Greg's lab. It came from the little servo-motors which drove the scanner mirrors he had integrated into his experimental infrared vision system.

The blimp could see in the dark. And it was looking for us.

"Stay still," I said to Irina. "The blimp's camera probably looks for things that move."

As if on cue from my words, the blimp halted and swung about. Instead of a longish profile, the blimp's shape had become round like a basketball, which meant it was headed straight at us.

A deep ruby glow lit up the blimp's nose. *Crack!* A pencil beam of laser light grazed my ear like a hot icicle. Greg's high-energy micro laser! An acrid, smoky smell rose from the deep tear in the fabric wall just behind my head.

"Are you ok?" Irina exclaimed.

"Don't say anything!" I whispered urgently. "It goes after voice, too."

I pointed to the piano. In a crouch, we crept along the wall toward the Bosendorfer for cover. The blimp hung in mid-air as if undecided where next to turn, then swung about and headed in our direction. I reached behind me and, grasping Irina's shoulder, pushed her to the floor, then pressed myself flat against the wall.

Crack! Another burst of red light cut through the darkness. A dagger of pain stabbed at my right jaw and neck. I ducked down and pressed my hand against the stinging flesh. The wound seemed bloodless—just hot and sticky.

While alerted by either movement or voice, the blimp seemed to shoot only for the face. How soon would it shoot again? I remembered Greg's student Tamara saying the laser's capacitors needed ten seconds to re-charge. I signaled to Irina, and we dashed the rest of the way to the black bulk of the piano.

Amidst the clutter of equipment—video monitors, oscilloscopes, keyboards, phones, patch-panels and such—that littered the space behind the Bosendorfer, I spotted a store-dummy head with glassy eyes. Greg and his students must have used it for testing out their face-and-eye tracking programs.

I snatched the head up and set it under the piano lid so that it looked out into The Block. If the blimp favored going after faces and eyes, then let it try blasting at that for a change.

The blimp drifted about The Block, its altitude about shoulder height. Its nose swung left and right, relentless yet indecisive—as if not sure of where next to search us down.

Irina quickly whispered a plan to me. It could work. I nodded yes.

Shielding her face from the blimp's scanners with one hand, Irina reached down with the other and picked up an extension phone that lay on the floor. Moving very slowly, she placed the phone under the piano lid next to where I'd set the dummy head. Then, ducking for cover, she gestured toward the piano lid. I nodded back, and got myself into position at the keyboard end of the Bosendorfer.

Irina reached under the piano lid and removed the phone's receiver. Working by touch, she tapped in a number, switched the instrument onto speakerphone, set it at peak loudness, and drew her arm back. After three rings, my recorded voice came on the line: "This is Bill

195

Rundle. I'm not in my office now, but if you'd…"

The blimp halted in mid-air, gunned its propellers, and swung about to face the Bosendorfer, the dummy head peering out from under its upturned lid. Having heard my voice, the blimp now surged toward the source, its video camera seeking a face and eye to match.

Irina and I crouched behind the piano, putting our hands over our faces and squinting through our fingers so that the only face image presented to the blimp was that of the dummy.

Crack! The laser beam seared through the right eye of the dummy head and ripped into the wood of the lid beyond.

The blimp glided forward, its nose now maybe twenty feet from the piano. I counted off the seconds to myself. Ten to recharge, and then the dummy would get it again.

There was another flash from the blimp's nose, accompanied by a crisp *crack.* The dummy's left eye blew away, leaving a smoldering hole.

By now, the blimp had a third of its length under the lid of the Bosendorfer. I leapt up and tripped away the mahogany strut supporting the piano's massive lid, which crunched down on the blimp like a sperm whale biting through a rowboat.

"Let's get that laser out," I said. "It may be our only hope when Greg gets back."

I heaved the piano lid back up while Irina pushed the strut back into place. With one hand she covered her face, and with the other, covered mine. Squinting through Irina's fingers, I reached over the blimp's wreckage and dragged the laser unit out, the camera coming along with it.

Was it still working? The camera's scanning mirrors were flapping frenetically like the fins and tail of a freshly gaffed fish. Quickly, I set the camera and laser on the floor next to the piano, and we both swung around to face away from it.

We'd won this round with Greg's blimp. But the next round would be with Greg himself. He had just re-entered The Block, kicked on the main lights, and was looking down at us from high up on the catwalk.

Chapter 27

"Rundle! Irina!" Greg called down to us. He seemed stunned. Baffled.

"How the hell did you…"

I could see his head turn from side to side, searching for the blimp.

"Save yourself the effort," I called. "I'm afraid the Bosendorfer swallowed your zeppelin."

He must have spied the remains of the blimp hanging over the side of the piano. "OK. I don't know what the hell you did, but whatever it was it must have been damn clever. But, I'm afraid, pointless."

He opened the briefcase he was carrying and held up a small, square-shaped packet. "You see, I've got the disks—right in here. They check out. It all runs OK. I finally got Justin's program."

He tucked the packet back into his briefcase and said, "OK—I was counting on the blimp to do the job for me. Now I guess I have to do what the blimp couldn't."

We stood below, silently. Greg was silent, too, for a long moment.

Greg cleared his throat. He fumbled in his briefcase and drew out a small dark object and held it up.

"Remember this, Rundle?" he asked.

"Yes, Greg. I remember." I guessed he was, again, using my last name as a way of distancing himself from me—and from all our lifelong friendship had once meant.

"Yeah. This is the Beretta I used when I was on the MIT pistol team. I showed it to you that time you were over the apartment. Haven't fired it in seven—maybe eight years. It's like bike riding, though. You never forget."

"No," I said, "I guess one doesn't forget—things like that."

Greg trained the pistol at us, aiming as best I could tell at a point between where Irina and I stood. I desperately tried to detect any glimmer of compassion or remorse, something to tell me that there was yet some corner of his being I might speak to, to persuade him to let us—or at least Irina—go. But I could detect none. I was mortally afraid of him.

I could hear ever so faintly the blimp's camera, its scanning mirrors making a soft whirring as it—spurred on by the sound of voices—searched wildly about for a face to strike at. Irina and I stood with our backs to it, so we didn't offer what it was seeking. Only Greg did, but Irina and I were standing in the scanner's line of sight and it wasn't locking on to him. Yet.

I had to give it a try. "Greg, you don't have to do this. Don't you see if you spare us and surrender to the police, what you did before—to Justin and to Alec—will all look different, that you did it under duress? You were afraid for your life. That would make all the difference."

"Rundle!" Greg shouted, anguish in his voice. "For God's sake, shut the hell up! It's all gone too far. It's too late. I've got to—to do what I have to."

Grasping Irina's hand to bring her with me, I took a couple of slow steps forward and into the beam from one of the spotlights above. I could hear the scanner mirrors still whirring about. We hadn't yet unblocked its line of sight to Greg, but we must be almost there.

Greg put down the briefcase and held the Beretta out in front of him with both hands.

"Rundle, you remember I won the intercollegiate match in my junior year at Tech. Highest individual scorer on the team. They gave me this trophy. On top of it was this little guy with a pistol in his hand. My name engraved along with 'highest individual scorer.' You know the secret of good shooting? You don't *pull* that trigger. You *squeeze* it. Let the shot surprise you." His voice became shrill. "Goddammit, you two! You know I have to do this."

It was over. I pushed Irina to one side and stepped out to the other. The mirrors whirred furiously. Greg yelled, "So you were hiding that goddamn thing…"

Greg fired off a shot at the deadly apparatus on the floor between Irina and me, but missed. He had no time to fire off another shot, as the laser beam knifed through the air, hit him just above and between the eyes, and burst on through his skull. His body teetered for a moment, then crashed to the floor of the catwalk.

I tore off my jacket and flung it over the camera with its whirring mirrors. They whirred on, but the camera couldn't see us.

I sprinted over toward the Bosendorfer, grabbed one of the chairs circled about it, rushed back to where the camera lay under my jacket, and slammed the chair down on it. A crash and tinkle of glass, and the whirring stopped.

Irina and I clung to each other, both of us shaking and trembling. When we were steadied, we went over to the phone by the piano—the one that had sent my voice out to Greg's blimp—and, for the fourth time in recent memory, I called 911.

Chapter 28

Time does indeed have a way of healing, but it took several weeks after our confrontation with Greg Evans in The Block before life for Irina and me began to settle into something like normality.

Lt. Haggerty was a brick. Not only did he apologize profusely to me for his suspicions and his gruff manner ("My professional face," he called it), but he did his utmost—in vain, it turned out—to keep Irina's and my names out of the papers. There was a lively curiosity on the part of the local press and TV about the "high-tech" way Greg had died, and we were badgered relentlessly and at all hours for the story behind the story. Both Irina and I were adamantly silent about it all, and gradually the clamor for interviews spent itself.

Better news for us was that Justin's program encapsulating his uncle's sailing skills was itself about to be encapsulated into a series of compact disks to be made available free of charge to junior sailing clubs both in the U.S. and abroad. John Creedon was underwriting the disks' production, just as he had picked up the costs of making the program in the first place. All of this was announced to the local press one Saturday in late February at a luncheon held, appropriately enough, at the Spinnaker Room atop Cambridge's Hyatt Regency Hotel.

Later that afternoon, Creedon invited those of us close to Justin and his uncle back for cake and coffee at his pied-à-terre at 1010 Memorial Drive, a high-rise luxury apartment complex affording an enviable view of the Boston-Cambridge skyline.

"If anything ought to diffuse the mad scramble over Justin's and your program, distribution of these disks ought to do it," said Creedon, holding his cup high and directing his eyes at Bennett Eames. "If your skills are out there for all, then that puts everyone at the same starting line—even if they want to have the program sail the boat for them!"

I thought of Kenichi Tsukamoto and the offer of hundreds of thousands he'd made to Greg. Now, anyone in a youth sailing program could have Justin's program with Bennett Eames' skills *gratis*.

"Oh, I suppose some people would be tempted to have me as 'virtual skipper' on their boat," said Bennett, looking appreciatively back at Creedon. "Not what I would want, though. How much better if they'd just use it to train with, and to pick up some pointers." He paused and added, "Everyone should—while they can—sail their own ship."

Bennett's last remark had a certain poignancy. Still trim and erect on his electric cart, even projecting a certain dash in the navy blue blazer he had worn for the occasion, he was clearly failing. His voice was much weaker than when I had visited him in Marblehead, and the hand that was not holding his cup was clutching the armrest of his cart with a trembling, white-knuckled grip.

The room was silent for a moment, as we all inwardly acknowledged what would inevitably—and perhaps not before long—befall Bennett.

Karen Hewitt broke the silence. "Yes, but they would still benefit from those pointers from you—and Justin's program." She had driven Bennett to the Hyatt Regency and from there to Creedon's place, and now was standing behind his cart. "I only wish Justin could be here to see the compact disks coming out."

"Bill, what happened to that Russian guy in Venice you said was after the program?" asked Creedon. "You talked about it on the way over, but I missed part of it."

"I just read about it in *Time Magazine*. Short piece they did on the reach of the Russian mob. Tells how Menshikov was murdered in his ski lodge in Switzerland, at Davos. Right after he'd moved nine million dollars from a bank in St. Petersburg to his personal account in Zurich."

I retrieved from my jacket pocket the article I had clipped out and handed it to Creedon. "Some unidentified person or persons got into his bedroom before dawn and put a half-dozen silenced gun shots into him," I said.

Probably not wearing his Kevlar vest beneath his pajamas, I added to myself.

"Good Lord," muttered Creedon, as he scanned the article. "That's a rough league people like him play in. This one probably'll never be solved."

One thing that would be solved, I reflected, as Creedon handed the magazine clipping back to me, was Jean-Paul Etherington's money problems—at least for the moment. No, it wasn't my proposal—which had finally gone out to the National Science Foundation and upon which we were awaiting word—that would be saving the day. Rather, Creedon, along with his announcement of Bennett's sailing tutorial disks, had disclosed his gift to the Cognitive Computing Lab of seven million dollars, plus a special memorial fellowship to be named for Justin.

"With Menshikov gone, Irina, where does that leave your cousin Sergei?" asked Harry Mirsky. A fading blemish over his left eye from where the stitches had been was the only remnant from his encounter with Kenichi Tsukamoto's buddies in MIT's East Garage.

"Sergei is back at Harvard. For good, now," Irina replied. "He'd quit Team St. Petersburg even before Igor Menshikov was killed. He'd finally realized what a ruthless man Menshikov was, how he might put himself in danger if he severed the connection, but was determined to risk it anyway."

Sergei had admitted to me he'd taken my hotel key from my pocket while I was unconscious from the hit by the boom on our Sydney Harbour sail, and that he'd passed it on to a confederate who'd ransacked my room and made off with my laptop. But that clout on the head in the first place? Sergei swears *that* really was an accident—and I've chosen to believe him.

"Bill," Creedon asked, "how about playing something on the guitar for us? The Torres is there, right behind you."

Creedon didn't know of the dog attack on me and how it had

affected my left arm, or I'm sure he'd never have suggested I play. The nerves and tendons had gotten a lot better. But still...

I glanced at Irina for help deciding. The expression on her face was both quizzical and caring, urging me to dare, yet signaling to not try if I felt I couldn't.

I picked up the venerable Torres—over a hundred and thirty years old—from its stand, and checked the tuning. I flexed my fingers a few times, took a deep breath, and plunged into Joaquin Turina's *Soleares*. It's a piece you really shouldn't try without some warm-up first, not to mention avoiding encounters with pit bulls. On the side of caution, I played it at two-thirds speed. Except for a few buzzed notes in the opening bars, I got through it.

A smattering of applause was followed by polite cries for an encore. To avoid tempting fate, I chose Fernando Sor's *Estudio #6,* elegant yet easy.

The Sor piece over, I started to put the Torres back on its stand, but Creedon gestured for me to place it back in its case, which was lying alongside. I obliged him, and when I closed the case I noticed a shiny brass plate set into its top. Engraved on the plate in script letters was my name.

"Really," I said, taken aback, "you can't do this..."

"Oh, yes I can," said Creedon. "Besides, it needs to be played much more often than the once a month I've been able to provide."

The only words I could muster were "Thank you."

It was now late afternoon, and Bennett Eames—who had been offering enthralling reminiscences of his Cup challenge races—was visibly tiring. Karen rose from her chair and made excuses for both him and herself, saying that she must be getting him back to Marblehead. With that as a signal, we all rose and readied to go.

Down at sidewalk's edge, Karen guided Bennett's motor chair through the side cargo door of his Ford Aerostar XLT van, while Bennett—having firmly waved off any assistance—slowly eased himself onto the front passenger seat.

I could see, mounted on the floorboard between the two front seats of the XLT a tall black box with a joystick protruding from it. Bennett must have caught my eye looking at it, for he said, "Neat gadget, that. It let me drive this thing myself for a while. Push it to either side to steer, push it fore or aft to accelerate or brake." He broke into a wan smile. "Trouble is, I can barely do even that nowadays." He glanced over at Karen, who had entered the driver's seat and started the engine. "I'm just as glad to have this young lady here today to work the regular controls."

With Bennett in place, I shut his door. He beckoned me closer. "I hope you're not going to let that young woman—Irina—get away from you," he said in a confidential tone. "If you do, I might have to come back here and have you keelhauled."

"No, sir...I mean Bennett," I said, quickly correcting myself. "I won't be letting her go." Looking into the man's steely eye—and into my own heart—I knew it was a commitment I'd be keeping.

We all gathered about the window of the van.

"Thanks for everything, John," Bennett said, as he reached out and shook Creedon's hand. "And thanks to you all—Bill, Irina, Harry—all of you," he said as he grasped our hands in turn. "Thanks for clearing things up about Justin. I knew for certain he'd never have taken his own life—but you all helped let everyone know that, not just Karen and me."

Bennett, with some effort, turned his head and shoulders around toward the rear of the wagon. The sky to the west had darkened to a deep russet hue, accented with a few wisps of fairweather clouds. "Now, there's a sky for you," he said, with a broad grin. "Sailor's delight, they call it. OK, Karen, let's cast off!"

With that, Karen put the van in gear and pulled away. I drew Irina close to me, and we all waved after Bennett and Karen until we could no longer see them.

About the Author

Holding a PhD in experimental psychology from Brandeis University, Richard Bolt was a founding member of MIT's noted Media Laboratory, where, as a Senior Research Scientist, he led groundbreaking research in multi-modal human/computer interaction. Since retirement from MIT, he has turned his hand to mystery and suspense writing. He and his wife Olga make their home in Arlington, Massachusetts.